AF505804

Radical Modernism and Sexuality

Radical Modernism
and Sexuality ⤺

Freud/Reich/D.H. Lawrence
and Beyond

David Seelow

RADICAL MODERNISM AND SEXUALITY
© David Seelow, 2005.

First published in 2005 by
PALGRAVE MACMILLAN™
175 Fifth Avenue, New York, N.Y. 10010 and
Houndmills, Basingstoke, Hampshire, England RG21 6XS
Companies and representatives throughout the world.

PALGRAVE MACMILLAN is the global academic imprint of the Palgrave Macmillan division of St. Martin's Press, LLC and of Palgrave Macmillan Ltd. Macmillan® is a registered trademark in the United States, United Kingdom and other countries. Palgrave is a registered trademark in the European Union and other countries.

ISBN 1–4039–6629–X

Library of Congress Cataloging-in-Publication Data

Seelow, David.
    Radical modernism and sexuality : Freud, Reich, D. H. Lawrence & beyond / David Seelow.
        p.cm.
    Includes bibliographical references and index.
    ISBN 1–4039–6629–X (hc : alk. paper)
    1. Lawrence, D. H. (David Herbert), 1885–1930—Criticism and interpretation. 2. Reich, Wilhelm, 1897–1957—Influence. 3. Freud, Sigmund, 1856–1939—Influence. 4. Radicalism in literature.
    5. Modernism (Literature) 6. Sex in literature. I. Title.

PR6023.A93Z868 2005
823′.912—dc22   2004050507

A catalogue record for this book is available from the British Library.

Design by Newgen Imaging Systems (P) Ltd., Chennai, India.

First edition: January 2005

10 9 8 7 6 5 4 3 2 1

Printed in the United States of America.

This book is dedicated to Dee Dee Brower for her unconditional love, passionate encouragement, and untiring support.

Contents

Acknowledgments

This book has been over ten years in the making without institutional support. However, I have had the privilege of working with a diverse and stimulating group of individuals who have contributed to the book's final form and, importantly, to my professional evolution. Professor Harvey Gross, a classic scholar and lover of verse, provided me a renewed opportunity at scholarship back in 1984. Jack Ludwig provided guidance. Jack's support and passion for great writing has been an inspiration to me. Elizabeth Anne Kaplan challenged early versions of the text and forced ever-deepening readings of Lawrence. My buddy, Ciro Sandoval, spent many hours of long conversation over Columbian coffee back in the late 1980s as we hammered out our mutual texts on the modern spirit. Randall Davis's friendship has been a sustaining element to my life since the first grade. My mother Doris Faulknor Fernandez has supported my intellectual growth in ways I can never repay.

Hugh J. Silverman has been a primary force in bringing this text to life. I met Hugh as a sophomore back in 1974. He was a new Assistant Professor fresh from Stanford University. His class on artistic consciousness initiated a lifelong friendship through which Hugh has acted as mentor. Professor Silverman's dedication to students is something all educators would do well to emulate. Harold W. Brightman's encyclopedic knowledge, facility with languages, and tireless support has improved both my thinking and writing. Professor Brightman first suggested the importance of Fourrier to my argument. More recently, Robert Corrington has provided important feedback and guidance on my project. His own book on Reich displays our mutual interest in "resurrecting" a maligned figure of modern thought. Arthur Efron entered the process late, but his many phone calls from Buffalo, keen editorial eye, and passionate embrace of both Reich and D.H. Lawrence have made my text stronger. I also thank my wonderful editors at Palgrave Macmillan, Farideh Koohi-Kamali and Melissa Nosal for their sharp eyes. Finally, I want to acknowledge Dee Dee Brower who helped refine my argument through her astute readings and whose keen intelligence, boundless creativity, and genuine love keep me focused and hopeful. Also, thanks to Veena Krishnan for her copyediting and to Jessica Fisher Neidel for her work on the index.

I would like to thank Pollinger Limited and the Estate of Frieda Lawrence Ravagli for permission to quote from the works of D.H. Lawrence. I acknowledge Sigmund Freud Copyrights, The Institute of Psychoanalysis and the Hogarth Press for permission to quote from *The Standard Edition of the Complete Psychological Works of Sigmund Freud* translated and edited by James Strachey, reprinted by permission of The Random House Group Limited. The quotations from the work of Wilhelm Reich have been reprinted by permission of Farrar, Straus and Giroux, LLC, on behalf of The Wilhelm Reich Infant Trust Fund: Excerpts from *Character Analysis* by Wilhelm Reich, translated by Vincent R. Carfagno. Copyright © 1945, 1949, 1972 by The Wilhelm Reich Infant Trust: Excerpts from *Children of the Future* by Wilhelm Reich, compilation and English translation © 1983 by Mary Boyd Higgins as Trustee of the Wilhelm Reich Infant Trust Fund. Excerpts from *Cosmic Superimposition* by Wilhelm Reich, copyright © 1951 by Orgone Institute, renewed copyright 1979 by Eva Reich. Excerpts from *Function of Orgasm* by Wilhelm Reich, translated by Vincent R. Carfagno, copyright © 1973 by The Wilhelm Reich Infant Trust. Excerpts from *Mass Psychology of Fascism* by Wilhelm Riech, translated by Vincent R. Carfagno, copyright © 1969, The Wilhelm Reich Infant Trust, translation copyright © 1970. The Wilhelm Reich Infant Trust: Excerpts from *Murder of Christ* by Wilhelm Reich; excerpts from *Reich Speaks of Freud* by Wilhelm Reich, copyright © 1967 by Mary Boyd Higgins, as trustee of the Wilhelm Reich Infant Trust: Excerpts from *Sexual Revolution* by Wilhelm Reich, copyright © 1969 by The Wilhelm Reich Infant Trust.

Introduction: Radical Modernism &

Radical altarity resists all incorporation, assimilation, and appropriation.

Altarity, Mark Taylor

IMPOSSIBLE MODERNISM

The opening of *Lady Chatterley's Lover* encapsulates the dilemma of modernity: "Ours is essentially a tragic age, so we refuse to take it tragically."[1] The parameters of modernity are impossibly fluid. Any reference to modernism must traverse both its aesthetic and its historical dimensions. In his deconstruction of Nietzsche's *The Birth of Tragedy* Paul de Man articulates this modernist dilemma:

> Within an organically determined view of literary history, Romanticism can appear as a high point, a period of splendor, and the subsequent century as a slow receding of the tide, a decay that can take on apocalyptic proportions. A reversed image of the same model sees Romanticism as a moment of extreme occlusion from which the nineteenth century slowly recovers until it can free itself in the assertion of a new modernity; Nietzsche himself, violently anti-Romantic in his cultural ideology, invariably adopts that perspective when he writes organic or, in his terminology, monumental history. The critical "deconstruction" of the organic model changes this image: it creates radical discontinuities and disrupts the linearity of the temporal process to such an extent that no sequence of actual events of no particular subject could ever acquire, by itself, full historical meaning.[2]

Paul de Man's deconstruction of the genetic model of literary history undermines the practice of literary classification and periodization. Further, de Man calls into question the validity of all historical narration.

The impossibility of writing a history of romanticism let alone modernism does not, however, preclude the "moment" of modernity. When Lawrence writes about a tragic age he shares a modernist preoccupation with apocalyptic thinking, but an age not acknowledged as an end, and, consequently, perpetually deferring the apocalypse. Nonetheless, history does not have to be read genetically. Michael Foucault's reading of Nietzsche discards the impossible search for origins and ends describing a history paradoxically located in the non-space of the interstice.[3]

Foucault's writing shifts from a genealogical model to an archeological one. In this later methodology modernism can be situated in the "non-space" of classicism's dissolution. For Foucault the modern episteme emerges from the rupture in Western thinking when resemblances are replaced by identities as a perceptual mode. The modern system unhinges foundational thinking and dislocates words from their representational significance.

Foucault describes *Don Quixote* as the threshold text that signals the closure of classical thinking and the beginning of another episteme. Interestingly, Foucault does not locate an end point for modernism. Although, he refers to Mallarmé and Nietzsche as examples of writers on the threshold of something other than modern, they, nonetheless, remain firmly within the modern episteme. In fact, Foucault raises the question of thinking the limits of thought afresh in the section on "The Anthropological Sleep."[4]

This new thought, or rather renewed thought would provide a final critique of reason. Foucault finds Nietzsche to be the crucial historical figure in thinking outside the limits of the human sciences. "Nietzsche rediscovered the point at which man and God belong to one another, at which the death of the second is synonymous with the disappearance of the first, and at which the promise of the superman signifies first and foremost the imminence of the death of man. In this, Nietzsche, offering this future to us as both promise and task, marks the threshold beyond which contemporary philosophy can begin thinking again; and he will no doubt continue for a long while to dominate its advance" (342).

Foucault's reading of the human sciences articulates some crucial ideas that this text draws upon. First, the human sciences are a product of modernity and, at the same time, a field of inquiry distinct from the natural sciences, "the human sciences are not an analysis that extends from what man is in his positivism (living, speaking, labouring, being) to what enables this same being to know (or seek to know) in what the essence of labour and its laws consist, and what way he is able to speak" (*OT*, 353). Within the domain of human sciences psychoanalysis, in Foucault's argument, has a privileged position as a counter science.

For Foucault, "psychoanalysis" advises and leaps over representation" and "towards what is there and yet is hidden, towards what exists with the mute selectivity of a thing, of text closed in upon itself, or of a black space in a visible text" (*OT*, 374). In other words, psychoanalysis makes clear the significance, rule, and norm that constitute the human sciences as a field of knowledge. Psychoanalysis joins ethnology and linguistics as "frontier-forms of human sciences" in situating "its experience in those enlightened and dangerous regions where the knowledge of man acts out, in the form of the unconscious and of historicity, its relation with what renders them possible" (381).

Here, one needs to pause and acknowledge the limitation embedded in the term "human sciences." Attaching the word science to human brings up numerous obstacles to an objective study of culture. None of the human sciences achieve anything like the validity of the natural sciences in terms of scientific theory. Although Freud and his contemporaries thought of themselves as scientists conducting a scientific project they, in effect, as Karl Popper states performed only pseudo-scientific endeavors that resemble "astrology more than they do astronomy."[5] Using Popper's basic definition, "as criterion of the scientific status of a theory is its falsifiability, or refutability, or testability," (Popper, 37) today's psychology remains unscientific. On a related note, neither Freud nor Reich would be opposed to a testable, scientific theory of the mind. On the contrary, both Freud and Reich would have benefited greatly from today's technology. Freud always maintained that at least half of all mental illness would be amenable to medical intervention. Reich, for his part, spent his years in Scandinavia and later the United States, searching for a way to test his theories. Although, his ideas on cancer and the like were naïve, he remained entirely committed to the scientific method and the need to connect clinical practice with proven theories.

Consequently, "human science" in this text should be construed in relationship to those disciplines analyzed in Foucault's *Les Mots et les choses* or the disciplines subsumed under the German term *Geisteswissenschuften*, which are analyzed in depth by Wilhelm Dilthey.[6] This methodological limitation regarding the word science does not, however, limit the truth value or significance of the human sciences to an understanding of culture.

Psychology needs to be thought of as a social science and not a natural science. Although Freud would, like today's psychologists, object to such a designation, the empirical facts remain. Even within medical science, psychology and psychiatry have lagged behind fields such as cardiology and neurology. Shifting psychology's truth claim then to hermeneutics does not lessen its theoretical or practical validity. Freud's own 1913 paper on

"The Claims of Psychoanalysis to Scientific Interest," bears relevance here.[7] The essay makes four particularly important claims for psychoanalysis. The first claim concerns the significance of dreams, which Freud maintains as, "the prototype of all psychopathological structures" (172). Depth psychology renders the unconscious conscious and making the latent manifest provides psychoanalysis with its cornerstone. As a result, hermeneutics has an essential relationship to psychoanalytic methodology. Second, the understanding of parapraxes, previously, "relegated to pathology" and the attempt made to find a "physiological explanation of them were eventually unsatisfactory" (166). In other words, Freud does not reject a medical intervention, he simply proposes a psychoanalytic intervention when all other techniques have failed. Third, Freud reiterates the overwhelming independence of sexuality (181). Sexuality, like the mind in general, remains resistant to understanding. Finally, psychoanalysis "indicates the subjective and individual motives behind philosophical theories which have ostensibly sprung from impartial logical work, and can draw a critic's attention to the weak spots in the system" (179).

The value of psychoanalysis inheres then in its critical attitude toward life, an attitude, ironically, that Freud himself rarely adapted regarding his discipline.

MODERNITY/MODERNISM

A second major theme outlined by Foucault's study concerns the parameters of the modern episteme. Although Foucault talks about thresholds and the closure of the modern he does not offer anything like a description of the postmodern episteme. Foucault's resistance to a postmodern archaeology supports my claim, in this study, that modernity and modernism remain active and viable concepts that the amorphous term postmodern fails to realize. Jürgen Habermas argues that modernity remains an unfinished product.[8] In a related fashion, Fredric Jameson describes the modernist paradox, "in which the foregrounding of continuities, the insistent and unwavering focus on the seamless passage from past to present, slowly turns into a consciousness of a radical break; while at the same time the enforced attention to a break gradually turns the latter into a period in its own right."[9] Modernity, in Jameson's reading, represents both a radical break and an integration into a larger "context from which it can be posited as breaking" (57). This leads Jameson to hypothesize modernity's fourth maxim as the need, "to come to terms with a postmodern break with the modern" (94). Such a break remains, however, a hypothesis. A genuine break would signify, as Perry Anderson argues, a revolution or, "an episode of convulsive political transformation, compressed in time and concentrated in target, that has a determinate beginning—when the old state apparatus is still intact—and a finite end, when that apparatus is decisively broken and a new one erected in its stead."[10] Modernity has no finite end, even if, one can posit a determinate beginning. Consequently, Jameson articulates a concept of late modernism to suggest a transition, but not a radical break, from the modernist enterprise.

Jameson puts forth Samuel Beckett as a representative late modern and articulates a concept of contingency as characteristic of late modernism against the equivalent role of chance and accident in high modernism (206–207). These subtle distinctions between high and late modernity remain tied to a chronological schema that fails to demarcate a true postmodernity. Thus late modernity (Beckett follows Joyce as Joyce follows Flaubert who follows Cervantes) expresses modernity's incomplete status and returns Jameson's argument to Habermas's earlier, and, more vital idea about modernity as an unfinished project.

Habermas makes an important distinction between modernity, modernization, and modernism. Modernity, according to Habermas, stretches from the Enlightenment to the present day. Modernism, on the other hand, represents an artistic/cultural movement beginning approximately with Baudelaire's writing in the 1840s. This avant-garde movement "explores hitherto unknown territory, exposes itself to the risk of sudden and shocking encounters, conquers an as yet undetermined future, and must therefore find a path for itself in previously uncharted domains" (Habermas, 40). Modernism, "rebels against norm-giving achievements of tradition" and nourishes itself on the subversion of the normative (41). Additionally, Habermas shows the frequent contradictions between modernism and modernity (42–48). Modernity and the process of modernization frequently create the very norms that modernism rebels against. For example, writers like Lawrence, criticize the industrialization that modernization produces. Simultaneously, such modern writers, often profess politics in direct contradiction to their more emancipated creative writing. This study focuses on the cultural movement of modernism in relationship to the historical confines of modernity. Freud, Reich, and D.H. Lawrence, all exhibit this subversive stance, articulated by Habermas, with respect to the tradition and, consequently, form a modernist triad within the modernist movement.

My text shares Foucault's idea of a threshold figure. Foucault uses both Nietzsche and Mallarmé as figures that express or point to a discourse outside the boundary of their own respective episteme. Thus Nietzsche and

Mallarmé border modernism and postmodernism. Since I am unwilling to grant postmodernism a clearly defined epoch I replace the term threshold with frontier. A threshold once crossed brings one into another clear distinct world whereas a frontier can keep moving without being crossed. Freud, Reich, and D.H. Lawrence are considered in this text to be frontier thinkers or what I shall call radical moderns and, consequently, they exemplify radical modernism, especially with respect to sexuality as the field of inquiry.

Sociologist Anthony Giddins has also used the term radical modernism as an alternative to postmodernism and Jameson's advocacy of late modernism.[11] For Giddens, postmodernity requires totally new and distinct social systems that have not yet emerged (Giddens, 47) and, "modernity turns out to be enigmatic at its core, and there seems to be no way in which this enigma can be 'overcome'" (Giddens, 49). Radical modernity, in Gidden's understanding of the term, retains modernity's promise of social transformation and individual emancipation in an increasingly global context. Interestingly, radical modernism features nation-states, which are bounded by borders and patrolled by state military power, but pushes toward the frontier as a boundless state. Thus radical moderns would possess the frontier thinking that I have posited as characteristic of the three figures discussed in this text. The radical moderns, however, have their own heritage that includes the Marquis de Sade, and Charles Fourier. Although Sade continues to be sexuality's most radical figure, Fourier's writing has much greater historical value than Sade's rather eccentric and isolated writings. Although, both pornographers and intellectuals have appropriated Sade, he has not had the wide scope of influence that Fourier has bequeathed in his own peculiar way to Western consciousness. Before moving to a description of this text's methodologies I want to briefly outline Fourier's contribution to the discursive nature of sexuality.

THE SEX RADICAL AS PROPHET

Fourier's life work provided a blue print for many utopian societies during the 1840s and after.[12] Additionally, Fourier's writings often anticipate, in their oddly systematic, but irrational way, the writings of Freud, D.H. Lawrence, Reich, and others. Fourier, like D.H. Lawrence, bitterly attacked civilization. He maintained that civilization caused mankind's discontent, but contrary to Freud, Fourier argued that discontent could be easily alleviated through the free expression of passion. Fourier advocated a life of gratified desire, which in turn, would lead to a happy society. Similar to Reich, Fourier's arguments presuppose an innate goodness in man directly the opposite of Freud's hypothesis regarding the innate self-destructiveness of the death instinct. Fourier actually describes an immensely detailed utopian society called Harmony that he offers as an antidote to civilized life. In Harmony people's passions proliferate and find expression and gratification in alignment with man's nature (as understood by Fourier).

Fourier's depiction of Harmony's libidinous arrangements predicts, and, in fact, exceeds Reich's extremely progressive ideas. In *Le Nouveau Monde Amoureux* (*OC, VII*), the author creates an architecture of desire and its gratification. In the Phalanx (a community of some 1,600 people) sexuality is fluid, and completely uninhibited. Social arrangements facilitate sexual pleasure for all members irrespective of age (except children whom Fourier did not consider to be sexual beings), orientation or physical disposition. Indeed, even the most downtrodden or sexually frustrated could find satisfaction at an orgy or through the revolving door of amorous relationships. Fourier did not believe fidelity could or should last more then four years.

Institutions, like the Angelic Couple, the society's most beautiful woman and most handsome man, would provide sexual philanthropy, that is, each would conduct a sexually free existence. Fourier, again like Reich, felt compulsory marriage to be an obsolete, coercive institution. Consequently, the Phalanx, unlike most utopias, facilitated travel and the travel facilitated fresh sexual partners for each community.

Fourier's descriptions of man's passions approximate Freud's description of instincts, but whereas Freud believes that civilization requires repression to succeed, Fourier's civilization requires an end to repression for man to triumph. Roland Barthes perfectly captures Fourier's erotic fantasy:

> That of availability: that every love demand at once find a subject-object to be at its disposal, either by constraint or by association; this is the province of the ideal orgy, or in French, partouze, a fantasmatic site, contra-civilized, where no one refuses himself to anyone, the purpose being not to multiple partners but to abolish the wound of denial; the abundance of erotic material, precisely because it is a matter of Desire and not of Need, is not intended to constitute a "consumer society" of love, but, paradox, truly utopian scandal, to make Desire function in its contradiction, namely: to fulfill perpetually.[13]

Fourier wrote before sexuality emerged as a field of inquiry for the human sciences and he also lacked the language subsequently developed by social scientists. Further Fourier's lack of education and his almost certain schizophrenia contributed to his writings' rambling and often delirious organization. Nonetheless, Charles Fourier brings to the fore the importance of sexuality to the utopian project and either the general well being or the dystopic misery of the human species (a misery, Fourier certainly shared). As I move on to discuss this text's radical methodology Charles Fourier's contribution to both psychoanalysis and Marxism, no matter how circuitous, remains important. Not only has Fourier displayed a version of utopian socialism, he has articulated his utopian vision around the significance of sexuality to human expression and social organization.

UNDERSTANDING AND ACTION: RADICAL METHODS

Psychoanalysis and Marxism are radical modernism's chief theoretical tools just as they are modernism's chief tools, but in radical modernism these tools are pushed to their theoretical limits. Wilhelm Reich, for instance, welds Freudian instinct theory and the unconscious, both radically modern conceptualizations, to Marxist theory. Consequently, Reich is a key and undervalued figure of intellectual history. Psychoanalysis, beginning with Freud, remains a century later, a potentially subversive tool precisely because, "the project of uncovering forces that underpin the individual personality is a radical one, akin to other attempts to show what appears to be natural and inescapable is in fact socially constructed."[14]

Psychoanalysis is a radical, critical theory, and expresses only negative, nonbinding communities. Rieff provides a fine description of Freud's negative therapeutics:

> We have seen that in the (classic tradition) of social theory the sense of well being of the individual was dependent on his full, participant membership in a community. The other traditional theory, also powerful and by now equally venerable was that men must free themselves from binding attachments to communal purposes in order to express more freely their individualities. A (third view) entered at this point that there is no positive community now within which the individual can merge himself therapeutically. Freud adheres to this third view.[15]

Analytic radicalism is the subversion of any possible community. Thus Freud's initial radicalism is his critical theory, which negates belief and authority.

A second application of Freud's radical critical theory concerns the intellectual and rationalist tradition. Paul Ricoeur finds in Freud's analytic principles a corrective to the Western philosophical tradition. He calls

Freud's analytic method the hermeneutics of suspicion: "This latter theory of interpretation begins by doubting whether there is such an object [an object of belief motivating inquiry] and whether this object could be the place of the transformation of intentionality into kerygma, manifestation, proclamation. This hermeneutics is not an explication that reduces but a tearing off of masks, an interpretation that reduces disguises."[16] In Ricoeur's reading, Freud's interpretations lead only to other interpretations; dream interpretation is an art of translation through which the question of truth loses its validity. Ricoeur's work, then, restates Rieff's interpretation from the philosophical perspective. For both Rieff and Ricoeur, Freud's radicalism is his negative, analytic position.

Psychoanalysis's radical negativity stems from its position vis-à-vis the unconscious. The analytic voyage is endless because the unconscious has no beginning, middle, or end. Likewise with therapeutics, if theory leads only to interpretation, therapy leads not to cure [the truth of therapy] but only to some relief from suffering. In Foucault's view, psychoanalysis eludes representation both as speculative philosophy and empirical science. And Freud's science is not a discovery, but rather, an uncovering of realities that always remain hidden from conscious knowledge. Radical analysis, however, remains, in psychoanalytic terms, only a critical theory and completely apart from a radical or revolutionary practice.

The Marxist radical, on the other hand, advocates change, the overthrow of social structures and class hierarchies. Marx's position inextricably links theory with praxis, for theory must liberate consciousness from ideology. Ideology is inherently conservative because it serves the interests of the dominant class; and unless ideology, which serves to promote false consciousness, is destroyed, radical change is impossible. Marx gives two excellent examples of ideologies' conservative nature. In one, Luther's radicalism is only theoretical, for he is a reformer not a revolutionary:

> Luther, without question, overcame servitude through devotion but only by substituting servitude through conviction. He shattered the faith in authority by restoring the authority of faith. He transformed the priests into laymen by turning laymen into priests. He liberated man from external religiosity by making religiosity the innermost essence of man. He liberated the body from its chains because he fettered the heart with chains.[17]

Luther substitutes one ideology for another, one form of servitude for another. In the second point, extrapolated from the analysis of Luther, Marx differentiates a radical revolution from a reformation. In a reformation, only part of society achieves power, and once in power the new party generalizes its specific interests, through ideology, to society as a whole. In reality the new dominant class reproduces the old, repressive structures of society, for example, the family, access to money. Thus, from Marx's perspective, critical theory is radical in so far as theory grips the masses; it must be realized in action through the gratification of needs. "Revolutions need a passive element, a material basis. Theory is only realized in a people so far as it fulfills the needs of the people."[18] Marx's critical theory moves, inevitably, from the negative position to a positive affirmation of change (i.e., from a radical theory to a revolutionary theory). A revolutionary theory enacts the "universal human emancipation" through destruction of private property ownership and class domination.[19]

Wilhelm Reich operates on the edge of both Freudian and Marxist thinking. He radicalizes Freud's libido theory and fashions an emancipatory or revolutionary theory of orgasmic potency. Reich binds his instinct theory to a trenchant analysis of how class structure impacts the individual's physical reality. An individual's development responds to, what Reich maintains are oppressive family dynamics, institutional structures, and moral strictures, that block the ego's instinctual thrust toward freedom. Consequently, the liberated self in Reich's vision requires the transformation of the social structures that oppress the self's biological core. Reich then describes, contrary to Freud, a body that thrives independent of a superego. Unfortunately, this revolutionary theory's materialistic foundation evaporated and left Reich advocating a transcendent vision of sexuality based on mystical intuitions and quasi-scientific experimentation.

Nonetheless, Herbert Marcuse picks up Reich's aborted Marxism in his classic study *Eros and Civilization* (1955).[20] Marcuse overturns Freud's basic social premise that man exchanges happiness for security. Although Marcuse does acknowledge the necessity of some repression, he formulates a theory of surplus repression that historicizes Freud's essentialist idea. Modern civilization, in Marcuse's reading, requires extraordinary degrees of repression that modern technology should have enabled man to overcome. Marcuse then advocates a non-repressive civilization, which he believes can be achieved through the elimination of alienated labor, the re-sexualization of the body, and an honest realization of death's inevitability.

In Freud's developmental model, an individual's regression to the pre-oedipal stage signifies chaos. Marcuse, contrarily, maintains that regression "in the light of civilization" (a contradiction for Freud) creates the possibility for libidinal gratification resistant to the co-opting power of institutional domination. Marcuse's model requires the dissolution of oppressive institutions such as monogamy, and the family, as well as, "the abolition of toil, the amelioration of the environment, the conquest of disease and decay, the creation of luxury" (193). Needless to say Marcuse's argument is utopian. Regardless, the utopian gesture returns radical analyses to praxis, which Freud's hermeneutical project failed to promote and rarely even, articulate.

In general, Marcuse's text retains the kernel of Reich's thought (a point rarely acknowledged). Marcuse, however, unlike Reich, accepts Freud's hypothesis regarding the existence of Thanatos. For Freud, "the inclination to aggression is an original, self-subsisting instinctual disposition in man, and I return to my view that it constitutes the greatest impediment to civilization."[21] The discovery of Thanatos conveniently fits Freud's theory of sublimation and repression, but fails to offer, in Freud's presentation, any hope for significant individual or social change. On the other hand, both Reich and Marcuse also theorize a strong biological core to individuality, but a core based on different assumptions than Freud's more pessimistic thinking allowed. What Reich and Marcuse's offer, though, is the possibility of radical change for individuals through a prerequisite and prior change in social structure. This change presupposes an acknowledgment of childhood sexuality and the explosive nature of its biologically driven content along with the possibility of non-alienated labor or the transformation of work into play.

D.H. LAWRENCE AND THE EROTIC IMAGINATION

D.H. Lawrence, like Reich and Freud, positions himself at the boundary of shifting attitudes about sex and human relationships. Lawrence belongs, however, to the Reich–Marcuse line of emancipatory thinking. In "The Novel and Feelings" (1925) Lawrence advocates a non-repressive civilization, which he symbolizes in the figure of old Adam.[22] "So great is the Freudian hatred of the oldest, old Adam, from whom God is not yet separated off, that the psychoanalyst sees this Adam as nothing but a monster of perversity" (204–205). Repression, in Lawrence's view, produces the guilt ridden modern man. Man's deeper nature, however, remains buried under "thousands of shameful years," untamed and waiting for liberation.

Lawrence believes that "real novels" speak the voice of old Adam. His fiction, especially during the 1920s links this old Adam with Pan. The character Renshaw, for instance, in "The Overtone" states that, "Pan is dead."[23] Elsa's response to Renshaw acknowledges that "Christ killed Pan" (14) and brings the conversation into the world of pre-Christian sexuality. Although the story itself is slight, the subject of pagan sexuality plays a large role in D.H. Lawrence's great novella of the period, *St. Mawr* (1924).[24]

This story explores pre-Christian sexuality symbolized by both the magnificent stallion named St. Mawr and Lawrence's evocation of the southwestern United States' landscape, which: "lived, and lived as the world of the gods, unsullied and uncovered. The great living landscape lived its own life, sumptuous and uncaring. Man did not exist for it" (146). The old satyr pictured as half man and half goat represents only the fallen god, but the true Pan remains invisible; a shadowy presence Lawrence's fiction discloses in contradistinction to Freud's highly visible and highly repressed modern neurotic.

Lawrence sees Freud as the epitome of the modern, scientific view of sexuality. Although Freud interprets sexuality through his patients' subjective experience, he renders the personal experiences objective. This objectification of sexuality, in Lawrence's reading, destroys the essence of sexuality. For Lawrence, Freud displays the rational attitude toward sexuality and this rational attitude destroys sexuality just as surely as censorship destroys it. In a letter to Mrs. Sterne, dated December 4, 1921, Lawrence describes his hatred of therapy: "I believe that a real neurotic is a half devil, but a cured neurotic is a perfect devil. They assume perfect conscious and automatic control when they're cured: and it's just this conscious-automatic control that I find loathsome."[25] Philip Rieff gives an excellent description of Lawrence's fundamental difference from Freud, regarding the experience of sexuality:

> . . . Held up to the light of the intellect, every motive, including the intellectual one, is seen through and thus put in question. To Lawrence, such approaches intellectualize the genuinely erotic out of life, thus destroying the possibility of achieving innocence—or, what amounts to the same thing, externality. (Rieff, 227)

Lawrence's work locates itself in the historical rift between the subjective experience of sex, and the scientific/analytic objectification of sex. His fiction emerges between repression and emancipation. The following metaphor expressed by Tommy Dukes in chapter 2 of *Lady Chatterley's Lover*, acts as a paradigm:

> . . . Real knowledge comes out of the whole corpus of the consciousness, out of your belly and your penis as much as out of your brain and mind. The mind can only analyze and rationalize—Set the mind and the reason to cock it over the rest, and all they can do is criticize and make deadness. I say *all* they can do. Therefore let's live the mental life and glory in our spite, and strip the rotten old show—But mind you, it's like this. While you *live* your life, you are in some way an organic whole with all life. But once you start

the mental life, you pluck the apple. You've severed the connection between
the apple and the tree: the organic connection. And if you've got nothing in
your life *but* the mental life, then you yourself are a plucked apple you've
fallen off the tree. And then, it is a logical necessity to be spiteful, just as it's
a natural necessity for a plucked apple to go bad. (*LCL*, 37)

The modern intellectual split between body and mind severs the organic
human connection with the world. The mind/body division recasts the
original biblical myth; it represents the individual's alienation from nature
and his or her nakedness (or true, sexual self). Although Freud might
appear, in *Lady Chatterley's Lover*, the modern reincarnation of Socrates,
Lawrence's novel is not an archetypical repetition of the Fall. Lawrence's
metaphor of the organic connection has historic specificity.

George Lukács uses the metaphor of the organic connection in differ-
entiating capitalist culture from previous cultural formations. For Lukács,
the organic connection means the unity of human production with the
products themselves; the products of culture grow out of the soil of social
being.[26] Each culture is, in turn, connected to its past. The capitalist culture, in Lukàcs's view, ruptures the organic basis of culture; culture is irrevocably severed from its past, and products become independent of human
creation. Under capitalism, Lukács states, economic life controls social life.
Indeed, Lukács asserts that capitalism destroys the very possibility of culture at its root: "The moment cultural productions become commodities,
when they are placed in relationships which transform them into
commodities, their autonomy—the possibility of culture—ceases" (6).

Lukács's essay "The Old Culture and the New Culture," like *Lady
Chatterley's Lover*, stands at a point of historical crisis. The old culture is
gone, and Lukács's new culture will, presumably replace capitalism just as
the proletariat replaces the capitalist. The future brings the possibility of a
new organic connection that restores the human individual's essential
humanness and creativity. Lukács's vision, of course, assumes the end of
economic misery, an end Lawrence's novel will refute.

Lawrence's goal, in *Lady Chatterley's Lover*, is to imaginatively recapture
an organic connection between man and nature in the midst of a capitalist
expansion. Lawrence states his goal as wanting "men and women to be able
to think sex, fully, completely, honestly and cleanly."[27] He will replace the
grey elders' "dirty-yellow" sex, and the jazzy youth's "nervous-white" sex
with blood-red sex. Lawrence wants to restore the organic essence of culture through touch: "A man must be self-conscious enough to know his
own limits, and to be aware of that which surpasses him. What surpasses
me is the very urge of life that is within me, and this life urges me to forget

myself and to yield to the stirring half-born impulse—up the vast lie of the world, and make a new world."[28] The "new world" is the symbolic world Lawrence creates in *Lady Chatterley's Lover*.

This text investigates the emergence of modern sexuality through the biological paradigm Dr. Richard von Krafft-Ebing describes in his monumental work, *Psychopathia Sexualis*, and how Freud, Reich, and D.H. Lawrence, modernity's three principal thinkers on sexuality, position themselves on the circumference of Krafft-Ebing's biological center. The conceptualization of sexuality by scientists, psychiatrists, and others is a determining feature of modern culture. Yet the key feature of modern culture is not just the intellectual preoccupation with sex, but also the way in which sexuality becomes the essential factor in each individual's personality structure and everyday experiences of the world. Thus, modern culture is best understood through sexuality approached through Freud and Lawrence's different inscriptions of the self's interiority and Reich's analysis of the cultural norms that determine how the interiority of sex is experienced. Chapter 1 outlines the emergence of sexual discourse in the mid-nineteenth century and its relationship to modernity. The chapter begins with Krafft-Ebing's struggle negotiating both environmental and hereditary models of sexual pathology and his eventual articulation of a biological paradigm. The chapter then moves to an in-depth investigation of how Freud inherits but then transforms the biological paradigm for understanding human sexuality into a more radical, intrapsychic model. For Freud, the theory of sexuality undergoes many changes, but all largely a result of his own clinical practice and how he conceptualizes intra-psychic processes. The text argues that Freud's ultimate vision espouses a masochistic substratum to human sexuality. Chapter 2 presents Reich's more optimistic and libertarian understanding of the body; the relationship between the body and the effects of capital. In this regard Reich appears much closer to Lawrence then his early mentor, Freud.

Lawrence, like Reich, but unlike Freud, negotiates the complex interplay between the sensual body and how cultural norms and practices determine the body's meaning and fate. Indeed, Reich's and Lawrence's fascination with the body represent two foci of radical thought, one social-analytic and the other, imaginative, about the body's place in modern thought. Chapter 3 engages a range of Lawrence's texts, including "The Blind Man," *The Man who Died, The Fox* and *Women in Love* in light of major contemporary theorists. This chapter reads the body in relationship to homosocial and homosexual impulses and also Christian belief.

Chapter 4 provides a close reading of *Lady Chatterley's Lover* as Lawrence's attempt to resolve the contradictions between a passionate, almost sacred vision of heterosexual love and the inevitable corruption and transformation of the man–woman bond by historical forces. Finally, chapter 5 interrogates the idea of postmodernism through the writings of George Bataille and Jean Baudrillard. Bataille's description of the interplay between erotic ecstasy and utilitarian productivity provides a provocative gloss on D.H. Lawrence's own version of the "accursed share." Finally, Baudrillard's articulation of the simulacra brings about the text's closure while offering a post-human configuration of desire.

The conclusion reconsiders the methodological questions raised by the text's arguments. Like Gadamer, I would challenge, though in a less ambitious fashion, the natural sciences' claim to some privileged notion of truth outside the reach of the human sciences.[29] The human sciences, including psychology and psychiatry (more so than any other branch of medical science), have emerged late in the history of scientific exploration, and these sciences are, necessarily, still evolving a methodology capable of describing and understanding the "laws" of human behavior. After all, as Gadamer so eloquently argues, all knowledge is necessarily incomplete, and the hermeneutic project investigates precisely what makes any knowledge, independent of its domain, possible and comprehensible to the fullest, but never total, degree possible.

Each chapter stands alone, but remains part of a larger intellectual project. Freud, Reich, and Lawrence are not read in a linear fashion nor are they understood simply as influencing each other in some traditionally historical notion. Nonetheless, the three share a radical agenda centered on the representation and deployment of sexual discourse. Reich and Lawrence remain closely aligned in their pursuit of a utopian community based upon individual emancipation. As Lawrence writes in planning his utopian community, Rananim: "I wanted a real community, not built out of abstinence or equality, but out of many fulfilled individualities seeking greater fulfillment" (*Letters ii*, 266).[30] This community assumes, "the goodness in the members, instead of the assumption of [. . .] badness" (*Letters ii*, 259). Ultimately, "each one may fulfill his own nature and deep desires to the utmost, but wherein the ultimate satisfaction and joy is in the completeness of us all as one" (*Letters ii*, 271). Both Lawrence and Reich argue passionately for a depersonalized ego that dissolves the armor of isolation and liberates a self always connected to others in a dance exemplified by sexuality's transforming power.

On the other hand, Lawrence's proclaimed antipathy to Freud betrays an underlying affinity between the two writers (Reich's relationship to Freud has the most direct connection among this text's three figures and forms part of the reading of Reich in Chapter 3). As radical thinkers Freud and Lawrence, as well as Reich, articulate a model of personal transformation for their patients and the modern self in general. Julia Kristeva locates Freud's foundational belief regarding psychic transformation in his "discovery" of the unconscious or the "unprecedented timeless" and the emergence of "analytic interpretation" as a "secular version of forgiveness."[31] Psychoanalysis, in Kristeva's view, "radicalizes it [guilt] to the point of moving away from it, in an opening of psychical space toward an always possible remission, restructuring, remanence, revolt" (17). In other words, psychoanalysis facilitates the ego's destruction in creating an imaginary space for the ego to reemerge as a new subject or, "the unconscious coming to consciousness in transference" (19).

Kristeva overturns many critical readings of Freud for as she writes about Freud's metapsychology, "the originality of Freud's position, which in 'The Unconscious' (1915) defines thus: 'to emancipate ourselves from the importance of the symptom of 'becoming conscious' " (27). Ultimately, Freud's concept of the death drive, in Kristeva's reading, becomes a trope of transformation that allows Freud's to remain congruent with Reich's and Lawrence's life affirmative positions: "Having put my analyst (the other) to death, I nevertheless assure his survival through the re-creation of the transferential dynamic with other others" (40). The "*homo analyticus* would [then] be the re-turn, the re-volt of the timeless in time" (41). This revolt, as Kristeva observes, finds its most complete expression in literature (12) and approximates Lawrence's notion of the unconscious as that "spontaneous origin from which it behooves us to live."[32] Kristeva's study features the troika of Aragon, Sartre, and Barthes while mine features the different triad of Freud, Reich, and D.H. Lawrence who represent a constellation of modernism, like Roland Barthes's *Sade/Fourier/Loyola,* as an organically linked, but nonetheless, disparate group who provide, in terms of this text, the best path to understanding sexuality in the modern era. The text delineates three central foci of radical thought on the curvilinear shape of modernity.[33]

1. The Analytic Radical: Freud and Modern Sexuality ∽

" 'Now we have agreed that love is in love with what he lacks and does not possess.' "

Socrates to Agathon, Plato's *Symposium*

"Call her one, me another flye We're Tapers too, and at our owne cost die."

John Donne, "The Canonization"

THE SEXUAL EPISTEME

Sexuality comes into being, paradoxically, sometime in the mid-nineteenth century Victorian era. Sex becomes an object of intellectual and scientific attention precisely when the official bourgeois culture attempts to silence the reality of sex. Just as sex enters public discourse as an independent subject of study (independent of reproduction), the individual's experience of sex becomes curiously secret. The social construction of sex as something hidden results, in Foucault's analysis, not in a repressive gesture but rather in an incitement to discourse.[1] The Victorian mind produces sex. Of course, there is sexuality before the Victorian period, but with the Victorian era comes a particular realization and awareness of sexuality's social importance and the necessity of approaching sex as a scientific object of study. This awareness of sexuality replaces the religious apprehension of sexuality with the scientific observation of sexuality. Also, the connection between reproduction and sex gradually severs such that the sexologist, scientist of sex, investigates both the psychological and social significance of sexuality. The preeminent Victorian sexologist, Sir William Acton, writes a book on the inseparability of sexuality and reproduction, *The Functions and Disorders of the Reproductive Organs* (1857), and another book investigating the growing social problems of prostitution. In order for sexuality to emerge simultaneously as an object of scientific study and a social problem, a number of factors had to emerge. First, population becomes a major social problem. With the growth of the middle class as an economic power base and rapid industrialization, the nuclear family becomes the chief source of social–moral value. An expanding population threatens economic stability and enforces state regulations on sexuality. As Jeffrey Weeks points out, these regulations had clear racial (eugenic) import.[2] Likewise, the ubiquitous presence of prostitutes on city streets provides an unavoidable sexual image undermining the moral facade of the middle class. Foucault sees the issue of sex emerging between the public discourse of scientific knowledge, which stresses regulations, and the private experience of sex as secret (Foucault, 20). To speak of sex as an issue is to invoke sexuality as a problem. A public problem naturally requires a solution and sexology arises as the scientific attempt to solve the "problem of sex." Given the nature of this social problem, the medical profession is the branch of science most equipped to attack this complex problem. Medical science brings forth a massive explosion of case studies, analyses, and interpretations, which systematize sexuality as a new, modern body of knowledge.

Parallel to the proliferation of medical discourse on sexuality is a proliferation of underground discourses expressing the secret side of sex. Just as sexology comes into being in this period, so too does pornography. In fact, pornography establishes itself as a minor industry. Thus, capitalism and middle-class values are linked from the outset with pornography. Steven Marcus makes the crucial connection between the two Victorians: between the hearth and the bed chamber.[3]

Marcus describes the development of two interlocking Victorian cultures. The Industrial Revolution brings rapid changes in social relationships. On the one hand, the woman becomes guardian of the home, an image of purity. On the other hand, the woman becomes a streetwalker, exchanging her body for capital. The woman exhibits the contradictory forces of the new urban environment. As wife, she provides an escape, a haven, from industrial competitiveness. As prostitute, she provides a release from sexual anxiety. The streetwalker sells sexuality and the wife buys goods. The female, then, is abstracted from industrialization and placed in the home, an angel. She is, at the same time, projected onto the urban landscape participating in the industrialization of sexuality itself. The official Victorian culture censures sexuality and the Victoria subculture produces more and more pornography. Marcus sees the connection between the two Victorian cultures as an expression of anxiety. The new middle class, in attempting to cope with a new social reality, fears the loss of its moral order. This new social environment provides a medical knowledge about sexuality. The city becomes a social laboratory contributing to the proliferation of discourses conceptualizing sexuality as a problem. Sex is a problem because, as Marcus states, sexuality threatens individual identity, family values, and the new solidifying class system. Sexology is the neutral discourse, attached to medicine, that will analyze the disorder wrought in the individual body and by implication the social body. The enormous growth of the discourse on sexuality would appear to support Foucault's contention that the Victorian period, rather than repressing sexuality, instead, saturates society with sexual discourse. Yet, Foucault fails to differentiate the scientific discourse, or sexology, from the fictional discourse, or pornography. Although pornography becomes an industry, the industry remains an underground, uncensored industry. Likewise, women are the objects of massive sexual repression and are exiled from sexual pleasure. The Victorian mind articulates not an explosion of sexuality, but rather, a contradictory attempt to grasp the reality of sexuality in a rapidly changing urban world. Sexology, as I show, always plays off its pornographic mirror image.

What then is the meaning the sexologists give to sexuality, and how do they arrive at the knowledge that they produce? As I have said above, the bourgeois mind conceptualizes sexuality as a problem allowing its incorporation within a medical framework. Sexuality is approached through its pathological manifestations. If sex is a problem, marking a doubt, a disturbance, the medical approach necessarily proceeds along the heath/pathology axis and psychiatry is the logical specialty equipped to investigate pathological sexual experience (Heath, 13). For the systemic approach to pathology to be effective, a theoretical framework must already be in place. Darwin provides the major theoretical background for sexological investigations. He gives to sexology both a taxonomical methodology and the emphasis on species and variation through which to describe the order of nature.[4] Jeffrey Weeks suggests that sexology seeks a biological essence to sexuality: "The sexologist's goal: was not less than the discovery, description and analysis of the laws of Nature."[5] What happens as medical science approaches the natural through the pathological is that the natural is quickly linked with the healthy and the healthy is defined as the norm around which the pathological circulates and deviates. Medical science sets up an equation whereby: the natural = the healthy = the normal. What happens, however, is that the sexological investigation of pathological individuals produces more pathologies so that the normal recedes from scientific observation. Sexology details a multiplication of sexualities all with a particular etiology. This expansion of singular sexualities must somehow be placed into an order of the human species. Foucault cites the homosexual as exemplary of how medical science produces a singular sexuality

(Foucault, 43). The homosexual is no longer just a sinner or deviant; he/she has a complex and unique sexuality. The contradiction set out in the investigation of sexual pathology is clear. How can there be a norm with so much variety? A statistical norm would at best indicate a preference for one form of perversion as opposed to all others.

With the preceding discussion as background, I now turn my attention to a specific investigation of the nineteenth century's most influential sexologist, Dr. Richard von Krafft-Ebing. Krafft-Ebing's book, *Psychopathia Sexualis* (1879), is the most comprehensive sexological work of its time.[6] The structuring of the book marks out the two Victorians at every moment. On the one hand, Krafft-Ebing catalogues every known sexual perversion providing a scientific explanation of each. On the other hand, he and his numerous supporting cases studies read like pieces of pornographic fiction. Krafft-Ebing's text displays the contradiction in Victorian sexuality between pornography and purity, between whore and angel. His main text represents the official culture. It attempts to order sexuality into scientific classification. The book's subtext, however, embodies the unleashing of uncontrollable sexuality, which threatens to overturn the official culture. Also, Krafft-Ebing's specialty in psychiatry brings his attention to bear on the psychological anxiety underlying the expression/repression of Victorian sexuality. Indeed, as I demonstrate, Krafft-Ebing, the psychiatrist, links sexual perversion with mental illness, preserving sexuality's subterranean power. The Victorian projects his fear of unleashed sexuality onto the streetwalker and then identifies with the angelic and sane wife at home.

The paradox of sexuality is clearest in Krafft-Ebing's discussion of "normal" sexuality. He maintains that the normal aim of sex is reproduction. The question he addresses is how does the normal aim come about? What in the nature of sexuality assures a reproductive drive between heterosexuals without causing deviation? Krafft-Ebing discovers the root of heterosexual attraction in the following description of a fetish:

> The germ of sexual love is probably to be found in the individual charm (fetish) with which persons of opposite sex sway each other.
>
> The case is simple enough when the sight of a person of the opposite sex occurs simultaneously with sexual excitement, whereby the latter is intensified.
>
> Emotional and optical impression combine and are so deeply embedded in the mind that a recurring sensation awakens the visual memory and causes renewed sexual excitement, even orgasm and pollution (often only in dreams), in which case the physical appearance acts as a fetish. (Krafft-Ebing, 18)

He describes fetishism as a physiological fact accounting for the nature of individual attraction and preference among sexual partners. What strikes me in Krafft-Ebing's analysis is the arbitrary nature of sexual attraction. In effect, the nature of normal, healthy sexual attraction proceeds through a sexual perversion: the fetish. Thus, reproduction assumes a secondary role to the primary one of an idiosyncratic sexual aim that can never be generalized into anything like a norm. So the normal function of sexuality is a consequence of a "perverted" sexual drive aroused through the distinctive marks of a particular fetish. Thus, a psychic process, easily construed as "abnormal," certainly unique to each individual's mental constitution, fuels the biological drive to reproduce. The indispensable role of the fetish dislocates any simplistic definition of normal, sexual desire. When analyzing the incredible diversity of sexual pathology, Krafft-Ebing discovers the only common ingredient of the pathologies to be hyperesthesias (i.e., excessive libido). The strength of the sexual drive constitutes the essence of sexual perversion. The chief ingredient of hypersexuality in turn is masochism; an ecstatic sexual experience, that annihilates pain. Thus, the driving force of Krafft-Ebing's text is a combination of fetishistic attraction, excessive libido, and the masochistic pleasure of all nonreproductive sexuality.

In articulating the triumph of the biological paradigm Krafft-Ebing, nonetheless, through his case studies and intellectual struggle with the sociological paradigm, brings to light the historical material that produces the Victorians' pornographic subculture. Perversion becomes an embodiment of a genetic disorder, but a genetic disorder produced at a particular point in the aftermath of the Industrial Revolution.

The movement from Victorian sexuality to modern sexuality often appears as an enlightened progression from sexual repression to sexual expression. Paul Robinson provides an excellent example of how historians explain the transition from Victorian sexuality to modern sexuality. He begins with a survey of the scientific approach to sexuality emerging in mid-nineteenth-century society to its expansion and gradual integration within early twentieth century culture. In Robinson's view, sexology triumphs over Victorian representations of sexuality. The triumph is entirely moral. Modern culture accommodates what Victorian cultures suppressed. Robinson sees modernism as progress. The transition from Victorian sexuality to modern sexuality retains the scientific paradigm changing only its moral context. Freud as I shall show both participates in and transforms Robinson's interpretation of sexual modernism. The following is Robinson's characterization of the modernists:

> Against the Victorians, the modernists held that sexual experience was neither a threat to moral character nor a drain on vital energies. On the contrary, they considered it an entirely worthwhile, though often precarious,

human activity, whose management was essential to individual and social well-being. Put bluntly—and I can think of no other way of putting it—the modernists were sexual enthusiasts. At the same time they sought to broaden the range of legitimate sexual behavior—to investigate and to apologize for those apparently deviant forms of sexuality that the Victorians, with their exclusive commitment to adult, genital, heterosexual intercourse, had been reluctant even to recognize. The modernists also rejected the nineteenth century conception of female sexuality. Where the Victorians had all but denied women a sexual existence, the modernists argued her sexual parity with the male, even at the risk of transforming her into an exclusively sexual being. Finally, the modernists entertained serious doubts about the traditional institutional contexts of human sexuality—marriage and the family—thereby raising to the level of explicit debate what seems to me the most vexing problem of human sexual psychology: the paradoxical need for both companionship and variety in erotic life.[7]

Robinson sees the modernists taking over the biological paradigm, by detaching the paradigm from its moral context. He implies that sexual perversion is synonymous with Victorian morality. Robinson believes that the Victorians interpret sexual behavior in a moral fashion. What the Victorians call perversion is, Robinson claims, just a form of sexual behavior, which is neither moral nor immoral. Thus, he sees sexual modernism as the emancipation of sexuality from Victorian morality. This perspective, in fact, notes four features that characterize modernism as sexual liberation: (1) the modernists' vision emphasizes pleasure, (2) recreational sex includes female sexuality and orgasmic equity, (3) monogamy is a social construction, and (4) marriage is an institution, not a natural state.

The next section and subsequent chapter take up Robinson's description of the modernist enterprise from the perspective of sexuality's preeminent psychoanalysts. Ironically, Reich turns out to be closer to Robinson's reading. He argues against the institution of marriage and advocates a utopian vision of sexual emancipation. Before looking at Reich's vision of the modern body, however, a close reading of Reich's mentor, Freud, displays another, entirely different vision of the sensual body described by nineteenth-century science. Although Freud inherits a Darwinian version of the human body, he transforms the biological paradigm of sexuality into a psychological model that discloses humanity's strangely masochistic drive.

FREUD AND THE ENIGMA OF HUMAN SEXUALITY

In Freud's *The Three Essays on the Theory of Sexuality*, the very title stands out as an indication of Freud's departure from the sexological tradition.

Freud devotes his attention to the theory of sexuality, showing virtually no interest in observation; he offers virtually no case studies of sexual pathology and little empirical evidence to support his line of argument. In fact, Freud builds his theory out of the empirical knowledge provided by the tradition he inherits.[8]

Freud's concern here is with a theory of sexuality and not with the observation of sexual behavior; the movement of his thought is speculative. One could almost go so far as to say that Freud creates fictions as a way to reach a truth that must, being psychic in nature, remain hidden from the scientific eye, the microscope, and laboratory. *The Three Essays* are also multiple texts. Freud publishes the first version in 1905, the same year he brings out his case study of Dora, completed years before, so that, with respect to publication date, these two major works appear simultaneously. Freud revises the text at a number of points throughout his career so that the text is, as Marcus remarks, a "palimpsest" (Steven Marcus, Introduction to *Three Essays*, xxv). Indeed, each version of the text appears within a different stage of Freud's changing theoretical work. The 1915 edition will juxtapose sexuality with the two major essays: "The Instincts and Their Vicissitudes," and "On Narcissism: An Introduction." The 1924 edition follows and includes information about the death drive presented in *Beyond the Pleasure Principle* (1921). My own reading of Freud's theory of sexuality focuses on *The Three Essays on the Theory of Sexuality*, while interpolating at each relevant moment Freud's later essays on sexuality in order to produce a critical palimpsest.

The complex historical dimension of the text must also be related to the enormously complex form of each individual version. Freud is as systematic a thinker as Krafft-Ebing, and the organizing principle of this complex system, as in Krafft-Ebing, is Darwinian. The first of the three essays focuses on sexual pathology because of the Darwinian methodology he inherits, and the fact that the sexological tradition privileges pathology as the entrance point for scientific investigations of sexuality.

Freud opens his text with an attack on the biological model of sexual instinct espoused by Krafft-Ebing and the four commonly held views about sexuality:

1. Sexuality does not exist in childhood,
2. Sexuality begins with puberty,
3. The sexual instinct is an overwhelming heterosexual, biological force that brings the sexes together,
4. The aim of the sexual drive is genital union with the opposite sex.

He then goes on to challenge accepted knowledge in all four areas beginning with an examination of aberrations of sexual instinct. The following is a close reading of Freud's section on aberration of sexual aim, emphasizing the place of the fetish in sexual pathology.

The fetish exists on the borderline between normal and abnormal sexual behavior:

> . . . No other variation of the sexual instinct that borders on the pathological can lay so much claim to our interest as this one, such is the peculiarity of the phenomena to which it gives rise. Some degree of diminution in the urge towards the normal sexual aim (an executive weakness of the sexual apparatus) seems to be a necessary precondition in every case. The point of contact with the normal is provided by the psychologically essential overvaluation of the sexual object, which inevitably extends to everything that is associated with it. A certain degree of fetishism is thus habitually present in normal love, especially in those stages of it in which the normal sexual aim seems unattainable or its fulfillment prevented: Schaffi' mir ein Halstuch von ihrer Brust, Ein Strumpfband meiner Liebeslust!" (*Three Essays*, 19–20)

The key phrase in Freud's analysis is "sexual overvaluation of the sexual object necessary in normal love." What distinguishes fetishism from normal sexual love? Freud does not give a very satisfactory answer; he suggests that fetishism becomes prevalent when normal sexual love is unattainable, but such a view offers little insight. Freud goes on to state that a fetish becomes perverse only "when the fetish becomes detached from a particular individual and becomes the sole sexual object." This definition of a fetish can be read in two ways: (1) an individual is obsessed with an object such as high heel shoes, and also has masturbation fantasies about such an object, or (2) an individual might be capable of making love only to a woman wearing high heel shoes. The distinction between a fetish and sexual variation is unclear. High heels, to use my example, often play an important erotic role in many normal sexual lives. If a major ingredient of the fetish is the anatomical extension of erogenous zones, the fetish is normal and contributes and compliments the eroticisation of the body exhibited in a sexually healthy individual. Nonetheless, Freud's beginning effort at understanding the fetish leads nowhere productive.

The real beginning of Freud's thinking on the fetish starts when he notes its symbolic role: "In other cases the replacement of the object by a fetish is determined by a symbolic connection of thought, of which the person concerned is usually not conscious" (*Three Essays*, 21). The emphasis on the role of the unconscious in producing the fetish is important to remember. Initially, Freud names two symbolic fetishes: fur and hair, which are both related to the vagina. In a 1911 footnote he adds the shoe/slipper as a substitute vagina; and a second 1910 footnote brings the sense of smell into connection with both hair and foot fetishes:

> . . . Psychoanalysis has cleared up one of the remaining gaps in our understanding of fetishism. It has shown the importance, as regards the choice of a fetish, of a coprophilic pleasure in smelling which has disappeared owing to repression. Both the feet and the hair are objects with a strong smell which have been exalted into fetishes after the olfactory sensation has become unpleasurable and been abandoned. (*Three Essays*, 1910, 21)

The historical and developmental repression of smell returns in the creation of fetishes. Smell, in relation to a fetish, remains sexual, but in the unconscious; its erotic quality returns, in modern times, displaced as the foot fetish. Freud discusses the role played by smell in producing sexual variation as early as an 1897 letter to Fliess.[9]

Freud writes this letter concerning sexual perversion when he is working on the material for *The Three Essays on the Theory of Sexuality*. While Freud borrows from Fliess the insight concerning the importance of smell in sexuality, what he does with it is highly original. He connects the role of smell with erotogenic zones; the repression of smell signals the primacy of genital sexuality. With the primacy of genital sexuality comes a de-eroticization of the body; the modern individual, and also the adult, as opposed to the child, is less sexual than his predecessor. Thus the acknowledgment of smell, and by extension the creating of a fetish, returns the body to its erotic status. The fetish implies that every part of the body can produce sexual excitement.

The second major insight of the letter concerns the relationship between sexual perversion (with its return to the sexuality of smell) and dreams. The fetish is like a dream, which expresses in symbolic terms the language of the unconscious. What a symptom is to the sexual life of a neurotic the fetish is to the sexual life of a "pervert." The symbolism of a fetish goes beyond the status of metaphor. The fetish (say high heels) does not simply replace the vagina as a source of sexual excitement because the sexual object remains the foot; what changes in the production of a fetish is sexuality itself. The sense of smell, originally sex positive, through historical development becomes sex negative. Freud discusses the role of repression in the transformation of sensuality in an extraordinary letter to Fliess dated November 24, 1897 (Letter 75, 229–235). The letter anticipates not only *The Three Essays*, but also the late philosophical book, *Civilization and Its Discontents*.

Outlined below is the double level of Freud's analysis in the letter mentioned above:

Historical Process (*Phylogenesis*)

Primitive Man	*Civilized Man*
Primacy of Smell	Primacy of Sight
Early man's posture close to animals in proximity to earth	Importance of mental processes
Organic connection between man, earth and animals	Alienation from nature; Organic repression of past

Developmental Process (*Ontogenesis*)

Child	*Adult*
Multiple erogenous zones	Single erogenous zone
Body as primary experience of world	Alienation from body

What my sketch of the letter indicates and Freud's writing implies is that the pervert exhibits a liberation of sexuality; he re-sexualizes the body. Perversion returns the self to childhood sexuality. Thus, the numerous peripheral sexualities (pathologies, aberrations) are less singular sexualities than an explosion of the component instincts present in the normal child. The pervert, like the child, experiences the world through the sensual body. The individual who becomes sexually excited when kissing a woman's anus, or the individual who has orgasms when having her toes licked, though classified a "pervert," actually releases the sexuality or sexual energy repressed in those parts of the body. Freud claims that sexualization of the body in adolescence or adulthood releases unpleasure, not pleasure. He implies that only a pervert experiences pleasure in nongenital sexuality; yet offers no evidence to support his claim that a return to abandoned erogenous zones releases some kind of internal unpleasure. This unpleasure must, by the logic of Freud's own argument, be socially produced.

Freud's thinking demonstrates that an entire shift in the sensual apparatus takes place in the replacement of the olfactory sense with the visual sense. In order for such a shift in sensual experience to occur, a complex psychic mechanism must be operating. The exaltation of feet as a sexual object, to take one example, must deny the smell of feet. Likewise, the erotic arousal of a fur coat (visual stimulation) entails a denial of vaginal odors (repression). As one aspect of the sexual object is idealized, another aspect, its material reality, must be denied; the foot is simultaneously exalted (sight) and repressed (smell). The historical shift from a coprophilic instinct to a scopophilic instinct necessitates such a splitting of the sexual object into an ideal and a real.

In 1915 he adds the footnote on scopophilia to the section on fetishism (the time of "The Instincts and Their Vicissitudes"):

> In a number of cases of foot-fetishism it has been possible to show that the scopophilic instinct, seeking to reach its object (originally the genitals) from underneath, was brought to a halt in its pathway by prohibition and repression. For that reason it became attached to a fetish in the form of a foot or shoe, the female genitals (in accordance with the expectations of childhood) being imagined as male ones. (*Three Essays*, 1915, 21)

The footnote helps explain the choice of a fetish. Freud locates fetishistic excitement in visual sexuality, and the favor of certain fetishes such as heels, stockings, garters, and lingerie, is elucidated by his analysis. The goal of the scopophilic instinct is the discovery and sight of the vagina. The fetish replaces the instinct's ultimate goal; it hints at this goal (sight of the vagina) and simultaneously covers it over. Thus, fetishes usually surround the genital region, which explains the erotic attraction of lingerie, miniskirts, stockings, and so on. Likewise, female strippers' erotic appeal is not the completely naked body, but the slow revelation of body parts and sexually exciting underclothing. I must add here that the entire direction of Freud's theme fails to analyze the fetish in relationship to the male as sexual object (i.e., from the point of view of the desiring woman). Freud goes no further, even in 1915, than the above observations.

He returns to the importance of the fetish in the important 1927 essay "Fetishism." In 1927 Freud begins just where he left off in 1915, picking up on the scopophilic drive to discover the vagina:

> . . . When the fetish is instituted some process occurs which reminds one of the stopping of memory in traumatic amnesia. As in this latter cause, the subject's interest comes to a halt halfway, as it were; it is as though the last impression before the uncanny and traumatic one is retained as a fetish. Thus the foot or shoe owes its preference as a fetish—or a part of it—to the circumstance that the inquisitive boy peered at the woman's genitals from below, from her legs up; fur and velvet—as has long been suspected—are a fixation of the sight of the pubic hair, which should have been followed by the longed for sight of the female member; pieces of underclothing, which are so often chosen as a fetish, crystallize the moment of undressing, the last moment in which the woman could still be regarded as phallic. But I do not

maintain that it is invariably possible to discover with certainty how the fetish was determined.[10]

The passage contains a number of complex ideas further developing Freud's earlier observations. In characteristic form, he refuses to state his discovery as fact, showing again his thinking about psychic problems in a new, uncharted fashion. The passage, in accord with his previous analysis, locates the fetish in developing childhood sexuality, but in 1927 the moment of revelation/concealment is related to a traumatic amnesia. Freud explains the moment of fetishism as the last moment in which the female can be considered as phallic. For the child, and Freud argues only from the point of view of a boy child, to actually see the woman's vagina would be to recognize the woman as different. She would then represent a possible future for the boy (a future without a phallus), and the trauma turns out to signify castration anxiety. Freud implies my supposition in the following passage:

> In every instance, the meaning and the purpose of the fetish turned out, in analysis, to be the same. It revealed itself so naturally and seemed to me so compelling that I prepared to expect the same solution in all cases of fetishism. When I announce that the fetish is a substitute for the penis, I shall certainly create disappointment; so I hasten to add that it is not a substitute for any chance penis, but for a particular and quite special penis that had been extremely important in early childhood but had later been lost. That is to say, it should normally have been given up, but the fetish is precisely designed to preserve it from extinction. To put it more plainly: the fetish is a substitute for the woman's (the mother's) penis that the little boy once believed in and—for reasons familiar to us—does not want to give up. ("Fetishism," 152–153)

The fetish is now always a substitute for the penis, in particular the penis the child believes the mother possesses. The fetish operates, in this fashion, as a preservation of loss but also a denial of reality, since the mother never possessed the phallus (154). The 1927 essay integrates Freud's earlier thinking with his now fully developed castration theory. He links fetishism and castration through the mechanism of psychic splitting; the creation of a fetish splits the object of desire. The external reality is denied (the woman has a vagina not a penis), but also replaced in the fetish; the fantasy now becomes the psychic reality.

Although Freud comes to the above insights in the mid-1920s, he has already prepared the foundation as early as the 1910 revision of *The Three Essays on the Theory of Sexuality*. During the time when he writes the 1910 footnotes Freud writes a remarkable, but often overlooked essay entitled "Formulations Regarding the Two Principles in Mental Functioning" (1911).[11] In this essay Freud develops the theory that all neurotic individuals seek to escape from some part of reality through a psychic process that denies a painful element of reality:

> The neurotic turns away from reality because he finds it unbearable—either the whole or parts of it. The most extreme type of this alienation from reality is shown in certain cases of hallucinatory psychosis, which aim at denying the existence of the particular event that occasioned the outbreak of insanity (Grieseinger). But actually every neurotic does the same with some fragment of reality. ("Two Principles," 218–226)

Freud places neurosis on a continuum with psychosis, and the essay's strategy is to place normal development on this continuum. What interests me here is that neurosis signifies a partial alienation from reality; my own reading of Freud's text displays perversion as an alienation from the body's genital organization. Neurosis, in the above essay, is a mental alienation from a realistic psychic organization of the external world. Thus, the essay outlines the institution of the reality principle as a secondary process. A full reading of what is one of Freud's richest essays would require many pages, so the following are but some essential points bearing on my argument.

Let's begin by outlining the pleasure principle, which exhibits primary processes. The conflict between two mental principles (pleasure vs. reality) expresses an underlying struggle between ego drives and sexual drives. In the normal individual, the reality principle remains superior, whereas, in the neurotic or perverted individual the sexual/pleasure principle overwhelms the reality principle. The neurotic responds to reality negatively, through illness, and the pervert progressively, through extreme pursuit of pleasure. The essay argues that psychic splitting is inevitable. If sex is the weak spot in civilized life, fantasy is, Freud remarks, the weak spot of our thinking process:

> In the realm of phantasy, repression remains all-powerful; it brings about the inhibitors of ideas in statu nascendi before they can be consciously noticed, should catharsis of them be likely to occasion the release to "pain." This is the weak place of our mental organization, which can be utilized to bring back the supremacy of our pleasure principle thought processes, which had already become rational. (18)

Phantasy making is inextricably linked to sexuality so that the stable ego, in Freud's analysis, is always under siege.

Now let's return via the detour on the splitting of mental processes, to a discussion of splitting exhibited by fetishists. His final analysis of fetishism forcibly locates its genesis within normal, psychic processes. The ego splitting taking place in fetish formation does not differ in any essential fashion from the ego splitting inherent in general mental life; the fetish bridges the normal and abnormal, fantasy and reality. Freud offers no explanation as to why some individuals create a fetish and others do not, because, as I suggest, fetishism is an indispensable ingredient of all sexual behavior.

I end this segment with Freud's movement from ego splitting to affective splitting: "Affection and hostility in the treatment of the fetish—which run parallel with the disavowal and the acknowledgment of castration—are mixed in unequal proportions in different cases so that the one or the other is more clearly recognizable" ("Fetishism," 157). Freud believes that the simultaneous expression of contradictory perceptions: she doesn't have a vagina, she does have a vagina, extends to the simultaneous expression of contradictory feelings: I hate her; I love her. The text moves toward the view that all relationships between the self and others are love/hate relationships whose ambivalence and instability spring from a sexual foundation. He ends the 1927 essay with a brief, but revealing comment on Chinese sexuality. The reverence of the foot in Chinese culture is normal, and Freud's citation implies, for the Occident as well: "Another variant [of affection/hostility], which is also parallel to fetishism in social psychology, might be seen in the Chinese custom of mutilating the female foot and then revering it like a fetish after it has been mutilated. It seems as though the Chinese male wants to thank the woman for having submitted to be castrated (157).

He does not comment on the fact that the Chinese custom represents a male sexual fantasy and conception of beauty that Chinese women must conform to. What the passage does represent is a highly sadistic view of sexuality: I will violate the woman, that is, make her foot fit the shoe, and love her through the violation. Fetishism's affective ambivalence and, at points, sadomasochistic quality moves logically into my final segment, a discussion of sadomasochism, the most complex and difficult, from Freud's perspective, sexual aberration.

Sadomasochism and the Human Spirit

Freud admits quite early that no satisfactory explanation of sadism can be offered. His initial movement into the perversion is consistent with Krafft-Ebing's and other traditional perspectives; he describes sadism as "an aggressive component of the sexual instinct which has become independent and exaggerated and, by displacement, has usurped the leading position." In commenting on masochism Freud repeats the traditional view that masochism is simply sadism turned around on it. Yet he brings up the traditional perspective, in my view, simply to dismiss the interpretation as naïve. The more revealing exploration of sadism–masochism develops out of the following comments about the scopophilic instinct: "In the perversions which are directed towards looking and being looked at, we come across a very remarkable characteristic with which we shall be still more intensely concerned in the aberration that we shall consider next: in these perversions the sexual aim occurs in two forms, an active and a passive one" (*Three Essays*, 23).

Freud's analysis moves from this point forward, in a structural fashion. The relationship between voyeurism/exhibitionism and sadism/masochism is one between activity and passivity; sadism is active and masochism is passive. Freud places such emphasis on sadism/masochism because he interprets the binary opposition as the most basic opposition in human sexual life: "Sadism and masochism occupy a special position among the perversions, since the contrast between activity and passivity which lies behind them is among the universal characteristics of sexual life" (*Three Essays*, 25).

The most startling discovery Freud makes in his investigation of sadism/masochism is that the binary opposition active/passive exists within a single individual. He makes quite clear that sadism cannot be separated from masochism, for the two sexual tendencies are a binary opposition within a single sign (here the human individual). Unable to explain the presence of a binary opposition within one individual, Freud collapses the opposition into a theory of bisexuality, which he suggests is the biological foundation of the contradictory impulses:

> We find, then, that certain among the impulses to perversion occur regularly as pairs of opposites; and this, taken in conjunction with material which will be brought forward later, has a high theoretical significance. It is, moreover, a suggestive fact that the existence of the pair of opposites formed by sadism and masochism cannot be attributed merely to the element of aggressiveness. We should rather be inclined to connect the simultaneous presence of these opposites with the opposing masculinity and femininity which are combined in bisexuality—a contrast which often has to be replaced in psychoanalysis by that between activity and passivity. (26)

The unity presupposed by biological bisexuality, however, is a myth. Bisexuality signifies another binary opposition: masculinity/femininity, which is then reinterpreted by Freud as activity/passivity. The transforming power of the activity/passivity opposition signifies many other binary opposition, such as loving/being loved, and love–hate/indifference (hating is, of course, an active process like loving, and the proper binary opposition would be indifference). In the 1915 essay, "The Instincts and Their Vicissitudes," Freud places the basic binary opposition of activity/passivity as one of three basic oppositions governing mental life.[12]

Reality model	Subject	Object
Economic model	Pleasure	Unpleasure
Biological model	Active	Passive

The binary opposition of activity/passivity symbolized by sadomasochism provides a window into the core of Freud's psychoanalytic thinking.

The following section examines the sadistic component of the polarity. Freud presupposes a prior force, a constant movement of energy, which generates all binary oppositions. Freud calls this force instinct, a frontier concept, but the force the instinct represents cannot be conceptualized. The emergence of instinct represents a biological process connecting the body to the mind (note above that activity/passivity is the biological, hence the original, antithesis).

In the original moment the body constitutes the human organism's world, and the organism's basic instinct is self-preservation. The organism experiences a source of stimulation and tension from within the body and also an assault of stimuli from the outside world. Freud characterizes an instinct as the internal, somatic force: "An instinct, on the other hand [contrasted to a stimulus], never operates as a force giving a momentary impact but always a constant one" ("Instincts," 118). Thus an organism always experiences the double play of internal and external forces.

The organism's goal is to reduce tension and satisfy itself through removal of the stimulus, for the reduction of tension is equated with pleasure and the increase of tension with unpleasure. In the first instance, the organism experiences satisfaction, or the reduction of internal tension, through its own body. Even the mother's breast, in the infant's experience, will be felt as part of the infant's own body. The initial experience of the instincts are what Freud refers to as primary narcissism, the continual production of instinctual demand Freud will later refer to as the ID.[13]

In primary narcissism the mind and body are welded together. The tension arising within the body produced by an outside stimulus is responded to by flight or denial: "External stimuli impose only the single task of withdrawing from them; this is accomplished by muscular movements, one of which eventually achieves that aim and thereafter, being the expedient movement, becomes a hereditary disposition" ("Instincts," 120). In other words, an external threat will also be responded to by flight, which is an instinctual response to a repeated stimulus. Yet the instincts do not just produce a biological reflex action; the internal stimulus is constant and requires complex responses if the organism is to master the stimulus. At the same time, Freud is quick to note that just as internal stimuli produce complex activities directed by the brain, so even the most complicated mental apparatus, that of humans, are subject to basic biological forces (the ID).

The development of the infant to a second stage, recognizing the external world, brings about the birth of objects, differentiation between self and other, and the emergence of affectivity. The object stage exhibits the pattern of sadism/masochism in the form of hate/love. The ego considers all objects with hate since the objects are synonymous with the external world; the object world evokes feelings of unpleasure. The ego either rejects the object or actively attempts to destroy the object in the interest of self-preservation.

Freud's hypothesis is that love develops out of hate, just as masochism develops out of sadism and passivity from activity in descending order with activity as the original moment responding to instinctual forces within the body. Although love develops out of hate (an affective vicissitude) the two necessarily comingle throughout the duration of an individual's life. Freud describes this process in a beautiful metaphor of waves:

> We can divide the life of each instinct into a series of separate and successive waves, each of which is homogenous during whatever period of time it may last, and whose relation to one another is comparable to that of successive lava. We can then perhaps picture the first, original eruption of instinct as proceeding in an unchanged form and undergoing no development at all. The next wave would be modified from the outset—being turned, for instance, from active to passive—and would then, with this new characteristic, be added to the earlier wave, and so on. (131)

In the above sense, masochism will always appear alongside of sadism and love alongside hate.

Two crucial elements must be foregrounded in elucidating Freud's analysis of sadism/masochism. The original moment of sadism or the active stage is not sexual; and the desire to destroy, a manifestation of activity, is connected, Freud states, with the ego's self-preservative instincts: "Psychoanalysis would appear to show that the infliction of pain plays no part among the original purposive action of the instinct. A sadistic child takes no account of whether or not he inflicts pain, nor does he intend to do so" (128). The experience of pain comes only in stage two and with it comes sexuality and fantasy (the narcissistic, reflexive stage).

The best way to grasp the nature of Freud's initial valuation of sadism and the role of masochism in emerging sexuality is through his own case studies of sadomasochism. The preceding discussion of the vicissitudes of sadomasochism or activity/passivity will act as a preface to Freud's important essay: "A Child is Being Beaten: A Contribution to the Study of the Origins of Sexual Perversions." I focus on this essay as the site of Freud's interpretation of sexual pathology, the title of which reinforces Freud's suggestion that sadomasochism is the crux of all sexual perversion.

Freud publishes the essay "A Child is Being Beaten" in 1919, four years after the metapsychological essay "The Instincts and Their Vicissitudes," but simultaneous with his beginning the most important of his metapsychological essays, *Beyond the Pleasure Principle*. The 1915 essay works entirely from hypothesis; he opens the essay with a defense of scientific speculation. Since instincts cannot be observed in themselves, abstraction becomes a basic tool in the science of psychoanalysis. The ideas, "derived from somewhere or other," do not, however, become "the basic concepts of science" unless some empirical data eventually supports the prior hypothesis.

The ideas hypothesized in the 1915 essay are concretized in the "A Child is Being Beaten," essay that derives its information from Freud's clinical practice. The paper "is based on the exhaustive study of six cases (four female and two male)." Freud considers the paper a contribution to the problem of masochism, which will be the focus of *Beyond the Pleasure Principle*, making "A Child is Being Beaten" an essay that marks the transition in Freud's thinking from the problem of sadism to the problem of masochism. And this transition represents a fundamental change in Freud's interpretation of sexuality.

There are three important elements to Freud's initial analysis of the beating fantasy: the sex of the child producing the fantasy, the child being beaten, and the individual doing the beating. The identification of the three individuals is initially unclear:

> The child being beaten is never the one producing the phantasy, but is invariably another child, most often a brother or a sister if there is any. Since this other child, may be a boy or a girl, there is no constant relation between the sex of the child producing the phantasy and that of the child being beaten. The phantasy, thus, is certainly not masochistic. It would be tempting to call it sadistic, but one cannot neglect the fact that the child producing the phantasy is never doing the beating herself. The actual identity of the person doing the beating remains obscure at first, only this much can be established: its is not a child but an adult.[14]

The second important factor in the fantasy concerns the child's family situation or environment. In a familiar dismissal of Binet, Freud points out the inadequacy of the environmental model, for his particular analysands never experienced any traumatic beating or seduction but nonetheless produced sadomasochistic phantasies (180). Finally, temporality plays an important role in the fantasy; although the fantasy comes to the attention of concerned adults during the child's first year of school (age five or six) the fantasy itself, Freud asserts, predates school. The child's witnessing of a teacher hitting/slapping a child brings out an already preexistent fantasy:

> Eventually it becomes possible to establish that the first phantasies of the kind were entertained very early in life: certainly before school age, and not later than in the fifth or sixth year. When the child was at school and saw other children being beaten by the teacher, then, if the phantasies had become dormant, this experience called them up again, or if they were still present, it reinforced them and noticeably modified their content. From that time forward it as "an indefinite number" of children that were being beaten. The influence of the school was so clear that the patients concerned were at first tempted to trace back their beating phantasies exclusively to these impressions of school life, which dated later than their sixth year. But it was never possible for them to maintain that position; the phantasies had already been in existence before. (179–180)

Freud's dating of the fantasy is crucial to his interpretation, for if the fantasy precedes the experience, not only is Binet's theory destroyed, but also external reality no longer plays a central role in the development of sexual perversion. Phantasy or the psychic life becomes primary in Freud's analysis, so when, then, does Freud date the phantasy's appearance?

He makes an interesting parallel between the origin and development of childhood sexuality and the stages of the beating phantasy:

> It is in the years of childhood between the ages of two and four or five that the congenital libidinal factors are first awakened by actual experiences and become attached to certain complexes. The beating phantasies, which are now under discussion, show themselves only towards the end of this period or after its termination. So it may quite well be that they have an earlier history that they go through a process of development that they represent an end product and not an initial manifestation. (184)

What Freud suggests in the speculative passage above is that the fantasies emerge simultaneous with sexuality. Further, the development of childhood sexuality, to which the fantasies are linked, are normal, implying, by extension the inevitability of sadomasochistic sexual fantasies. Since the sadistic component of sadomasochism is independent of sexuality, the beginning of libidinal desire must be attached to the masochistic stage of the beating fantasy. This connection between sexuality and masochism is already explicit in the following passage from the 1915 text:

> A sadistic child takes no account of whether or not he inflicts pain, nor does he intend to do so. But when the transformation into masochism has taken place, the pains are very well fitted to provide a passive masochistic aim; for we have every reason to believe that sensations of pain, like other unpleasant sensations, trench upon sexual excitation and produce pleasurable conditions, for the sake of which the subject will even willingly experience the unpleasure of pain, when once feeling pains has become a masochistic aim, the sadistic aim of causing pains can arise also, retrogressively; for while these pains are inflicted on other people, they are enjoyed masochistically by the subject through his identification of himself with the suffering object. In both cases, it isn't the pain itself, which is enjoyed, but the accompanying sexual excitation—so that this can be done especially conveniently from the sadistic position. The enjoyment of pain would thus be an aim which was originally masochistic, but which can only become an instinctual aim in someone who was originally sadistic. ("Instincts," 128)

Jean Laplanche explicates the above passage from Freud as indicative of masochism's primacy: "Thus, whether what is under discussion is fantasy or sexuality, in both cases the masochistic moment is first. The masochistic fantasy is fundamental, whereas the sadistic fantasy implies an identification with the suffering object, it is within the suffering position that the enjoyment lies."[15]

Laplanche's close reading of the text reveals the contradiction at the heart of Freud's analysis. The sadist's pleasure is, properly speaking, not sadistic; his pleasure comes from assuming, through identification, the masochist's position (passive). Freud's passage can be reformulated by saying that the masochist experiences "real" pleasure in suffering pain and the sadist experiences refracted pleasure. The sadist introjects the suffering object and suffers as he masturbates. Thus, the identification of the sadist with the sexual victim suggests that sadomasochistic pleasure is the foundation of sexuality itself.

Let me now turn to the three clear stages of sadomasochistic phantasy:

1. "My father is beating the child,"
2. "I am being beaten by my father,"
3. "A child is being beaten."

The second stage is of special interest because it is perfectly consistent with Freud's metapsychological scenario regarding the transformation of masochism into sadism. In stage one, the child fantasizing remains outside the fantasy. In stage two, the child enters the fantasy as an actor in the passive role. The child of stage one has been introjected by the, now erotically charged, child in stage two. Freud points out that only with stage two does the fantasy become sexual and promote masturbation. Stage two is, as Freud says, "of an unmistakably masochistic character." The most extraordinary characteristic of stage two, however, is its entirely fantastic existence: "The second phase is the most important and the most momentous of all. But we may say of it in a certain sense that it has never had a real existence. It is never remembered; it had never succeeded in becoming conscious. It is a construction of analysis, but it is no less a necessity on that account" ("A Child is Being Beaten," 185). What Freud actually means is not that the event or experience never had a real existence, but rather that the event does not exist in the individual's conscious life. During phase two the individual represses the experience, and Freud's construction of phase two is an attempt to restore a missing piece in the individual's life history. The above passage, then, forms a perfect compliment to Freud's defense of speculation in "The Instincts and Their Vicissitudes." What in the 1915 essay plays a primary role in a theoretical argument, by 1919 has become the cornerstone of psychoanalytic technique. In fact, by the end of his career, Freud compares psychoanalysis with archaeology: "His (the psychoanalyst) work of construction, or if it is preferred, of reconstruction, resembles to a great extent an archaeologist's excavation of some dwelling place that has been destroyed and buried or of some ancient edifice."[16]

The only real difference between the archaeologist's constructing a building from fragments and the psychoanalyst's constructing of a life story from dreams and free associations, Freud suggests, is that fragments of psychic life are never completely lost in the way a material fragment could be lost (e.g., in fire): "All of the essentials (in psychic life) are preserved, even things that seem completely forgotten are present somehow and somewhere, and have merely been buried and made inaccessible to the subject. Indeed, it may, as we know, be doubted whether any psychical structure can really be the victim of total destruction" (276).

Thus, Freud's discussion of the beating fantasy centers on repression and the subsequent reconstruction of the lost/repressed memory. The fantasy can now be constructed in three stages. In stage one, the child fantasizes the beating of a rival in love. If the father is beating another child the father must love me (the producer of the fantasy). In stage three, or the present, a teacher or father substitute does the beating, and the fantasy brings about masturbatory satisfaction. The repressed material from stage two supplies the power of fantasy. The mother has split the child's incestuous love for the father apart. The child feels guilt over his desire for sexual union with the father and represses the sexual desire by turning it into the masochistic fantasy in which the child receives the punishment he or she deserves from the transgressive desire, but which continues to produce masochistic pleasure. The "I am being beaten" replaces the "I am being loved by my father," that is, the fantasy of having sex with the parent. The beating substitutes for sex. This entire phase exists only in the individual's unconscious. In the following passage Freud makes the connection between guilt and sexuality explicit:

> This being beaten is now a convergence of the sense of guilt and sexual love. It is not only the punishment for the forbidden genital relation, but also the regressive substitute for that relation, from this latter source it derives the libidinal excitation which is from this time forward attached to it, and which finds its outlet in masturbatory acts. Here for the first time we have the essence of masochism.
>
> This second phase—the child's phantasy of having itself beaten by its father—remains unconscious as a rule, probably in consequence of the intensity of the repression. ("A Child is Being Beaten," 189)

The essence of masochism is the fantasy of incestuous sexual relations; the child assumes, in other words, the role of the wife/mother in sexual intercourse with the father. The child imagines sex with the parent through the beating fantasy, as Laplanche remarks: "What is repressed is not the memory, but the fantasy derived from it or subtending it: in this case, not the actual scene in which the father would have beaten another child, but the fantasy of being beaten by the father" (Laplanche, 102).

The masochistic drive is what makes the fantasy a fantasy. Jean Laplance gives, what is to my mind, the most succinct interpretation of Freud's discussion in his analysis of how fantasy is produced:

> To shift to the reflexive [stage two of sadomasochism, above] is not only or necessarily to give a reflexive content to the "sentence" of the fantasy; it is also and above all to reflect the action; internalize it, make it enter oneself as fantasy. To fantasize aggression is to turn it round upon oneself, to regress oneself: such is the moment of autoeroticism, in which the indissolvable bond between fantasies as such, sexuality, and the unconscious is confirmed. (Laplanche, 102)

Laplanche's commentary reinforces my own reading of Freud's thought as it turns from sadism to masochism, which is the moment of fantasy and sexuality that no sooner comes into being than it undergoes repression and enters the unconscious. The only problem with Laplanche's interpretation is that, unlike Freud, he leaves out questions of gender, and fails to sufficiently account for the final section of Freud's essay. A brief examination of this final section of Freud's essay, "A Child is Being Beaten," is necessary to account for the place of gender within the fantasy.

The reader should recall that Freud considers four male cases and two female cases. A comparison of how males as opposed to females experience the fantasy will show the fantasy's asymmetry:

Little Girl's Fantasy
I.   Adult beating child,
II. Father beating self (girl), unconscious phantasy,
III. Father figure beating male child (sadistic), (substitute self),

Little Boy's Fantasy
I.   Adult beating child,
II. Father beating self (boy), unconscious fantasy,
III. Mother beating self,
IV. Mother beating male child (masochistic), (substitute self).

The asymmetrical development of the two fantasies upsets the reader's and Freud's expectations. The boy's fantasy has one additional stage, which corresponds to the second stage of the girl's fantasy.

The content of each fantasy sequence is also different. The little girl replaces herself with a boy child so that the fantasy concludes with a male beating a male child; she removes herself from the fantasy desexualizing the content and giving the fantasy a sadistic form. The male child replaces himself with another boy keeping the fantasy's sexual component alive; however, since the active figure in the male fantasy is a woman, the fantasy remains masochistic:

> In the case of the girl what was originally a masochistic (passive) situation is transformed into a sadistic one by means of repression, and its sexual quality almost effaced. In the case of the boy the situation remains masochistic, and shows a greater resemblance to the original phantasy with its genital significance, since there is a difference of sex between the person beating and the person being beaten. (198–199)

There are important conclusions to be drawn from Freud's reinsertion of gender into the beating fantasy. In the girl's fantasy, masochism is converted into sadism allowing the girl an escape from "the demands of the erotic side of her life altogether" (199). She becomes active, but active in fantasy only. In reality she will remain passive, tied to the father, and ultimately receive a child from the father figure. The boy has a more difficult time escaping the perils of sexuality; he remains tied to the father through the castration complex. In reality the boy will have to move into an active position through work and achievement, but in fantasy he will remain linked to the position of the mother (i.e., passive in receiving intercourse/love from the father). Freud makes this observation with respect to the fantasies of adult men: "For the fact emerges that in their masochistic fantasies, as well as in the performance they go through for their realization, they invariably transfer themselves into the part of a woman; that is to say, their masochistic attitude coincides with a feminine one" (197).

In Freud's reading, to be masochistic is not only to be sexed but also to be feminine. Thus, Freud's essay on sadomasochistic fantasies shows not only the bond between sexuality, phantasy, and the unconscious, but also the inextricability of these associations with gender. The male's sadism is converted into activity in the outer world (either as aggression or work), but his sexuality emerges with masochism.

The direction of Freud's thought brings him directly into a theoretical confrontation with masochism: if masochism is linked with sexuality and sexuality with pleasure then Freud's most fundamental hypothesis, the pleasure principle, comes under question. Freud addresses such a question in the 1924 essay, "The Economic Problem in Masochism": "For if mental processes are governed by the pleasure principle in such a way that their first aim is the avoidance of unpleasure and the obtaining of pleasure, masochism is incomprehensible."[17] Still Freud is unsatisfied with the above explanation of masochism. He considers "feminine masochism" the outer layer of masochism's core, and the original form of masochism erotogenic: "The feminine masochism which we have been describing is entirely based on the primary masochism, on pleasure and pain" (162).

Freud discusses this primal "erotogenic masochism" in *Beyond the Pleasure Principle*. The essay traces the feminine form of masochism to its original point in passivity, then proceeds in a structural analysis of three dimensions of passivity: infantile life, neurosis, and war anxiety. The structural unity Freud discovers in these three apparently disparate forms of passivity leads him to posit the death drive. In his analysis of passivity Freud begins with a presentation of traumatic neurosis. And in analyzing the dreams of patients suffering from this neurosis, he discovers that patients' dreams continually return the patient to the traumatic situation that produced the neurosis. These dreams are always nightmares, with the patient returning time and time again to an experience he wants to escape.

Freud's analysis of dreams occurring in traumatic neurosis lead him to modify his basic interpretation of dreams as wish fulfillments. Individuals ordinarily dream the fulfillment that reality denies. The traumatic dream, however, returns the patient to a terrifying reality: a rape scene, war experience, or the like, and such dreams force the patients to psychically reexperience the most intense unpleasure.

He is able to move from this observation on the dreams of severe neurotics to a more general observation drawn from his entire analytic experience. He points to individuals resistant to the analytic principle. If the goal of analysis is to liberate the patient, through memory, from his past, the resistant patient, failing to remember, that is, bring to consciousness repressed material, must repeat the past (the repressed material remains in the unconscious perpetuating the neurosis): "He [the resistant patient] is obliged to repeat the repressed material as a contemporary experience instead of, as the physician would prefer to see, remembering it as something belonging to the past."[18]

The resistant patient, of course, represents all patients beginning analysis. Through the analytic process of transference, patients relive their past in a fashion that confirms, for the patient, the analyst's interpretation of his past experience. If transference fails, the patient will continue to repeat the past and most likely break off analysis. What strikes Freud as remarkable is how often patients repeat, in the analytic situation, experiences that can only recall pain. The fact that such repetitions occur so frequently suggests their compulsive character. This repetition compulsion must be independent of the pleasure principle precisely because the past experiences are painful: "The compulsion to repeat also recalls from the past experiences which include no possibility of pleasure, and which can never, even long ago, have brought satisfaction even to instinctual impulses which have since been repressed" (*Beyond the Pleasure Principle*, 20).

If the compulsion to repeat also begins with painful experiences, Freud concludes, the instinctual drive must be regressive. He redefines his theory of instincts based on the analysis of repetition compulsions: "It seems, then, that an instinct is an urge inherent in organic life to restore an earlier state of things which the living entity has been obliged to abandon under the pressure of external disturbing forces; that is, it is a kind of organic elasticity, or, to put it another way, the expression of the inertia inherent in organic life" (36).

Freud explores "the earlier state of things" in his famous analysis of a childhood game, for when he turns to examine play, Freud is exploring both a normal and universal behavior. What most interests me in Freud's analysis concerns the child's transformation of himself vis-à-vis the game from a passive role to an active role. The passive situation precedes the active control or mastery of the game: the child repeats experiences of unpleasure. On one level play represents an activity independent of the pleasure principle; although the child may be avenging himself on the mother by sending her away, the game's deeper significance suggests the child's desire to merge with the mother. The game, on this level, symbolizes a regressive trend apparent even at the age of one-and-a-half. Freud extrapolates from the child's play rhythms of sending off and returning the very rhythm of sexuality in its sadistic and masochistic forms:

> One group of instincts rushes forward so as to reach the final aim of life as swiftly as possible; but when a particular stage in the advance has been reached, the other groups jerk back to a certain point to make a fresh start and so prolong the journey. And even though it is certain that sexuality and the distinction between the sexes did not exist when life began, the possibility remains that the instincts which were later to be described as sexual may have been in operation from the very first, and it may not be true that it was only at a later time that they started upon their work of opposing the activities of the "ego-instincts". (41)

The struggle between two groups of instincts symbolizes the struggle within sexuality itself (a single, primal instinct) through the division of the sexes into an active male and passive female. Just as the child wants, through play, to return to the mother, the sexual drive similarly represents a drive to return to an original unity in which the two sexes would be a single being. The only explanation Freud can offer for his hypothesis is Aristophanes's myth of the origin of love offered in Plato's *Symposium*:

> Science has so little to tell us about the origin of sexuality that we can liken the problem to a darkness into which not so much as a ray of hypothesis has penetrated. In quite a different region, it is true, we do meet with such a hypothesis; but it is of so fantastic a kind—a myth rather than a scientific explanation—that I should not venture to produce it here, were it not that it fulfills precisely the one condition whose fulfillment we desire. For it traces the origin of an instinct to a need to restore an earlier state of things. (57)

Thus, a poetic myth becomes the mode of discovering the deeper significance of sexuality. In this passage Freud most emphatically merges the empirical observation of the repetition compulsion with total speculation producing the insight that the origin of an instinct is the drive "to restore an earlier state of things." What comes to represent a masochistic aim, repeating a painful experience, appears as an active, that is, sadistic instinct.

The unifying factor, in Freud's theory, is the experience of passivity; and my argument has been stressing the intricate connection between masochism and sexuality. Thus, the organism's regressive, self-destructive movement must be experienced as sexually pleasurable. Freud made just this point in concluding his essay "The Economic Problem in Masochism." From an ontogenetic perspective the masochistic trend pulls the individual back into the phase of infantile sexuality, while necessarily disrupting ego structures. Leo Bersani makes this developmental aspect of sexuality the focus for his discovery of the masochistic foundation of sexuality:

> Sexuality would be that which is intolerable to the structured self. From this perspective, the distinguishing feature of infancy would be its susceptibility to the sexual. The polymorphous perverse nature of infantile sexuality would be a function of the child's vulnerability to being shattered into sexuality. Sexuality is a particularly human phenomenon in the sense that its very genesis may depend on the decalage, or gap, in human life between the quantities of stimuli to which we are exposed and the development of ego structures capable of resisting, in Freud's terms, of binding those stimuli. The mystery of sexuality is that we seek to get rid of this shattering tension but also to repeat, even to increase it. In sexuality, satisfaction is inherent in the painful need to find satisfaction. It is therefore not a question of deciding whether or not cruelty—or more specifically now, masochism, as the "ground" of all the forms of the cruel—operates independently of all erotogenic zones, or even seeking out the "mutual influences" to which cruelty and sexual development would somehow both be subject. Rather, sexuality—at least in the mode in which it is constituted—could be thought of as a tautology for masochism.[19]

Freud's earlier claim that sexuality represents the individual's weak spot finds its most powerful support in the analysis of the repetition compulsion. Sexuality emerges with masochism, which pulls the individual back into the chaos of infantile sexuality. Therefore, masochism is no longer an aberration but rather an inherent part, a tragic flaw, in human sexuality. The force of Freud's argument leads him to a revelation about his work and the positing of a primary masochism:

> Clinical observations led us at the time to the view that masochism, the component instinct which is complementary to sadism, must be regarded as sadism that has been turned round upon the subject's own ego. But there is no difference in principle between an instinct turning from an object to the ego and its turning from the ego to an object—which is the new point now under discussion. Masochism, the turning round of the instinct upon the subject's own ego, would in that case be a return to an earlier phase of the instinct's history, a regression. The account that was formerly given of

masochism requires emendation as being too sweeping in one respect: there might be such a thing as primary masochism—a possibility that I had contested at that time. (*Beyond the Pleasure Principle*, 54–55)

We can now understand why sadism/masochism occupies the privileged position in Freud's analysis of sexual pathologies. This duality returns in his analysis of the relationship between the super ego (sadistic) and ego (masochistic), but most important is the general division, not between the sexes, but between mastery of understanding and disruptive instincts. Bersani bears out my analysis in a brilliant passage linking the masochistic experience to Freud's entire project in *The Three Essays on the Theory of Sexuality*:

> Sexuality is the temporal substratum of sex, although the teleological argument of the *Three Essays* represents an attempt to rewrite sexuality as history and as story by reinstating structures of organ—and object—specificity. Freud's work is a textual recapitulation of the psychoanalytic body's existence. The phases of infantile sexuality and the climactic Oedipus complex give a narrative intelligibility to a text otherwise tormented, so to speak, by knots of tautological and self-canceling formulations. In the same way, the ego will domesticate, structure, and narrate those waves of excitement, which simultaneously endanger and yet also protect the first years of human life. That process is described and exemplified in the textual body—in corpore freudiano—of psychoanalytic discourse. (Bersani, 1989: 40)

Psychoanalysis attempts to give narrative order to life history (i.e., to master, to understand the other) and the experience of sexuality resists such order. Freud laments the inadequacy of psychoanalytic language in understanding the nature of instinctual life: "The deficiencies in our description would probably vanish if we were already in a position to replace the psychological terms by physiological or chemical ones" (*Beyond the Pleasure Principle*, 60). The irony of this statement will not escape Freud; *Beyond the Pleasure Principle* is a biological myth speaking psychoanalytic truths. If the above lament will be answered by modern biology's and neurophysiology's scientific descriptions of the mind's operations, Freud's own work in 1895 already attempted and discarded such an impossible dream. Freud concludes the above lament in a half-ironic vein: "It is true that they too are only part of a figurative language, but it is one with which we have been familiar and which is perhaps a simpler one as well" (60).

One can sympathize with Freud's frustration but should not take his desire for simplicity too seriously. As he remarks, even a biological language remains within the play of figuration; language can never adequately represent the bodily forces. Ricoeur points to this interdiction between the body and the textual body as the essence of Freud's theoretical enterprise: "Psychoanalysis never confronts one with bare forces, but always with forces in search of meaning; this link between force and meaning makes instinct a psychical reality, or more exactly, the limit concept at the frontier between the organic and the psychical."[20]

Krafft-Ebing was content with a biological explanation of sexuality; and Freud began where Krafft-Ebing left off, only to return to the insolvable play between the body and the psyche. If Freud yearned for simplicity he did so after twenty years of psychoanalytic thinking; he realized the impossibility of an ultimate, deep truth, either psychological or biological. Thus psychoanalysis itself became the frontier science moving between the physical and psychical, and pushing the possibility of knowledge to its limits where only myth can still speak. Wilhelm Reich would literally take this frontier science to the threshold of myth. In fact, Reich, as chapter 2 demonstrates, created his own sexual mythology.

2. The Social Radical: Reich and Sexual Utopia ❧

Psychoanalysis ought to be song of life or else be worth nothing at all. It ought, practically, to teach us to sing.

Gilles Deleuze and Felix Guattari, *Anti-Oedipus*

REICH'S OEDIPUS COMPLEX

Steven Marcus has remarked that Wilhelm Reich ends his career as a "latter-day member of the visionary company."[1] Just as Robert Langbaum considers D.H. Lawrence a late romantic, Marcus places Reich toward the end of a romantic tradition, and most critics of Reich are happy to comply with this view of Reich as a "prophet in the wilderness," if they even grant him this Blakean designation. How does an apparently modern figure such as Reich, who is inevitably thought of as the first radical come to be conceptualized as a romantic? To some extent Reich's own grandiose style and oppositional nature contribute to his alienation. He was expelled from both the International Psychoanalytic Association and the Communist Party, and ended his long career by organizing his own community in Forest Hills, New York, and then later in Rangley, Maine. Reich did not lack admirers and, he was, partly romantic in his devotion to the natural world and his holistic vision. Like D.H. Lawrence (see chapter 3), he searched for an organic community as an alternative to modern industrial society.

Reich is radical in the revolutionary sense; he wants to change society and the change must involve a revolution of values. He must, as Rieff describes, take on a spiritual role and sacramental language to produce his utopian visions.[2] This chapter describes the core of Reich's revolutionary vision, which will be presented against a Freudian backdrop, for Reich always thought of himself as Freud's true heir.

One obstacle to understanding Reich is the historical failure to take him seriously. The critics' presuppositions are frequently extreme, making Reich particularly difficult to approach on neutral ground. Further, his flamboyant lifestyle helped promote the critical tendency to read his work from a biographical perspective. My project does not seek to uncover some ultimate true Reich, but rather to bring out a fuller, more complex sense of the man than his critics present. Critics, positive and negative, divide Reich's life and work into clear-cut entities and use these divisions to either praise or dismiss Reich's work.[3] Severe critics like Charles Rycroft divide the early work from the late work: the post-analytic work becomes embarrassing nonsense; the work of a bitter, paranoid mind. Reich's followers, such as Raknes and Boadealla, attempt to rescue the late Reich at the expense of the early Reich.[4] Others, led by Bertall Ollman, who focus exclusively on the Marxist Reich, neglect the fact that his radicalism, the orgasm theory, predates his Marxism by ten years.[5] Reich's career charts many paths: psychoanalysis, Marxism, character analysis, vegetative therapy, and finally orgone therapy, and all of these phases work as part of a complex integrated whole expressing the vision that body and soul are one.

Reich's own work in sexology follows the biological tradition that Freud's work inherits. He reiterates Freud's rejection of Jung and Adler on grounds of their rejection of libido theory, and eventually takes up, what he considers to be, the true Freudian theory and asserts himself as a disciple. In his own eyes, Reich will remain Freud's disciple to the end. It is important to note that Reich's intellectual relationship to Freud emphasizes the importance of libido in human activity and thought. Reich, like Freud, is trained in natural science; he believes entirely in the libido's biological basis. For Reich, the libido theory forms the core of psychoanalysis; he concurs with Freud that to reject the libido theory is to reject psychoanalysis. And Reich, the natural scientist, criticizes the sociological analysis of sexuality; he destroys the false opposition between drive and society as a simplistic myth. For Reich, socialization happens at birth and his developmental perspective always includes a social psychological dimension.[6]

Reich maintains that psychoanalysis abandoned the libido theory following Freud's publication of *The Ego and the Id* in 1923. For Reich, "ego psychology" operated in a mechanical fashion, which turned libido theory into a figure of speech.[7] Reich interprets the turn in Freud's thought as a response to external pressures, including the rebellion of Jung and Adler, and later, Freud's own identity crisis. He believes that Freud suffered a tremendous conflict between his Jewish origin and his identification with German culture (*Reich Speaks of Freud*, 60–61), and with the growth of National Socialism Freud's internal conflict turns to crisis. Finally, Freud develops cancer of the jaw, and Reich sees the cancer as directly related to Freud's emotional turmoil. In Reich's interpretation, disarray in the International Psychoanalytic Association, the Nazi terror, and then cancer all contribute to Freud's sense of tragic resignation. Reich does not see the movement toward ego psychology as a fundamental change in Freud's thinking. He believes that Freud modifies the libido theory in resignation; weary not only of the burden he carries, but also in preparation for his own death.

In the 1920s Reich takes up the libido theory, almost single-handedly, to carry through Freud's most fundamental vision. Here Reich receives the impetus for his radical politics. He also begins his character analytic work and speculations on cancer biopathy. Reich speculates that Freud's cancer of the jaw makes literal his struggle with language, and, subsequently, Reich then begins to interpret emotional illness somatically.

Ironically, in 1927 Reich undergoes a serious battle with tuberculosis. The same year, or so, Freud rejects Reich's request for personal analysis. On one level, Reich's TB, which follows Freud's professional rejection of him, is psychosomatic. Nonetheless, following a sanitarium stay Reich emerges ready to carry out his own historical mission independent of Freud. Freud's rejection catalyzes Reich's personal liberation, and in 1927 he organizes a preventive psychiatric movement. Thus, the mid-1920s bring about a complex convergence surrounding Reich's relationship with Freud.

In summary, Reich's relationship to Freud operates on two continuous levels. He is very attached to Freud's libido theory and will defend this libido theory to his career's end; he also looks at Freud as a father figure. The combination of Reich's personal attachment to Freud and his professional interest in Freud's theory of sexuality plays itself out in Reich's own intensely experienced Oedipal conflict.

Reich describes his childhood as an early initiation into sexuality, and reports incidents of "dry intercourse" with a nurse at age four.[8] He describes feelings of excitement watching people copulate, and he talks in detail about masturbating over thoughts about his mother. When he is twelve Reich discovers his mother having a sexual affair with his young tutor. (One can sense Reich's vicarious identification with the tutor throughout his description of the incident.) Reich reveals his mother's affair to the father, and their marriage falls apart. The mother commits suicide and the father catches TB by deliberately standing in water. He subsequently dies of TB, as does Reich's brother.

Reich's career hinges on this early experience.[9] His advocacy of childhood sexuality and the sexual rights of youth are a partial result of his own premature sexual exposure and also an overcompensation of his own guilt about his parents' suicides. And Reich's later scorn of established rules follows his early exposure to sexual transgression. But most important for this essay is how Reich's childhood exhibits Freud's theoretical work. Reich's attraction to Freud launches him on a path of self-discovery. When Freud rejects Reich's request for personal analysis during his recovery from TB, at Davos he loses his symbolic father. From this point on Reich becomes increasingly radical, which is to say uncompromising in his advocacy of the libido theory. He establishes himself as a symbolic father with respect to his own followers. With this complex set of personal and professional events in mind, I now turn to Reich's orgasm theory.

LIBIDO UNBOUND

Reich's immediate interest in libido theory is that of a natural scientist: "With the libido theory, psychology hooked on to natural science for the first time in the history of science" (*Reich Speaks of Freud*, 126). He is interested in Freud's attempt, represented in the *Project for a Scientific Psychology* of 1895, to construct a physiological psychology.[10] Fundamental to Freud's biological vision and Reich's elaboration of the scientific system are Freud's two theses. Freud's quantitative thesis states what is now called the homeostatic position.[11] In the primary process, energy presses for immediate discharge, whereas the secondary process stores energy for future actions. The primary process is a force driving for release of tension; however, reality (the discrepancy between desire/drive and perception) necessitates the storage of energy in memory neurons. The secondary process modifies the primary process in the direction of the least possible tension. Thus, the theory elaborates a complex control mechanism through which the biological system maintains its homeostatic status, that is, self-regulation.

Freud's second thesis describes his neuron theory. The essential point, for my perspective, is the role of contact barriers. The resistance to energy's flow by the contact barriers retains or binds energy in mnemic cells (U), and the ego develops in accord with this bound energy. In other words, the ego stores energy (the buildup of excitation) until a real object presents itself to consciousness. In such a model, pleasure must be delayed gratification. The secondary process's biological ego parallels the quantitative model of regulated energy: the ego promotes regulation, that is, resistance to force and energy conservation. In contrast, the primary process follows an automatic reflex action belonging to infantile states (i.e., pre-ego, hallucinatory, and psychotic).

Reich pays close attention to Freud's early work on anxiety. The following passage from Freud's "Sexuality in the Aetiology of Neuroses" provides the spark for Reich's work in the 1920s: "In the anxiety-neurosis there may regularly be found conditions relating to the sexual life which all have in common such as coitus interruptus, abstinence with strong libido, so-called frustrated excitation, and so forth."[12] Reich takes up Freud's psychological theory and extrapolates an alternative explanation for anxiety formation. He conceptualizes energy as entirely sexual, and pursues a quantitative approach to libido. Freud, it will be remembered, distinguishes libido from the general circulation of energy on a qualitative basis. In distinguishing between libidinal and other forms of psychic energy, Freud is giving expression to the presumption that the sexual processes occurring in the organism are differentiated from the nutritive processes by a *special chemistry* (Freud, *Three Essays*, 85). Contrarily, Reich maintains that all energy is libido. He retains a qualitative dimension to analysis only in that quality is pure quantity; that is, the undisturbed flow of energy from the body outward. Reich reverses the role that contact barriers play in Freud's systems. For Freud, contact barriers promote ego growth and reality testing; for Reich, contact barriers block the flow of energy, stagnate "ego growth" and promote emotional and physical problems, that is, instability. Although in both Freudian and Reichian systems the secondary process evolves out of the primary process, in Reich's thought the secondary process is unnecessary and unnatural.[13] Reich translates "contact barriers" into somatic tension. The key point is that Reichian analysis strives to unlock the biological core and Freudian theory seeks to modify the primary process.

Reich promotes the primary process as the key to mental health. His reinterpretation of Freud is clear even in his earliest sexology papers, where he begins with a scientific description of sexual activity that anticipates the work of Masters and Johnson.[14] Reich's observation on the temporal dysfunction of male and female orgasm (i.e., one partner climaxing before the other partner) prompts him to reinterpret the temporal dysfunction as unnatural. He then interprets the dysfunction in orgasms as a product of the split between affect and desire, which an emotional connection between partners can heal.

Reich's description of sexual activity as a primary process brings me back to his modification of Freud's energy concept and its relationship to anxiety-neurosis. In Reich's system, energy pushes toward discharge. This pulsation of energy begins in the organism's biological core and moves through the body to the genitals, where it must be discharged into the external world. Thus, the orgasm formula: Tension>Charge>Discharge>Relaxation (*FO*, 272), becomes fundamental in Reich's theory. Any resistance to the libido's flow contributes to the formation of secondary systems, frustration, and anxiety production. Reich renames Freud's diagnosis of "anxiety neurosis" and "psychoneurosis" as "stasis anxiety," which describes immobile or locked up libido. This trapped libido or stasis anxiety produces all forms of psychic disturbance: "*The severity of any kind of psychic distur-bance is in direct relation to the severity of the genital disturbance. The prospects of cure and the success of the cure are directly dependent upon the possibility of establishing the capacity for full genital gratification*" (*FO*, 96).

At the heart of Reich's orgasm theory is blocked libido. Orgasm, in his theory, becomes the realization of health. Reich defines orgasm in a very specific fashion: It must be a complete and involuntary surrender of both partners to the sexual experience. The ability to achieve true orgasm is a function of an individual's orgastic potency: "*Orgastic potency is the capac-ity for surrender to the flow of biological energy, free of any inhibitions; the capacity to discharge completely the dammed-up sexual excitation through involuntary pleasurable contractions of the body*" (*FO*, 102). Reich feels that neurosis can only be treated through the establishment of orgastic potency. The orgastically potent individual, whom Reich will later name the genital character, lives in harmony with his or her biological core. Such biological living forces a radical understanding of ego: "The ability to focus the entire affective personality upon the orgastic experience, in spite of any contra-dictions, is another characteristic of orgastic potency" (*FO*, 108–109). The ego is submerged in the body, and Reich's perspective leaves little role for the superego. Indeed, Reich's orgasm theory maintains that body and mind are unified in the organism's biological core. I use the word organism pur-posefully, for the genital character lives in unity with the environment: "Orgastic potency constitutes the biological primal and basic function which man has in common with all living organisms. All experiencing of nature is derived from this function or from the longing for it" (*FO*, 108). Later Reich will expand this unity to include the cosmos as well.

This biological vision radicalizes Freud in a fundamental way. The orgastically potent person achieves orgasm through the orgasm reflex, that is, involuntary bodily movement, and this automatic reflex action signals the primary process. Reich advocates what to Freud would be tantamount to pursuing chaos as a therapeutic goal: reaching the primary process allows the organism's biosystem to express itself naturally and spontaneously. Man is unified with nature, the body with spirit and mind.

The orgasm theory becomes the nucleus for his entire oeuvre. Reich's clinical development and vision regarding a unified mind–body theory (1922–1926) began with his work on the orgasm. Reich's presupposition of man's essential unified nature along with his belief that the primary process is directly accessible to therapy led him to focus his work on the body.[15] To begin with, the organism's biological core always strives toward release. This plasmatic movement toward release is not simply a release into nothing, but an attempt to establish contact with what is outside the organism. The contact can be with another individual, an object, or anything other than the organism itself. In sexuality, the organism strives for contact with the opposite sex. In childbirth the baby strives for contact with the mother. The movement is reciprocal, as in the mother's desire for contact with the child. In a late essay on the living orgonome, Reich articulates a model of biological thriving that characterizes his general biological model of the life process: "*Orgastic longing, which plays such an enormous role in animal life, now appears to express this 'striving beyond one's self,' this 'yearning' to escape from the narrow confines of one's own organism.*"[16] He understands emotion (affect) as the organism's natural mode of expression; emotion moves outward as spontaneous expression and communication of an organism's needs. The blocking or holding back of emotion signifies the organism's pulling back into itself, away from contact and, therefore, producing anxiety.

An interesting facet in Reich's analysis of emotion is its resistance to language.[17] If emotion is a natural expression of biological processes, emotion cannot be described or analyzed within language. Reich's departure from Freud evidences itself in this account of language. If the living organism expresses itself in a fundamentally pre-linguistic style, then any therapeutic attempt to work on the neurotic or restrained organism must operate in a nonverbal fashion.

When the organism does not strive, that is, turns back into itself, another self develops replacing or, more accurately, superimposing itself on the true (living) self. This static, anxious, nonliving self develops a character structure to assist its false, that is, non-healthy, lonely, living style; he or she resists contact with the world. When the biological flow resists discharge or expression, the retention of energy producing anxiety must express itself somewhere within the body. Character formation functions somewhat differently than Freudian expression:

> By character, we mean here not only the sum total of all the ego shapes in the way of typical modes of reaction, i.e., modes of reaction characteristic of one specific personality. By character, in short, we mean an essentially dynamically determined factor manifest in a person's characteristic demeanor: walk, facial expression, stance, manner of speech, and other modes of behavior. This character of the ego is molded from elements of the outer world, from prohibitions, instinctual inhibitions, and the most varied forms of identifications. Thus, the material elements of the character armor have their origin in the outer world, in society. (*CA*, 171)

The formation of a character trait resolves the symptom but replaces the symptom by a trait resistant to treatment. The relation between character and repression can be observed in the following process:

> The necessity of repressing instinctual demands initiates the formation of the character. Once the character has been molded, however, it economizes upon repression by absorbing instinctual energies—which are free floating in the case of ordinary repressions—into the character formation itself. The formation of a character trait, therefore, indicates that a conflict involving repression has been resolved: either the repressive process itself is rendered unnecessary or an inchoate repression is transformed into a relatively rigid, ego-justified formation. Hence, the processes of the character formation are wholly in keeping with the tendency of the ego to unify the strivings of the psychic organism. These facts explain why repressions that have led to rigid character traits are so much more difficult to eliminate that those, for example, which produce a symptom. (*CA*, 172)

In all cases Reich argues that armoring emerges from a conflict between instinct and the social world. Additionally, Reich calls attention to: "the stages of development during which the character-forming conflicts occur; and which instincts are involved" (*CA*, 160). Character resistances "derive their special character not from their content but from the specific mannerisms of the person analyzed" (*CA*, 45). Consequently, therapy requires attention to the form at least as much as the content of the patient's illness. In affect, a person's everyday self becomes a defensive structure for interacting with the world. Therapy can no longer simply focus on making the unconscious conscious because the embedded character resistance wards off each new piece of unconscious material. Character analysis had to move beyond a topographical and dynamic approach, in Reich's thinking, to an economic perspective. "It is quite clear that the patient suffers from an inadequate, disturbed libido economy; the normal biological functions of his or her sexuality are in part completely negated—both contrary to the average healthy person" (*CA*, 12). Reich builds his comprehensive character typology around this distinction between the healthy or genital character and the unhealthy or neurotic character.

The table below graphically summarizes the chapter in *Character Analysis* entitled "The Genital Character and the Neurotic Character" (169–193).

Neurotic character	*Genital character*
Rigid Armor; Blocked contact with world	Flexible Armor; open contact with the world
Sickness	Health

(Continued)

Neurotic character	Genital character
Unregulated libido economy	Regulated libido economy
Inadequate binding of anxiety	Adequate binding of anxiety
Pre-genital fixation: oral eroticism, anal eroticism, voyeurism etc.	Resolved Oedipal complex
Id conflicts with Superego	Id harmonizes with Superego
Ego ideal deeply divided from ego	Ego ideal approximates the ego
Reaction formations predominate	Sublimation predominates
Rigid moral code	Post ethical sexuality
Guilt mechanisms	Sublimated aggressions and increased social cooperation
Compulsory monogamy or asceticism	Voluntary monogamy or polygamy
Success = the performance of masculinity	Success = narcissistic gratification

Although each of the neurotic character types present differentiated symptoms the therapeutic goal remains dissolution of the respective characters' armor and the restoration or establishment of genital potency. If a patient's armor cannot be loosened and his or her character restructured, then the analysts must help the patient obtain a greater ego syntonic armor, that is, a greater openness to the world. The genital character's libido on the other hand flows openly to the object world and this character lives a self-regulated life:

> As far as our clinical practice is conceived, there can be no longer be any doubt every successful analytic treatment, i.e. one which succeeds in transforming the neurotic character structure into a genital character structure, demolished the moral arbiters and replaces them with the self regulation of action based on a sound libido economy. (*CA*, 185)

The successful character analysis requires dissolution of armor, the development of the fear of orgastic contact and "complete overcoming of the orgastic inhibition and establishment of totally uninhibited, involuntary movement at the moment of climax" (*CA*, 322). Despite his modifications of Freud's techniques Reich maintains, at least into the early 1930s, that character analysis remains consistent with psychoanalysis, "Freud's libido theory, unrestricted and consistently thought through, is the only legitimate foundation for psychoanalytic characterology" (*CA*, 193).

Nonetheless, by 1934 Reich's analysis had, in fact, moved away from Freud's psychoanalytic foundation and character analysis had metamorphosed into vegetotherapy.[18] This theoretical modification of character analysis represents six points of departure from Freudian psychoanalysis. One: Reich describes the role of secondary emotions: for example, desire gives way to rage. Aggression is reactive and unnatural. Two: Blocked energy is expressed through the body. Anger, for example, can be expressed through a stiff neck. Three: forces from the outside world block energy. Four: Character traits develop as an entire defensive character structure replacing individual symptoms. Five: Character structure and disorders develop in response to pressure from the social world. Six: Treatment must focus on both the human body and the social body.

Reich's post-analytic technique builds on his theoretical model, and he eventually replaces Freud's free association with somatic interpretation. Reich reads the individual's distorted affect through the patient's bodily attitude, postures, and movements. He outlines an entire layering of character defenses. The blocked energy lodges in some part of his body; for example, the urge to cry or let out emotion becomes bound in the neck producing muscular anxiety and expressing itself verbally through rage and somatically through a stiff neck. Reich divides the body into seven major segments where the organism's affective life can become trapped. Therapy unlocks the blocked energy, loosening the muscular armor and releasing the primary drive toward spontaneous movement and growth. Reich makes language concrete and provides affective life with the language of natural science; therapy, then, must also be concrete. Consequently, Reich extends Ferenczi's active therapeutic techniques to their most direct application through massage and breathing exercises.[19] The liberation of energy restores the individual's true, naturally expressive self.

The second and third editions of *Character Analysis* indicate Reich's increasing departure from his psychoanalytic roots. When vegetotherapy becomes biotherapy Reich leaves psychology behind. Nonetheless, Reich's late work in orgonomy follows, logically, his development of the orgasm theory and character structure. He elucidates the opposition between active and reactive living over and over. The active individual or organism (Reich compares humans to jellyfish) is orgastically potent (genital), and strives toward uninterrupted contact with the world. Reactive organisms (neurotic characters) retreat from the world into a character armor existing in a contactless state of being (i.e., dead, lonely, immobile). Reich connects the active/reactive antithesis to the cancer cell and expands this antithesis to explain God and the devil.[20] A cancer cell is constrictive (i.e., reactive) and sensitive to invasion by toxic substances, and the devil is a reactive character formation (a secondary drive).

The major difference between Reich's early and late works is his discovery of orgone energy. In his late work, natural somatic drives begin in the cosmos and move through the natural world. Thus, orgonomy brings a metaphysical dimension to Reich's analytic and scientific work. Although he attempts to give his metaphysical work a scientific basis through inventions like the orgone accumulator, he does not achieve much credibility.[21] Much of his late work remains scientifically naïve, and the work on cancer, as Sontag shows, can, at times, be morally repugnant.[22] Nonetheless, Reich's work in the area of child development and character structure is revolutionary and groundbreaking.

The groundbreaking work of the Orgonomic Infant Research Center coincides with Reich's savagely ridiculed work with the orgone accumulator.[23] And his work on infant development anticipates the work of contemporary, pediatric and child research experts like T. Berry Brazelton, by some twenty years.[24] Reich's therapeutic approach to growing emotional disturbances is preventive. The preventive technique begins in the infant's first three months; and orgonomic intervention happens during the birth experience. Reich begins with the emotional situation of pregnancy; he then attempts to construct a positive birth environment, which must be followed up by positive childrearing practices. A negative birth environment forces the infant into reactive living from the start, producing compulsive, at-risk development. Thus, Reich's interventions are neonatal, taking place both on an individual scale, that is, treating the infant through orgonomic first aid (basically a caring environment) and on a social scale, that is, the entire birth environment must be changed to create healthy childbirth. He promotes frequent contact between mother and infant and less use of impersonal nurseries.

Anticipating future research, Reich locates emotional difficulty in the lack of *contact* between mother and child.[25] Poor mother–infant contact creates a condition of "anorgomin," where the child develops in a field lacking positive, warm contact and parental modeling. The orgonomist, whether nurse, doctor, or childcare worker, must learn to read the infant's language in an effort to restore its positive contact with the world. In a dramatic passage on "The Source of the Human No!" Reich describes modern society's destruction of the infant's vitality at the moment the baby meets the shock of life (*Children of the Future*, 3–4). The infant responds to life with a cry, and the world responds to the infant by taking away its mother and putting the baby on a fixed feeding schedule. Contactlessness, emotional vulnerability, and forced docility begin at birth.

Behind Reich's presentation of the anorgomic infant rests the possibility of change. He believes in early intervention, and toward his career's end comes to believe that only early intervention at birth can promote healthy infant growth. By healthy growth Reich means spontaneous, natural growth, free of the severe parental oppression, which frequently follows the hospital's oppressive structure and is replicated in the oppressive, rigid social–educational system. Mother and child contact creates the bonding relationship essential for healthy growth; this relationship is always reciprocal, with the mother and infant participating in an interpersonal dance. Reich's theory presupposes an active, striving infant at birth that the world oppresses and turns into something other than its true self. This belief in the active infant reverses the traditional concept of the infant as a passive body molded by society. "This infant is not, as so many erroneously believe, an empty sack or a chemical machine into which everybody and anybody can pour his or her special ideas of what a human being ought to be. It brings with it an enormously productive and adaptive energy system which, out of its own resources, will make contact with its environment and begin to shape that environment according to *its needs*" (*Children of the Future*, 20).

Reich's theory of contact becomes Bowlby's theory of attachment.[26] So what begins in orgasm theory as the striving for mature contact in love, concludes, before his arrest and persecution, as attachment theory, the original striving for contact with the world in the form of the mother's warm body and caring gaze.

I return to Reich's post-analytic work at this chapter's conclusion. Now, I want to explore Reich's revolutionary embrace of Marxism, an embrace, he appears to largely abandon after 1934. Reich's social-oriented sex-economic work redirects Freud's intrapsychic model to the psyche's infiltration by a complex, highly stratified, and historically conditioned social world. Reich rejects the Oedipal complex and turns therapy into a radical praxis that anticipates the work of Gilles Deleuze, Felix Guattari, and R.D. Laing in the 1960s.

A MARXIST THERAPY

Reich's turn toward infant research brings out his lifetime concern with the socialization of psychic processes. This "Marxist phase" focuses on the application of dialectical materialism to the study of character formation; however, Reich's emphasis on the sociology of psychology precedes and extends well beyond his more purely Marxist phase (a Marxism always linked with Freud). For instance, in studying infants, Reich emphasizes the immediacy of socialization on infant armoring. He believes that the human "no," or the interaction between child and life-denying social processes starts at birth. Reich's late work demonstrates the belief that life-denying messages must be counteracted at birth in order to prevent severe character armor, which could emotionally disable children before puberty. This would co-opt the adolescent's rebellious sexual impulses through programmed preadolescent socialization.

Given Reich's firm belief in the sociological component of psychic development, his therapeutic techniques must always involve social praxis. For this reason, Reich's therapy focuses much more on prevention than analysis. He is a forerunner of community psychiatry and the mental health movement; he brought the clinic to the people. Reich's preventive work brings him into contact with the young and the working class, expanding therapy to much wider circles than traditional psychoanalysis. Through his preventative focus, Reich's social interventions occur on many levels. In childbirth, the social intervention, for example, would involve changing hospital care practices and humanizing obstetrical practices, and the individual intervention would involve fostering contact, perhaps through a mother's birth companion. The individual and social components of therapy always work together.

Reich's basic premise is that blocked energy, a consequence of social reality, develops into character armor, thus any liberation of energy must ultimately coexist with a change in social structure. Reich focuses his advocacy foremost against the modern family. He sees the family as initial supporter of an oppressive educational apparatus molding docile children, the infrastructure of authoritarian political systems, and preserver of reactive moral values, which naturalize the economic interests of the dominant, capitalist class.

Reich analyzes the family as the institutional apparatus supporting the economic interests of the ruling class. The foundation of the family is compulsory morality, that is, sex-negative morality.[27] Compulsory marriage demands the premarital chastity of females and their subsequent marital fidelity. Reich clearly delineates the function of patriarchal marriage, which oppresses feminine sexuality. The family assures feminine subjection because of the wife's economic dependence on men, and the woman's sexual slavery follows from her economic dependence. By excluding women from the social world, patriarchal marriage co-opts any possibility of a true sexual revolution—a moral revolution that is sex affirmative. The natural sexual process becomes a function of social ideology: "Compulsive marriage is part and parcel of the authoritarian economic system and is therefore maintained in spite of all its critical conflicts" (*SR*, 147–148).

Reich's sexual–political campaign attacks the foundation of marriage. His initial intervention advocates the liberation of women from marital bondage. Reich also argues for "enlightened" adolescent sexuality (through his sex hygiene clinics where, he is fifty years ahead of contemporary society's sex education programs) and housing units suitable for adolescent sexual gratification. Reich also seeks to detach adolescents from family authority ("The Sexual Rights of Youth," *Children of the Future*, 161–221).

In order to better grasp Reich's interpretation of ideology, something must be said of Marx's position on the subject. Marx and Engel's interpretation of ideology allows for no possibility of natural relations.[28] From the Marxist perspective, consciousness is always social; man is burdened with history. To survive, man must join with others (primitive family), and for individuals to join together communication is essential. Two points are particularly important to note in Marx's analysis. Man's consciousness is social consciousness and preeminently practical. Primitive men communicated by forming groups to preserve themselves from hostile natural forces, thus, language is a material reality. Ideology in its simple form mystifies social consciousness; it represents social/material relations as natural relations. Capitalist ideology develops from the divorce between intellectual and physical labor. In Marx's second interpretation of ideology, consciousness's material base disappears. Consciousness is no longer connected with material reality, and theory replaces communication. Ideologies are abstracted from immediate, sensual, and practical realities. These modern ideologies represent the dominant-class interest providing their material power with a spiritual justification. And those who wield established social and juridical order also wield "spiritual" power. The representations, that is, the consciousness of society, are elaborated into a systemic idealizing of existing conditions, those conditions that make possible the economic, social, and political primacy of a given group or class. Man acts in the world, however, what he understands about his actions comes through consciousness, that is, language and ideology. Therefore, man can easily act against his own material interest while simultaneously believing his action to be in his own best interest.

Reich is very sensitive to Marx's description of ideology's spiritual power, and he focuses on how ideology enters consciousness.[29] Society, in Reich's interpretation, produces character structure (individual psyche). The dominant class creates the very psychic structure it needs to perpetrate continual economic dominance over the working and middle classes. Morality, for Reich, is pure ideology; it justifies the economic interests of the ruling class. Reich repeatedly asks himself the question: "why the majority of those who are hungry don't steal and why the majority of those who are exploited don't strike."[30] His answer is that institutions reproduce themselves in the individual psyche. The working class develops its passive posture toward authority as a defense (i.e., ideology) protecting itself from real material deprivation.

The middle class fares no better than the working class. A middle-class worker identifies, through a career, with the dominant class; the idea of honor and duty (the dominant class's ideology) produces middle-class submission. The middle class aspires only to be part of the ruling class. In consumer society the working-class individual will aspire through commodity consumption to be part of the middle class, solidifying the power of the ruling class. Capitalist character structures disable revolt because the worker identifies with his exploiter. Although Reich focuses attention on fascist systems, he considers the capitalist state's more dispersed authority equally repressive. In every instance reactionary character structures develop through the family institution, which filters the state's authoritarian structure into the individual character formation.

Reich aptly calls the family a factory for the manufacture of authoritarian ideologies (*MPF*, 60). The ideology is socially produced but psychologically binding even when economic arrangements change. Man is simultaneously master and slave; he is slave to the economic elite, but master of his household. Thus, the master/slave economic superstructure reproduces itself within the household, showing that the patriarchal family supports authoritarian systems. At the same time, the woman gains economic security, but relinquishes her sexual freedom. The idea of female monogamy (and premarital chastity) creates socially imposed, reactionary, moral proscriptions for women.

Reich's description of family ideology makes clear how a change in economic arrangements does not necessarily mean a change in family structure. Social changes allow women some economic independence; however, the psychological dependence on authority remains. The rise of professional parenting experts, for example, replaces the husband's authority with another form of authority.[31] The point is that in giving up responsibility the self must live reactively. The independent woman may overcome the male-oriented family, but remains bound to the capitalist system. Her independence, then, consists in identifying with the very superstructure that demands her submission.

Thus, Reich gives to Marxist ideology a psychological dimension, and brings to therapy a social praxis. If Reich's orgonomy liberates an individual's neurotic character armor only to return the individual to authoritarian social structures, the therapeutic triumph will be subverted. Thus, his theory/practice works on multiple levels across individual developmental stages. For adults, Reich advocates a form of work democracy. He strives to overcome "alienated labor," not through a nostalgic and utopian return to agricultural social models, but through a return to worker participation in business. Each worker, for instance, would be part owner with a direct stake in the corporate process.[32] For Reich, gratifying work requires the consciousness of one's skills as a worker, a nonclass specific identification with other people performing vitally necessary work (i.e., life sustaining) in an interlocking network (e.g., an optician relies on a glass grinder, a registered nurse on a nursing assistant etc.), a reduction in working hours, better working conditions, variety in work duties, and most importantly, a direct relationship between the worker and his product (*MPF*, 296). Class, Reich writes, often undermines the worker's development. For instance, the estrangement of the industrial worker from the technician creates hostility among workers with similar goals. Similarly, unions might admit a white worker, but not a black worker (true at the time Reich writes about work democracy).

Reich also advocates complete economic independence of women, which requires changes in parenting structures, divorce laws, legal statutes, and sexual practices. The female must have equitable access to marital finances, sexual freedom equal to the male's, and daycare must be sufficiently available to allow women full participation in the economic sphere and adequate time to fulfill herself in the social and sexual spheres.

Ultimately, Reich's position demands both the abolition of the authoritarian family institution and the modern school system. He proposes, in place of the family and traditional school, early preschool education, including sex education, and innovative childrearing. Reich's therapy and social praxis require a massive reeducation of the population. His practical techniques and tactics bring him, ultimately, to a radical, utopian position. This position then diametrically opposes Freud's argument in *Civilization and Its Discontents* (1930).

ANTI-OEDIPUS

Reich's desire to demolish social institutions brings him to a ground zero, where he seeks to replace the current institutions with new, flexible forms of social organization. He moves, therefore, from anarchy to utopia. Reich believes in the possibility of a healthy society in which the human organism can live a self-regulatory, active life. Implicit in this argument is his belief that individual satisfaction is possible once external oppression is removed. Reich sees the future society populated with orgastically potent individuals living productive, fulfilling lives. From the Freudian perspective, Reich's attempt to construct or envision a new society is an illusion. Freud criticizes any religious system: the idealism involved in the notion that removing external obstacles will allow individuals more happiness. Freud refuses to let psychoanalysis develop a world picture; he sees man's unhappiness as internally constituted and resistant to a change in the material world. The human organism's resistance to happiness comes from the double nature of guilt, and in Freud's system, guilt is an inescapable human dimension. In ruminations on the relationship between historical contingencies and ancient Judaic morality, Freud defines the dynamic doublings of guilt: "We (psychoanalysts) know of two origins of the sense of guilt: One arising from a fear of an authority, and the other, later on, arising from fear of the super ego. The first instance upon a renunciation of instinctual satisfactions; the second, as well as doing this, presses for punishment, since continuance of the forbidden wishes cannot be concealed from the super ego."[33]

With the institution of the superego, guilt becomes inescapable. Yet the above account of guilt presupposes an initial externally induced guilt. The fear of authority is fear of external authority; Freud traces this personal fear back to the primal father. He later refines the story of the primal father recounted in *Totem and Taboo* to an account of primitive guilt's internal (i.e., instinctual) derivation.

In a famous passage from *Civilization and Its Discontents* (79–80) verification of primal murder does not matter. Guilt is part of a psychic process independent of external realities; it comes out of primal human ambivalence. This ambivalence originates with the beginning of the family (any group, two or more, living together to secure survival). The Oedipus complex evolves simultaneously with the family and its internalization of guilt. Janine Chasseguet-Smirgel in a comparison between Freud and Reich stresses Freud's emphasis on internal, intrapsychic, determinants of behavior.[34]

Thus Chasseguet-Smirgel joins Freud in her condemnation of Reich's social analysis as a utopian, essentially religious system. Two key points must be made regarding Reich's critics. First, Freud's system, like Reich's cannot be anything but a system of faith. Freud lives as a father figure within psychoanalysis, tolerating little deviation from his own system of ideas. Second, Freud's theory, regardless of the primacy accorded internal factors, proceeds from a hypothesis about the primal father, the universal character of the Oedipus complex, and family organization. Reich's own myth making will challenge Freud's theory by providing an alternative to the Oedipal hypothesis.

Reich's rejection of the original Oedipal complex follows his rejection of the family as a capitalist institution. Reich reverses Freud by understanding the family as the consequence of sexual repression, and not the genesis of repression. This anti-Oedipal hypothesis borrows from Malinowski's research on sexual life in Trobiand society. Reich's book *The Imposition of Sexual Morality* reads Malinowski's anthropology from a Marxist perspective.[35] He discovers in Malinowski's data a sex-affirmative society; a society in transition from a matriarchal system to a patriarchal system (i.e., Oedipal) symbolized by the institution of the marriage dowry (primitive capitalism). Reich's reading of Malinowski presupposes an original matriarchal society later replaced by the patriarchal system. This matriarchal society has horizontal models of authority; social processes are fluid, natural, communal, and antiauthoritarian.

Erich Fromm, following Bachofen's work on mother right, and clearly, indebted to Reich's hypothesis on primal matriarchy, rereads the Oedipus legend.[36] Fromm understands Sophocles's trilogy as the dramatic conflict between matriarchal society, represented by Antigone, and patriarchal society, represented by Creon. Oedipal civilization brings with it authority, obedience, rationality, monogamy, and the legal system. Within matriarchy, maternal love or nurturance fosters dependence, as with Antigone, and sacrificial acts; paternal love replaces unconditional love with respect, responsibility, and duty to something outside the self. The conditional basis of love necessitates guilt, which in turn demands punishment, further guilt, and strict obedience to a higher order. In patriarchy, the maternal becomes submissive to paternal authority. Thus, both Reich and Fromm understand matriarchal society as fundamentally different from, and historically prior to, patriarchal society. They locate the Oedipus complex within a specific historical matrix. The Oedipus complex's historical context situates Sophocles's (through whom Freud reads the myth) dramatization of historical shifts within Greek society from mythic loyalties to developing city-states.[37] The Oedipus complex emerges simultaneously with the polis. Thus, the intervention of authority must be read in relationship to a historically constituted system of authority, instituted through the development, codification, and application of civil laws.

Reich's replacement of an Oedipal civilization with a matriarchal civilization (replacing one myth with another) represents only one phase in his rewriting Freudian theory. Freud would agree with Reich that the family is a historically specific form; however, Freud considers the family a historical necessity. In his view, civilization demands that the family survive and likewise, the family demands instinctual renunciation and repression in order to survive. Civilization, in the Freudian system, is a repressed civilization. Reich rejects the necessity of repression: If matriarchy precedes patriarchy, then nonauthoritarian kinship systems precede the guilt-producing Oedipal family. Reich believes that when the patriarchal family is abolished along with its social superstructure, a new non-repressive society will emerge. The new society will return civilization to a more matriarchal, natural, and mobile structure. Reich's vision of society turns instinctual repression into instinctual expression. He is not interested in relieving some of society's inevitable mental suffering; he wants to prevent mental suffering by cutting off social repression at the root. He shifts psychoanalysis from its analytic base to an educational methodology, social praxis, and cultural prophylaxis.

Reich's reversal of Freud's cultural position follows his belief that the family produces the Oedipus complex and vice versa: destroy the family's authoritarian family structure and the Oedipus complex will disappear. Reich believes that with the reorganization of the social structure, culture no longer requires repression. He does not argue against culture, but he does argue against instinctual repression as a necessary prerequisite for cultural development. Freud's position on instinctual repression is clear; he stresses the replacement of the individual by the community. Civilization requires sacrifice at the expense of individual happiness. If an individual lives out his or her instinctual desire, the community's cohesion is jeopardized and chaos is likely to ensue. Freud's position presupposes a natural aggressiveness in humans, and Reich sees aggression as a secondary, culturally constructed force developing in response to libidinal renunciation. The human organism able to express and gratify sexual needs will be able to sublimate aggressive impulses. For Reich, aggression follows repression. He feels that the free expression of sexuality will in turn produce a culture independent of repression. Like Marcuse, Reich strives for a guilt-free, anti-Oedipal culture. The release of sexual energy, he believes, will also release and enhance cultural development.

Reich finds confirmation of his position in Freud's early paper " 'Civilized' Sexual Morality and Modern Nervous Illness" (1908).[38] This paper outlines three stages of civilization based on three levels of sexual repression. Primitive society allows sexuality free reign and gratification; developed society restricts sexuality to the aims of reproduction; and civilized society requires almost total sexual repression: "Only legitimate reproduction is allowed as a sexual aim" (189). This complex essay appears to contradict Freud's later advocacy of sexual repression. In his 1908 essay he marks the limits of repression that the individual psyche can absorb. He particularly stresses adolescents and females (the two groups Reich also emphasizes) as undergoing the severest instinctual repression. The adolescent unable to sublimate his or her sexual desire suffers emotional harm. The repressed woman enters marriage, but civilized sexual standards forbid her sexual satisfaction (194–196). The woman's only response to sexual frustration becomes neurosis: "Thus the married state, which is held out as a consolation to the sexual instinct of the civilized person in his youth, proves to be inadequate even to the demands of the actual period of life covered by it. There is no question of its being unable to compensate for the deprivation which precedes it" (195–196). Freud might ask himself why, if marriage does not compensate adolescent repression, does it continue?

Freud understands woman's removal from culture as a consequence, not a result, of sexual repression (199). He also makes this important observation: "The sexual behavior of a human being often lays down the pattern for all his other modes of reacting to life" (198). Freud's reflections on modern nervousness lead him to question the value of sexual repression. Although he refrains from advocating a social position in the essay, he implicitly conveys his support of a social policy that would release some of modern civilization's sexual controls (Freud here foreshadows what Marcuse will later call surplus repression).

Reich's work picks up on Freud's 1908 essay and carries it to its logical conclusion. Repressed men identify, in Reich's interpretation, with work as a national symbol (duty); women, unable to work, identify with the domestic symbol (duty to obey their husband, i.e., the ideology of motherhood). Reich's attack on Oedipal civilization is an attack on the Oedipus complex. He believes that in reeducating society's authoritarian disciples (the parents) the child will mature in a self-regulatory fashion, meeting its needs as they arise during the developmental process. The superego of the genital character is chiefly distinguished by its important sexually affirmative elements, and a high degree of harmony, Reich asserts, exists between the id and superego. Thus, for the genital character, there are no superego prohibitions of a sexual nature, and the genital libido, since it is gratified directly, is not concealed in the strivings of the ego ideal. Hence, social accomplishments are not, as in the case of the neurotic character, proof of potency; rather they provide a natural, non-compensatory, narcissistic gratification. Since there are no potency disturbances in the genital character, an inferiority complex does not exist, and ego ideal and ego coexist harmoniously (*CA*, 179).

Reich's critics dismiss the orgasm theory as a naïve utopian gesture. The orgasm, however, does not, in Reich's theory, return the individual to the oceanic feeling of primary narcissism. Although the self merges with the other in the sexual act, this merger is not narcissistic; the genital character's permeable ego allows this sexual and erotic contact without a loss of self. The desire is rational, active, and outward, and the contact Reich advocates, through the orgasm, is in reality pre-ego (pre-Oedipal as well as anti-Oedipal). Social contact comes out of a natural, biological striving. Therefore, Reich's position is that of holistic awareness (Berman, 168–169).[39]

Unfortunately, Reich's venture into radical social therapy did not last. His turn to biophysics dilutes his radical sex-economic work and, like Heinz Hartman's development of ego psychology, continues a conservative trend with the history of psychoanalysis.[40] However, Robert Corrington makes a valuable argument that preserves a radicalism for Reich's late work. Corrington sees orgonomy as a manifestation of ecstatic naturalism.[41] The "radical naturalist will go a step further [then the naturalist] and also assert that the 'one' nature manifests (and is) a deep pulsating energy that spawns new life out of itself-that is nature is conceptually expressed by Spinoza's notion of *natura naturans* or nature creating nature out of itself alone" (193). Corrington's presentation of Reich's radical naturalism as "an inevitable product of his views on sexuality" (205), which forms a religious metaphysics, makes an important contribution to understanding Reich's overall project. This religion of sexuality in turn makes an excellent bridge to the work of D.H. Lawrence.

Lawrence and Reich have a deep affinity, which can best be understood through a mutual reading of each writer's late engagement with the figure of Christ. Both Reich's *The Murder of Christ* (1953) and Lawrence's *The Escaped Cock* (1929) represent radical revisions of the gospels and their meaning; a preeminently sexual vision of Jesus's life and significance.

READING REICH THROUGH LAWRENCE OR
A GENITAL JESUS

Late in his book *The Murder of Christ*[42] Wilhelm Reich draws explicit attention to D.H. Lawrence's last novella, *The Escaped Cock*.[43] Reich laments the official church's misreading of Christ's life, which he believes Lawrence's story corrects: "no trace of the very essence of Christ's life (in the official accounts of Jesus's life), of the women who loved Christ's body. A lonely, persecuted writer will, two thousand years later, understand this deepest secret and write a little book, 'The Man Who Died,' which will present Christ in a truer, more Christ like light" (*MC*, 151–152). Reich finds in Lawrence a kindred spirit and each writer composes a powerful reworking of the canonical gospels.

On the surface Reich sees himself, quite accurately given the historical circumstances of his life at the time, as a persecuted figure and *The Murder of Christ* operates, in part, as an allegory of Reich's own life (see especially chapter XIV, "Gethsemane," 126–131). On a deeper level, both Reich and Lawrence perceive Jesus as a cosmic messenger who delivers their respective metaphysics or worldviews. Each writer's vision stresses the resurrection over the crucifixion and valorizes a very sensual, human Jesus.

The Escaped Cock has a definite intellectual genealogy, but Lawrence's summarizes the story's purpose in a letter to Earl Brewster on

May 3, 1927:

> "I wrote a story of the Resurrection, where Jesus gets up and feels very sick about everything, and can't stand the old crowd any more—so cuts out—and as he heals up, he begins to find what an astonishing place the phenomenal world is, far more marvelous than any salvation or heaven—and thanks his stars he needn't have a 'mission' any more." (*Letters* vi, 50)[44]

Lawrence's Jesus finds his new post resurrection life liberating: " 'my mission is over, and my teaching is finished, and death has saved me from my own salvation' " (*EC*, 24).

Reich also stresses how the people burdened Jesus with his mission and seduced him into leadership because of their need for an idol (*MC*, 38). For Reich, Christ does not cultivate the messiah's role; he waits for the people to come to him (67). Indeed, where the people hunger for salvation Reich finds Jesus taking joy in "carpentry or microscopy or healing people's wounds or tending fields" (38). Lawrence makes precisely the same point about Jesus's new life as Reich in his essay "The Risen Lord" (1927): "And if he (Jesus) remembered His first life, it would neither be teaching nor preaching, but probably carpentering again, with joy, among the shavings" (114).[45] The risen lord aligns himself, as Reich says with, "the inner freedom of the animal man which is part of the lawful freedom of the whole creation" (*MC*, 35).

Both Reich and Lawrence represent Christ, as I've mentioned above, as cosmic messengers. Reich compares Christ, in a provocative metaphor, to a ripple on an ocean wave: "The meaning of the existence of a wave ripple on the surface of the ocean is exactly what it does: *Being aware*, rolling onward, spraying a beautiful gust of water all around itself and vanishing again" (85). The principle remains, Reich continues, as long as the ocean lasts. Lawrence makes nearly the identical comparison of Jesus and the ocean through Jesus's consciousness, "And the man who has died watched the unsteady, rocking vibration of the bent bird he saw, but one wave-tip of life overlapping for a minute another, in the tide of the swaying ocean of life. And the destiny of life seemed more fierce and compulsive to him even than the destiny of death. The doom of death was a shadow, compared to the raging destiny of life, the determined surge of life" (*EC*, 22).

Each writer then sees Christ as a life force and, subsequently, they privilege the resurrection over the crucifixion. Robert Corrington nicely describes Reich's vision of the risen Jesus, "Reich wanted to align himself with a triumphant and healthy person for whom the cross was not so much fulfillment as a symptom of the horrors of the emotional plague. Put differently, Reich would have been uncomfortable with any sense that Christ has a death drive or accepted a way out of life as part of a divine plan he had made with a supernatural father" (229). Likewise, in "The Risen Lord" Lawrence juxtaposes "Christ Crucified" with "Christ the Man." Lawrence writes out of the world war's aftermath and he emphatically wants a Christ for the new postwar generation. The maiming of young men, Lawrence claims, "broke the image of mother and Christ-child, and left in its place the image of Christ crucified" (107). This version of Christ, however, remains, "Untrue to the inner experience and feeling of the young" (110). What youth need, Lawrence proclaims, is a Jesus of "flesh and blood," a "man on earth," "among other men" (112).

For both writers the risen lord lives a nomadic life. A displaced person in constant movement Jesus hates being shut in, confined or classified, "His [Christ's] whole behavior is so much at variance with all kinds of isms that no one accustomed to 'place' people, could tell where he belongs"(*MC*, 37). The man who died spends the first part of the novella wandering the countryside, "He still hated to be shut up" (21). This nomadic life signifies an affiliation with nature and discontent with the structure of human society.

Perhaps the deepest affinity between Reich and Lawrence concerns their valorization of a physical Jesus and, especially, his penis. Attributing man's biblical fall to sex strikes Reich as preposterous and he laments the idea that, ". . . the symbol of wavy, living life and the male sexual organ had seduced them [Adam and Eve]" (14). In fact, Reich understands Eden as inhabited by the spirits of two gods. The bad God, not man, produces the exile from Eden, while the good God, that is, Jesus, embodied a natural sexuality. Reich's version of Noli me Tangere, DO NOT TOUCH IT, refers to the church's prohibition against genital touching and childhood masturbation. For Reich, the church's condemnation of the body begins the process of armoring and the spread of emotional plague or sin, that is, the failure to live a life attune to nature's and the body's rhythms. Consequently, *The Murder of Christ* addresses itself preeminently to the prevention of childhood pathology.

Although Lawrence does not imagine dual gods presiding over Eden, in a letter to the psychologist Trignant Burrow, he does imagine two Edens, which correspond to dual modes of consciousness, the sexual and the cognitive (*Letters* vi, 113–114). Lawrence also stresses the sexual mode of knowing and his versions of the sacred phallus and sexual Christ figures dominate his poetry. In "Snake" (*CP*, 349–351) he represents the phallic snake: "Like a king in exile, uncrowned in the underworld, / Now due to be crowned again."[46] In "Manifesto" the Christ figure comments:

> Let them praise desire who will,
> but only fulfillment will do,
> real fulfillment, nothing short.
> It is our ratification,
> our heaven, as a matter of fact.
> Immortality, the heaven, is only a projection of this strange
>   but actual fulfillment,
>   here in the flesh. (*CP*, 262–268)

The late lyric, "The Risen Lord" evokes how, "man rises again / with mouth and loins and needs, he lives / again man among men" (*CP*, 459–461). The poem "Resurrection" (*CP*, 743–746) associates the risen lord with the natural world of cyclamens and crocuses. For Lawrence, Christ must be touched and his fleshy Jesus necessarily requires a woman.

In a letter to Laurence Pollinger about *The Escaped Cock* Lawrence stresses the relationship between Jesus and women, "And church doctrine teaches the resurrection of the body; and if that doesn't mean the whole man, what does it mean? And if man is whole without woman—even Jesus—then I'm damned" (*Letters*, vii, 122).[47] Reich makes a similar point in his reading of the gospels' displacement of women, "It is self-evident that the women who had loved *Christ in the body*, and not his admirers and disciples who had only sucked life from his body, should be present at his last agony. Accordingly, the women will recede into the background when man will take over Christ's tragedy for the purpose of deification, and the absent disciples will be put in the foremost foreground" (*MC*, 151). The second half of *The Escaped Cock* reinserts the woman's role in Christ's life through a complex superimposition of the Osiris myth onto the Jesus narrative.

This work directly engages notions of transgression and the sacred by retelling the story of Jesus as man and not as the risen Christ described in the gospels. In the story Jesus (never actually named) refuses his Christ role. Rather, the man who dies wanders the countryside with a companion cock healing people. The cock serves as both historical signifier (Peter's denial of Jesus) and sign of manhood. Lawrence stresses the resurrection of the body and plays, sacrilegiously for many, with resurrection's reference to the penis.

In stressing Isis as searching, Lawrence calls attention to the myth's resurrection motif. Isis must collect and put together the dismembered god's body. Osiris's missing part, of course, is his penis, hence the original title of Lawrence's story as *The Escaped Cock*. When the man who died says: " 'surely thou art risen to the Father, among birds' " (28) the double entendre is obvious. Further when he gives his victorious cock to the man at the inn, the man who died inverts Christian belief: " 'Thou at least hast found thy kingdom, and the female to thy body. Thy aloneness can take on splendour, polished by the lure of thy hens' " (33). The risen/restored cock responds only to the touch of a woman. The resurrection is sexual and Jesus's penis becomes the story's chief symbol of humanity.

The story's climax brings the man who died into sexual contact with Isis's priestess. After massaging the man's lower body the priestess enfolds his wounded side and they then proceed to consummate their relationship: "Then slowly, slowly, in the perfect darkness of his inner man, he felt the stir of something coming: a dawn, a new sun. A new sun was coming upon him, in the perfect inner darkness of himself. He waited for it breathless, quivering with fearful hope. 'Now I am not myself, I am something new . . .' " (56–57). More appropriate for the Osiris myth, Lawrence's inscription of Jesus's transformation as a sexual initiation rejects all modes of transcendence.

Lawrence's revision of the Noli me Tangere motif further represents his radical textuality.[48] The gospels' "Touch me not, for I am not ascended to my father" (John 20:17) becomes, in Lawrence, " 'Don't touch me . . . Not yet! I am not yet healed and in touch with men' " (23). The healing comes through the female body. Thus Lawrence pushes modernism to the limit. The limits are the limits of the body: "I wanted to be greater than the limits of my hands and feet, so I brought betrayal on myself. And I know I wronged Judas, my poor Judas. For I have died, and I know my own limits. Now I can live without striving to sway others any more. For my reach ends in my finger-tips, and my stride is no longer than the ends of my toes" (24). In Lawrence's corporeal textuality resurrection is subsumed into regeneration: " 'No man can save the earth from tillage. It is tillage, not salvation' " (24).

The Lawrencian hero remains firmly on the ground. Over a decade prior to writing *The Escaped Cock* Lawrence imagined a utopian community called Rananim. In a letter about the community to Lady Ottoline, Lawrence imagines the armorless individual described by Wilhelm Reich as the apogee of health: "Every strong soul must put off its connection with this society, its vanity and chiefly its fear, and go naked with its fellows, weaponless, armourless, without shield or spear, but only with naked hands and open eyes. Not self-sacrifice, but fulfillment, the flesh and the spirit in league together, not in arms against one another" (*Letters*, ii, 271–273). Reich could have written this letter; for both writers Christ signifies the fulfilled self. Unfortunately, both Reich and Lawrence lived in a time of world war, and, in Reich's case, the Nazi Holocaust. Chapter 3 charts Lawrence's radical vision of the body in his early fiction and his masterpiece *Women in Love* (1920).

3. The Sexual Radical: D.H. Lawrence's Embodied Fiction ∽

All sexual rivalry is thus structurally homosexual.

René Girard, *Desire, Deceit and the Novel*

Lawrence's radical engagement with the body preoccupied his imagination, as chapter 2 suggested, right up to the late novella, *The Escaped Cock*. More than any other modern fictionalist Lawrence writes about the body's experience of the world. When he calls man a "thought-adventurer," Lawrence means the adventure of the body.[1] Man must risk the unknown self or "the black touchstone at the center of me" (217). The opposite of the corporeal self is the modern personality of the conscious, fully rational self:

> Today men don't risk their blood and bone. They go forth, panoplied in their own idea of themselves. Whatever they do, they perform it all in the full armour of their own idea of themselves. Their unknown bodily self is never one moment unsheathed. All the time, the only protagonist is the known ego, the self-conscious ego. And the dark self in the mysterious labyrinth of the body is cased in a tight armor of cowardly repression. (217–218)

Lawrence's writing seeks to unlock this dark self and shatter the armor of the Cartesian ego. As Paul Poplawski writes in a collection on Lawrence's writing: "By the end of his career, the body for Lawrence is not just the focus of an artistic and moral struggle for verisimilitude in representation and for rebellion against bourgeois materialism and censorship, but also, and perhaps, more importantly, it becomes the site of a philosophical struggle with the very nature of language, art, and reality."[2] Actually, Lawrence's writing about the body engages what Peter Brooks calls an "epistemophilic project" from the beginning of his career.[3] In other words; the body becomes site of both desire and knowledge, which Lawrence represents in multiple configurations. This chapter analyzes Lawrence's figures of embodied desire from early short fictions to his masterpieces, *Women in Love* and *Lady Chatterley's Lover*.

First, "The Prussian Officer" represents a point Lawrence shares with Reich, that "cruelty is a form of perverted sex."[4] Next, a short story from the same collection, "The Sick Collier," displays the male body as narrative object. Another story, "The Blind Man," also inscribes the male body as site of desire and narrative springboard, which leads me to a discussion of homosocial/homosexual desire in *The Plumed Serpent* and *Women in Love*. Discussion of triangular desire in *Women in Love* is then followed by a close reading of how "The Fox" depicts triangular desire through two women, Banford and March, thus inverting, *Women in Love*'s depiction of two men, Birken and Gerald, caught in the escalation of mimetic desire. Finally, the chapter ends with an extended discussion of *Lady Chatterley's Lover* in the context of Luce Irigaray's philosophy. Maria Ferreira's comment that in his "last writings, Lawrence is rethinking his sexual politics and making way for the (re) emergence of woman, and more specifically, the desiring woman, such as the priestess of Isis and Lady Chatterley, in a new post-Christian context," provides the occasion for this chapter's poststructuralist readings of Lawrence.[5]

THE FASCIST BODY

"The Prussian Officer" appeared in the August 1914 edition of the English Review, the very month and year World War 1 broke out.[6] The story, written a year prior to its publication, anticipates not only the horrors of the great war, but also captures the psychodynamics that produced the fascist personality emerging from the war's aftermath. Barbara Mensch[7] has used Wilhelm Reich's work on fascism as well as Adorno's monumental study *The Authoritarian Personality*[8] to discuss Lawrence's often-ambiguous relationship to authority. Although Mensch focuses on Lawrence's "leadership" novels *Aaron's Rod, Kangaroo*, and *The Plumed Serpent* she provides an important entry way into Lawrence's mid-career novels with a discussion of Gerald Crich, in *Women in Love* (71–118), as an authoritarian personality. Mensch observes how closely Crich's behavior approximates the officer's behavior in the much earlier "The Prussian Officer" story. Similarly, Hugh Stevens notes the close affinity between the story and novel. Stevens considers Lawrence's postwar experience as a second Oedipal crisis where by, ". . . nation state as father figure who brutally treated the wayward son, crucified him, marked him out as symbolic and sacrificial victim in order to consolidate its own militaristic, brutalizing modernity and the psychotic discourse of modern nationalism."[9]

Wilhelm Reich's work becomes especially helpful in illuminating the sexual aspects of this "brutalizing modernity." Reich stresses the libidinous affect of militarism emphasizing the "sexual effect of the uniform" and "exhibitionistic nature of militaristic procedures" (*MSF*, 32). The military, in Reich's view, offers substitute gratification for sexual urges. Man's natural drives are distorted by the military into the sadistic impulses that fuel imperialistic nation-states. Sadism, in Reich's understanding of the phenomenon, emerges as a reaction formation to the repression of the natural sex drive. Although not natural, sadism becomes a kind of second nature fundamental to the fascist personality's everyday functioning.

The Prussian officer represents what Reich would call a highly armored neurotic personality whereas his much younger servant would represent an unarmored, genital character, "[t]here was something so free and self-contained about him [the servant], and something in the young fellow's movement, that made the officer aware of him" (*PO*, 3). Contrarily, the officer's rigidity intensifies through the story. Even after a brief sexual liaison the officer, "returned to duty with his brow more tense, his eyes still more hostile and irritable" (2). The sexual tension between the master and servant bubbles just underneath the surface. The servant admires the officer's muscles during rubdowns and the officer, ironically, becomes tighter the more he interacts with the youth. Apparently, the officer defends against his erotic feelings toward his servant (whose name Schöner means beautiful in German), but he also refused the youth's request to visit his sweetheart thus maintaining their exclusive male bond. Then during one dining experience a spilt bottle of wine leads to a transformation of the pair's relationship. The officer seems more aggressive toward the servant and the servant's natural ease evaporates to be replaced by an ever present anxiety: "And from that time on an undiscovered feeling had held between the two men" (3).

This incident marks the beginning of the servant's armoring. Simultaneously, "the influence of the young soldier's being had penetrated through the officer's stiffened discipline, and perturbed the man in him" (4). As the young soldier begins to deny natural impulses he necessary develops an underlying and festering sadistic urge against the officer who, in turn, requires greater efforts of sexual suppression to defend against his libidinous tie to the youth. The officer's increasing repression can only find an outlet in directly sadistic acts that commence when the officer flings a heavy glove in the soldier's face. Simon Casey draws attention to how the soldier's physical disfigurement parallels his instinctual disfigurement.[10]

The more the soldier denies his natural impulses the greater his sadistic urges become. In other words, the soldier's near suffocation from his anti-social behavior reflects his denial of natural instincts. In a mirror-like fashion, the officer only shows emotion when he stops suppressing his instincts.

Reich describes how the prolonged denial of sexual release turns sexual excitation into a torturous, destructive experience, which results in the manufacture of a diabolic expression of sexuality (*MSP*, 149). The officer, in Lawrence's story, then experiences sexual excitation as degrading and must defend against these feelings both through intense sadism and the construction of a pure, gentlemanly behavior: "[w]hen he saw the youth start back, the pain-tears in his eyes and the blood on his mouth, he felt at once a thrill of deep pleasure, and of shame" (*PO*, 6). The story then escalates quickly toward its dramatic climax. The young soldier's intensifying sadism finally erupts when he breaks the officer's neck. The soldier experiences this sadistic act as a sexual release, which the narrator describes in almost orgasmic terms: "[h]eavy convulsions shook the body of the officer, frightening and horrifying the young soldier. Yet it pleased him too to repress them. It pleased him to keep his hands pressing back the chin, to feel the chest of the other man yield in expiration to the weight of his strong young knee, to feel the hard twitching of the prostrate body jerking his whole frame, which was pressed down on it" (15). Ironically, the soldier delivers the officer an orgasm without the officer suffering guilt (see Reich's comment below), but simultaneously, the servant "presses down" and maintains rigidity within him even as he releases the officer to an orgasmic death.

Stevens refers to the murder as a "scene of homoerotic sacrifice" (57). Reich provides a more compelling context for discussing the homoerotic tension exhibited by the officer and soldier's sadomasochistic relationship:

> Clinical experience in sex-economy shows that the desire to be beaten or to castigate oneself corresponds to the instinctual desire for release without incurring guilt. There is no physical tension that will not evoke fantasies of being beaten or being tortured as soon as the person concerned feels himself incapable of bringing about the release. Here we have the root of the passive ideology of suffering of all genuine religions. (*MSF*, 148)

The officer's physical tension, as I have indicated, increases each time he interacts with the soldier. Although the story does not represent the officer's fantasies, the fiction's dynamics suggest that the officer's inability to experience release must culminate in an intense sexual explosion that simultaneously ends in death. In Reich's reading of sadomasochism the officer's repressed desire would lead to a fear of desire that eventuates in a mystical longing (the masochistic feeling of suffering). Reich describes the transformation of orgasmic convulsion into sadistic compulsions in the essay "The Rooting of Reason in Nature":

> It is safe to assume that the impelling drive to overcome the basic natural function of the orgastic convulsion that rendered man helpless was later justified by the development of ugly, secondary, perverse, sadistic, cruel drives in man. The first struggles of the founders of many religions were quite obviously directed against these distortions of nature. Since no distinction between primary, natural genital drives and secondary, perverted, cruel, lascivious drives was possible, the most essential root of man in nature, his orgastic convulsion, fell prey to suppression, physiological blocking, and, finally, together with the secondary anti-social drives from which the primary drives were not distinguished, to severe condemnation. (*CS*, 284)

Similarly, the soldier's suppression of natural desire created his own sadism, which ultimately results in his own mystic longing experienced as he looks at the snowy mountains, "his face illuminated" (*PO*, 19). The soldier moves toward the mountains in a delirious state and passes out in a kind of ecstasy: "He stared till his eyes went black, and the mountains as they stood in their beauty, so clean and cool, seemed to have it, that which was lost to him" (20). Kingsley Widmer described decades ago how the youth's break with the natural continuum leads to this ecstatic identification with the mountains.[11] Widmer concluded that the soldier's "guilty longing for the ultimate beauty, innocence, and purity beyond life becomes the annihilation of life" (10). True to Reich's reading of fascism, the denial of natural impulses transforms sexual desire into either an unnatural sadistic impulse to destroy or an equally destructive, mystical longing for the end.

Ultimately, the soldier dies in a hospital. The story places the two characters together even in death: "The bodies of the two men lay together, side by side, in the mortuary, the one white and slender, but laid rigidly at rest, the other looking as if every moment it must rouse into life again, so young and unused, from a slumber" (*PO*, 20–21). Just as in life, the officer's corpse now rests armored, as the soldier's corpse seems poised for regeneration, a natural body twisted into perversity by the Prussian military, which Reich correctly identified as the harbinger of German fascism.

UNDERGROUND MEN

Lawrence's preoccupation with the collier is, naturally, a product of his own childhood as the son of a collier. Lawrence engages the colliers' plight in numerous stories, essays, letters, and novels. An early pre-figuration of Mellors's masculinity is the early story, *A Sick Collier*.[12] Composed in 1912 and revised in 1914 this story encapsulates issues of class and sexuality.

The story immediately indicates class distinction: "She was too good for him, everybody said" (165). The collier is a short, dark muscular man. The young woman is drawn to the man's "physical brightness." After the couple's marriage the man sets the tone of a colliers' married life: " 'Set th' table for my breakfast, an' put my pit-things afront o'th' fire. I s'll be gettn' up at ha'ef pas' five. Tha nedna shift they-sen not till when ter likes' " (165).

Lawrence's ear for working-class dialect is already superb, but even more impressive is Lawrence's depiction of working-class masculinity. The collier, Willie, symbolizes physical vitality: "When he washed himself, kneeling on the hearth rug stripped to the waist, she felt afraid of him again" (166). Lawrence here evokes the "man adventure," a figure of self-assured, spontaneous corporeal selfhood. Willie's masculinity, however, is challenged when he falls seriously ill at work.

The six weeks Willie spends in bed become a time of vulnerability. This powerful collier now screams with pain: " 'I canna' elp it, it's th' peen, it's th' peen,' he cried again. He had never been ill in his life. When he had a smashed finger, he could look at the wound. But this pain came from inside, and terrified him" (167). The pain drives Willie into a state of madness where he shouts incomprehensible, violent threats toward his frightened wife. The temporary insanity coincides with Willie's observation that his friends, now out on strike, are on their way to a football match that Willie cannot attend. Willie has been deprived of his male companions, and his physical strength. In a moment of emotional breakdown, Willie: "bit his lip, then broke into tears, sobbing uncontrollably, with his face to the window" (170).

Lawrence brilliantly captures the complex vulnerability of wounded, working-class masculinity. Although Willie's verbal skills are limited, he clearly acknowledges his sense of vulnerability and deep self-fear symbolized by his sudden attack on his wife. The rage buried underneath the surface of masculine confidence can be unleashed by any threatening crisis: illness and unemployment being two crises represented in the story. This powerful man is ultimately helpless to control his own destiny. The further tragedy concerns the rapidly dwindling compensation paid the sick collier. As his nameless wife remarks, pay has already been cut down, and Willie's outburst can only bring about his total alienation: " 'If it gets about as he's out of his mind, they'll stop his compensation, I know they will' " (171). The story simply trails off since the implied conclusion is obvious; capitalism has conquered the mining town and working-class masculinity.

A Silk Collier illustrates the struggle between social identity and self-awareness outlined by Peter Middletown in his discussion of *The Rainbow*.[13] A sick collier has by definition lost a sense of masculinity, which Lawrence struggles with in a series of personal reflections. Lawrence describes the commercialization of the new working class in a letter to Lady Ottoline, dated December 27, 1915, a full ten years before the coal miners' strike.[14] In this letter, Lawrence recalls his passionate boyhood and also intimates his future mission. He admires the colliers' sensuality and their intimate connection with the land, yet all the workers' sensuality is consumed by industrialization. The workers strike only for money, in an effort to climb out of their class and into the consumer and business class. The workers are only part of a vast machine. Their organic connection to the land has been replaced by the inorganic machinery that owns the land: "The strange, dark, sensual life, so violent, and hopeless at the bottom, combined with this horrible paucity and materialism of mental consciousness, makes me so sad, I could scream. They are still so living, so vulnerable, so darkly passionate. I love them like brothers—but, my God, I hate them too: I don't intend to own them as masters—not while the world stands. One must conquer them also—think beyond them, know beyond them, act upon them" (*Letters*, ii, 488–490).

Here Lawrence simultaneously loves the sensual vibrancy and hates their intellectual void. Lawrence, as writer, cannot identify with this working class, nor can he ever leave them; the struggle within Lawrence is most pronounced in his *Autographical Sketch*.[15] His identification with his father is clear, and although his background is working class, Lawrence also identifies with his mother's lower middle-class position. He locates the mother's "superiority" precisely in terms of language, since the mother never speaks the father's dialect; the couple is irrevocably split by language. The working class supplies Lawrence's vitality, the material of his craft, and much of his life's substance, but Lawrence's language owes itself to another class division within himself, the transfer of class being impossible and yet necessary. For Lawrence, to leave the working class would be to leave the body and the land, yet if he does not leave the working class, he does not write. The dilemma is deeply felt, and in speaking of the colliers from the Erewash Valley, Lawrence reiterates the double pull of class: "They are the only people who move me strongly, and with whom I feel myself connected in deeper destiny. It is they who are, in some peculiar way, 'home' to me. I shrink from them, and I have an acute nostalgia for them" (*Phoenix II*, 596).

One gets the sense that Lawrence finds himself in the middle of a tug-of-war; he is home only between classes, and the ambivalence of home shows itself in Lawrence's wandering life. This encounter with his personal past, his family, class, and nation provides the impetus that eventually culminates in *Lady Chatterley's Lover*.

CASTRATED BODIES OR OEDIPAL ECSTASY
IN THE MIDLANDS

Linda Williams's *Sex in the Head* interrogates Lawrence's representation of gender in some provocative ways.[16] She sees Lawrence as a painfully divided writer: "Lawrence is not simply the dark masculine soul he would persuade us of, he is also the eager feminine voyeur that he disavows; more sexually divided than heterosexual prophet, the Lawrence who would close the eyes of his culture is also the orgiastic picture-maker" (x). Lawrence's split writing divides along the axis of dark and light, body and mind. Dark love is a passionate, physical, and phallic hymn to the body. The world of sight reveals conscious control of instinctual life affirming urges and repression of the body: "What he advocates is any experience which strips one of sight, as a way of pre-visual bliss, the immersion of the self (at the risk of losing it) in an experience of unmediated darkness. Blindness is an aid to truth, a guarantee of insight" (32).

Williams sees the pervasive split in Lawrence's writing in the story, "The Blind Man."[17] She reads the story as inversely foreshadowing, *Lady Chatterley's Lover*. The early fiction tells the story of a married couple, Maurice and Isabel Pervin, and the visit of the wife's Scottish friend Bertie. Maurice is the inverse of Clifford Chatterley. Like Clifford, Maurice's disability results from a World War I injury. The Freudian parallel between Clifford's penis and Maurice's eyes, however, is not symmetrical. Maurice's blindness rather than being a sign of castration signifies potency. The war, in a sense, produces Maurice's virility just as the war causes Clifford's impotence. Maurice thrives in his new, dark world: "It was a pleasure to him to rock thus through a world of things, carried on the flood in a sort of blood-prescience. He did not think much of trouble. So long as he kept this sheer immediacy of blood-contact with the substantial world he was happy, he wanted no intervention of visual consciousness" (54).

Williams correctly reads Lawrence's valorization of the body, but to suggest that Lawrence: "advocates any experience which strips one of sight, as a way back to pre-visual bliss—the immersion of the self in an experience of unmediated darkness" (32) is overstated. The presence of Bertie isolates Maurice and opens the story to a triangular model of desire. The rivalry between Maurice and Bertie, however, plays out in unexpected ways.

Cast, structurally, in the Mellors's role, as outsider threatening the marital relationship Bertie does not, however, play a sexual role vis-à-vis Isabel.

In fact, Bertie is not even a sexual being: "He was ashamed of himself, because he could not marry, could never even approach women physically" (58). A highly intelligent, successful barrister, Bertie appears more like Clifford than Mellors. Bertie responds to Maurice's quest to touch him as if Maurice has worked a spell: "Now Bertie quivered with revulsion. Yet he was under the power of the blind man, as if hypnotized. He lifted his hand, and laid the fingers on the scar, on the scarred eyes" (62). The image's radical nature stems from Bertie's reciprocal action. He reluctantly, touches Maurice and establishes a physical intimacy initiating their "friendship":

> Then suddenly Maurice removed the hand of the other man from his brow, and stood holding it in his own. "Oh my God," he said, "we shall know each other now, shan't we? We shall know each other now." Bertie could not answer. He gazed mute and terror-struck, overcome by his own weakness. He knew he could not answer. He had an unreasonable fear, lest the other man should suddenly destroy him. Whereas, Maurice was actually filled with hot, poignant love, the passion of friendship. Perhaps it was this very passion of friendship which Bertie shrank from most. (62)

The narrator's language suggests a very passionate friendship. Further, the displaced sensual imagery reveals Maurice's eye cavity being touched by Bertie. The men's symbolic intercourse leaves the previously virgin Bertie, "like a mollusk whose shell is broken."

Consequently, Lawrence's story valorizes darkness, the world of the mines, in relationship to the male body. His challenge to clearly defined gender roles, and their reflection of sexuality is also evidenced through the privacy of the two men, and Isabel's ultimate invisibility. This reading contradicts Ronald Granofsky's reading of the story as representing a triangular relationship, which displaces Maurice in favor of Isabel's coming child.[18] Granofsky sees Isabel as the story's central figure, one who manipulates a confrontation between the men in order to further her own survival. This Darwinian reading sees Isabel as Lawrence's surrogate and Isabel's giving birth as a metaphor for Lawrence "about to give birth to a new form of fiction" (150). Granofsky generates his reading from his understanding of: "Lawrence's worries about his own survival both in terms of the intellectual self whose ego boundaries have been smashed in by the hostility of his country and of the reading public and in terms of the dark, strong, sexual self he would like to believe in but whose existence is belied by his illness and his physical decline" (154).

Michael Ross allows for a different reading of the story to emerge from Lawrence's life. He sees the relationship between Bertie and Maurice as an allegorical working through of Lawrence's relationship with Bertrand Russell during the years 1915–1916.[19] In Ross's interpretation Bertie would represent Russell and Maurice would represent Lawrence. The blind man then, as the story indicates, achieves potency and triumphs over the effete intellectual. This reading accords, as Ross shows, with Lawrence's praise of darkness or "blood consciousness" as opposed to "mental consciousness" and Lawrence's further advocacy of the lower self articulated in the writer's psychology book. After all, Lawrence, who once thought of Russell as a partner in his Blütbruderscaft (*Letters*, ii, 363, 12 July 1915 to Lady Ottoline Morrell), eventually resented the Cambridge intellectual's rational approach to social dilemmas. Lawrence described Russell as an isolated ego, "ready-defined self intact, free from contact and connection" (*Letters*, ii, 378, 16 August 1915 to Lady Cynthia Asquith). Russell, in Lawrence's scheme, represents the shell Bertie dissolves into at the story's conclusion. Bertie's triumph, however, rings hollow since contact with a shell or armored ego to use Reich's terminology precludes intimacy. Ross reads the story's ironic conclusion as, "a clear dream-reversal of Lawrence's own experiences, a willed denouement whose ringing finality serves to compensate for the frustrating, inconclusive outcome of the actual friendship between Lawrence and Russell" (Ross, 308).

Although Ross's interpretation of "The Blind Man" has a Darwinian echo (Lawrence's surviving a ruined friendship), he does not show Isabel as triumphant. Contrarily, Ross reads the story as a pessimistic indictment of failed hopes. Interestingly, neither critic broaches the question of homosexuality. Yet, Maurice's physical gesture in guiding Bertie's exploration of his "cavity" carries, as I indicated above, sexual undertones. Given Lawrence's revulsion at Russell's group of Cambridge friends and their open homosexuality (note Lawrence's comment on seeing John Maynard Keynes in his night shirt) the homosexual tension of the stories takes on a complicated dynamic that frustrates any attempted resolution. The dynamic plays itself out in the relationship between Birkin and Gerald in *Women in Love*, where a broken Blütbruderscaft points to catastrophe, and the later, ironic triumph of a pregnant Connie (Isabel's later refiguring) over the crumbling worlds of Mellors and Clifford in *Lady Chatterley's Lover*. For now, I draw attention to Judith Puchner Breen's comment on "The Blind Man" as a subversive story wherein, "Lawrence has encoded his secret plot of homosexual love within the parameters of more permissible plots" (73). I now turn to a fuller consideration of Lawrence's subversive art through a reading of *The Plumed Serpent*, *Women and Love*, and *Lady Chatterley's Lover*.

THE DARK BODY

In a provocative reading of the crisis in masculine subjectivity from 1900 to the 1930s Mauriza Boscagli challenges any claim to monolithic male authority: "The marks of eroticism and desire that it bears contradict its claim to phallic plenitude and rather present an image of dispossessed masculinity that gestures toward gender instability and abjection."[20] Boscagli focuses on how artists appropriate Nietzsche's work on the body or instinct as privileged over the rational mind. For example, the discovery of manhood as outside civilization applies to *A Sick Collier*. Willie's sickness, the story implies, results from the condition of the mines. Capitalism's rapid growth across the British landscape signals the difficulty of ever getting outside the sickness.

Lawrence turns, as Boscagli suggests, to the outsider figure of his "Indian" fiction. What interests me here, however, is how the alien body represents a complex version of homosexual desire. For Boscagli, Lawrence's primitivism (exemplified in *The Plumed Serpent*) hides a strong homosexual dynamic. This dynamic's apotheosis occurs in the ritualistic encounter between Ramón and Cipriano ("*The Living Huitzilopochtl*"):

> Ramón knelt and pressed his arms close around Cipriano's waist, pressing his black head against his side. And Cipriano began to feel as if his mind, his head were melting away in the darkness, like a pearl in black wine, the other circle of sleep began to swing, vast. And he was a man without a head, moving like a dark wind over the face of dark waters.[21]

The ritual submission of the Indian, Cipriano, to Ramón is clear. Likewise, the homosexual component of the submission is unmistakable: "Ramón bound him fast around the middle, then, pressing his head against the hip, folded the arms around Cipriano's loins, closing with his hands the secret places" (368). Both characters appear highly sexualized and the scene of: "divine possession is in fact a scene of seduction: under Ramón's influence Cipriano becomes a pliable and submissive body ready to be aroused" (Boscagli, 202).

Boscagli's emphasis on Lawrence's hymn to masculinity and Lawrence's diffusion of homoeroticism through the narrator, Kate Leslie's perspective captures a powerful Lawrentian dynamic. *The Plumed Serpent*'s hidden "homoerotic plot, the central story of the fellowship of Cipriano and Ramón," is already anticipated in *Women in Love* and revised in *Lady Chatterley's Lover*.

HOMO(SOCIAL)SEXUALITY IN WOMEN IN LOVE

Eve Kosofsky Sedgwick's adaptation of René Girard's model of triangular desire contributes a fresh perspective on Lawrence's inscription of homoerotic desire.[22] Girard's model discloses an intense bond between male rivals for the female love object.[23] Sedgwick reads the triangular model as structuring men's relations to other men. Women serve, in this model, as a mediator for male desire. Sedgwick stresses the class basis of such desire. She further argues that homosocial and homosexual desire exist as a continuum among women, but not men. In other words, female friendships are not, in Sedgwick's reading, troubled by sexuality, whereas male friendship cannot tolerate a sexual component.

Male friendship and homosexual desire play a decisive and complicated role in *Women in Love*. Homosexual desire emerges in three different, but interrelated ways during the novel's unfolding. First, homosexuality is represented through socially acknowledged homosexual traits. Loerke is an unabashed homosexual presented as a symbol of decadence.[24] His sexuality is established both through his relationship to Leitner, a young, handsome companion, and also through Loerke's disdain for women. The sculptor prefers young girls as subjects for his art: " 'I don't like them any bigger, any older. Then they are beautiful, as sixteen, seventeen, eighteen-after that, they are no use to me' " (433). Although Loerke appeals to Gudrun, both Gerald and Birkin detest him. Lawrence's narrative links Loerke with dirt, scum, vermin, crime, and deformation, "he looked like a lop-eared rabbit, or troll" (422). In addition, Loerke preaches the gospel of futurism: "As a matter of fact sculpture is always part of an architectural conception. And since churches are all museum stuff, since industry is business, now, then let us make our places of industry our art—our factory—area our Parthenon-ecco!" (424). Consequently, the novel's representation of Loerke's public homosexuality remains stereotypical and, like futurist art, condemned.

The novel's second, and more complex, inscription of homosexual desire occurs in the famous chapter "Excurse" (302–320). The chapter begins with Birkin asking Ursula to go on a leisurely drive through the countryside. A heated argument ensues when Birkin indicates his desire to visit Hermione. Ursula bursts into a vitriolic diatribe over Birkin's suggestion, " 'I jealous! I—jealous! You are mistaken if you think that. I'm not jealous in the least of Hermione, she is nothing to me, not that!' And Ursula snapped her fingers. 'No, it's you who are the liar. It's you who must return, like a dog to his vomit' " (306). The harangue continues with Ursula calling Birkin, " 'scavenger dog, you eater of corpses,' " and to Birkin's truth as

" 'offal smelling.' " Ursula concludes by defining her partner's desire for death, " 'you want yourself, and dirt, and death-that's what you want. You are *perverse*, so death-eating' " (307).

Perversion, then, links together a metonymical chain of signifiers: vomit, shit, dirt, and death (also linking Birkin and Loerke). Yet, Birkin and Ursula's heated argument undergoes a strange sea change as they reach the Saracen's Head Inn. The sound of church reminds Ursula of her childhood dream world. She then enters a trance state, "New eyes were opened in her soul, and she saw a strange creature from another world, in him" (312). Subsequently, Ursula proceeds in, "tracing the back of his [Birkin's] thighs, following some mysterious life flow there" (313). Incredibly, the narrative's perverse twist turns Ursula's previous condemnation of Birkin as "offal smelling" into her exaltation of Birkin's asshole!

Ursula digitally explores Birkin's ass in a remarkable passage:

> She traced with her hands the line of his loins and thighs, at the back, and a living fire ran through her, from him, darkly. It was a dark flood of electric passion she released from him, drew into herself. She had established a rich new circuit, a new current of passional electric energy, between the two of them, released from the darkest poles of the body and established in perfect circuit. It was a dark fire of electricity that rushed from him to her, and flooded them both with rich peace, satisfaction. (349)

Doherty reads this passage as indicating the narrative's transformation of metonymic associations into metaphoric associations.[25] The passage, however, discloses even more than this topological transfer. First, Ursula initiates the sexual encounter making Birkin the sex object. A further symbolic reversal concerns the displacement of the phallus in favor of the anus: "And now, behold, from the smitten rock of the man's body, from the strange marvellous flanks and thighs, deeper, further in mystery than the phallic source, core of the floods of ineffable darkness and ineffable riches" (314). The passage dislodges the phallic signifier and hence calls into question its privileged status.

On yet another level, the narrative's re-inscription of the life-affirming anus must be read along a gender axis. Homosexuality would, after all, generally find the anus an erotic zone. Consequently, Ursula's usurpation of a male role displaces a frequently homosexual activity with a heterosexual context. In other words, the narrative radicalizes sexual ecstasy and destabilizes its gender moorings.

Jonathan Dollimore describes this displacement of desire as a sublimation of one form of sexuality into another.[26] The displacement is typically from the acceptable, that is, heterosexual to the unacceptable, that is, homosexual. Such a displacement of sexual desire, however, necessarily depends on the interconnectedness of both forms of desire. "In short, Lawrence finds ecstasy not in heterosexuality per se but its radical perversion, and he does so by reactivating the perverse dynamic at the heart of desire" (275).

G. Wilson Knight has explicated the role of anal sex in Lawrence,[27] but Lawrence's praise of anal love finds its strongest language in an early version of his essay on Whitman for *Studies in Classic American Literature*.[28] In the essay's 1919 version Lawrence replays his psychology from *Fantasia of the Unconscious* in a curious twist on the star equilibrium Birkin effuses about in *Women in Love*. Lawrence discusses the life circuit of man and woman polarized in the hypogastric plexus and the sacral ganglion (365). However, this life circuit provides only a gateway to the self's deepest sacral center, the cocygeal, "[h]ere is the dark node which relates us to the center of the earth, the plumb-centre of substantial being" (365). Lawrence continues through his exposition of Whitman to privilege the manly life circuit over the male–female life circuit: "[t]he last perfect balance is between two men, in whom the deepest sensual centers, and also the extreme upper centers, vibrate in one circuit, and know their electric establishment and readjustment as does the circuit between man and woman. There is the same immediate connection, the same life-balance, the same perfection in fulfilled consciousness and being" (366). In *Women in Love* the male-to-male bond of Birkin and Gerald becomes subsumed by the anal encounter between Birkin and Ursula as if Birkin has translated his homosexual desires into a heterosexual encounter that echoes homosexual intercourse. The complexities of Birkin's desire then must be rethought in terms of the novel's initial prologue and the Whitman essays.

In the chapter "Male to Male" Birkin proposes a Blütbruderschaft to Gerald, in which two men:

> "Make a little wound in their arms, and rub each other's blood into the cut?" said Gerald.
>
> "Yes—and swear to be true to each other, of one blood, all their lives—That is what that is what we ought to do. No wounds, that is obsolete—But ought to swear to love each other, you and I, implicitly, finally, without any possibility of going back on it." (*WL*, 206–207)

This male fellowship, which Lawrence once believed he nearly had with Bertrand Russell, replaces the star polarity Birkin discusses at the chapter's beginning. Birkin had desired a perfect balance between a man and woman, "leaving two single beings, constellated together like two stars"(201). Birkin's ideal heterosexual union meets with disappointment, first with Hermione, and then with Ursula, because of women's possessiveness: "always a man must be considered as the broken-off fragment of a woman, and the sex was the still aching scar of the laceration. Man must be added to a woman, before he had any real place or wholeness" (200). The laceration image foreshadows the cut of Blütbruderscaft, but here indicates not an equitable relationship, but, contrarily, a subservient one. Further the laceration image reverses the biblical story of Eve being taken from Adam's rib now showing man as the appendage to woman. This mythical reversal indicates, on a textual level, that male friendship appears stronger than the idealistic star equilibrium of man and woman.

In an exceptional essay on the novel Kristopher Craft examines the vicissitudes of male bonding in Lawrence's letters written during the composition of *Women in Love*.[29] Craft begins by discussing Lawrence's letter to Amy Lowell (*Letters*, iii, 645) wherein Lawrence exclaims a Blütbruderschaft with his new typewriter (a gift from Lowell). The letter goes on to describe how the typewriter mutates into a naked beach scene between Lawrence and Frieda. Craft reads the letter as a metaphor encapsulating gender inversion, "where man was, there woman shall be" (166) and concludes his discussion showing how the inversion trope, "refuses to countenance the masculinity of male homosexual desire, a refusal shared, we should note, by Lawrence's title *Women in Love*, which silently ingests, all the better to occlude, the open secret of the novel's secret subject: men in love" (166). As Craft continues, the inversion figure demands: "The elimination of at least one male, either by murder or 'castration' " (166). In *Women in Love*, a "castrated" Gerald ends up in dead among the Alps. The road to castration requires, however, more explication.

Lawrence's thinking about homosexuality occupies a more fluid space than his critics will allow. In addition, to the Whitman essay, Lawrence's letters indicate shifting perspectives on homosexuality. In an oft-quoted letter to Henry Savage, dated December 2, 1913 Lawrence poses a provocative question, "I should like to know why nearly every man that approaches greatness tends to homosexuality, whether he admits it or not: so that he loves the body of a man better than the body of a woman—as I believe the Greeks did, sculptors and all, by far. I believe a man projects his image on another man, like on a mirror. But from a woman he wants himself re-born, re-constructed" (*Letters*, ii, 115). Despite the stereotypical assumptions Lawrence makes and the irony that he would also be included as an artist who approaches greatness, the letter espouses that the creative thrust of homosexuality springs from its fundamental narcissism. The self projects itself on the other like a mirror reflecting itself back in a loop of natural creativity. Mark Kinkead-Weekes observes the letter's ambiguity; ". . . the letter to Savage clearly implies that the greater otherness in heterosexuality makes it more transforming, though (failing that) a homosexual relationship might have saved Middleton [a suicide] from fatal solipsism."[30] This comment nearly replaces Lawrence's heterosexual vision with a barely latent homosexual option that threatens to erase the heterosexual vision. Later, writing about *Women in Love*, Kinkead-Weeks writes that, "[t]he whole point here is less to distinguish 'homosexual' from 'heterosexual' relationships, than to begin exploring the difference in both alike between relationships that can transfigure, and those that are deathly because they disintegrate the self and destroy the other" (330). Here the fluidity of desire emerges emphatically and Lawrence's biographer delineates a coequal circuit of desire, male-to-female and male-to-male.

Ultimately, Kinkead-Weeks's argument evolves from an early assumption about Lawrence's modernity, ". . . where Modernist emphasis fell on the artist-self as creator, Lawrence emphasized transformation of the self at the hands of the Other—hence the vital importance of sexual relationships" (137). This transformation, as indicated above, can be homosexual or heterosexual, and the self can be his mirror image, the same or homo: "the man for the man who stands not merely as himself for the homo: but also as the representative, even the guarantor, of the same, of the same man, of the man, that is, whose self-sameness must not be overthrown or degraded by the 'feminine' cast of his desire" (Craft, 170).

These comments frame my discussion of the physical undercurrents of Birkin and Gerald's friendship. Lawrence locates the literary bonding of male opposites (e.g., northern and southern men, officer and servant, blind and sighted) in his reading of James Fenimore Cooper's Leatherstocking novels. Lawrence sees the relationship between the White Man, Natty Bumppo, and the Red Man, Chingachgook, as the nucleus of a new society:

> That is, he [Cooper] dreamed a new human relationship. A stark, stripped down relationship of two men, deeper than the depths of sex. Deeper than property, deeper than fatherhood, deeper than marriage, deeper than love. So deep that it is loveless. The stark, loveless, wordless unison of two men who have come from the bottom of themselves. This is the new nucleus of a new society, the clue to a new world-epoch. (*SCAM*, 58)

This rather mystical statement certainly privileges the male bond over the male–female bond. Male friendships' erotic current resurfaces in the Whitman essays and also in the *Women in Love* chapter entitled

"Gladiatorial" (266–276). Interestingly, the wrestling metaphor, (wrestling being the chapter's key event), with its archetypal significance represents Lawrence's own grappling with both Whitman, in particular, and the censors in general. Lawrence worked on *Studies in Classical American Literature* and *Women in Love* (their composition overlapped) more than any other of his published books and he considered *Studies in Classical American Literature, Women in Love*, and *The Rainbow* as his dearest and most dangerous books (*Letters*, iii, 546–547).

In facing boredom and emptiness for the first time Gerald grasps for an activity to fill his inner void. The two friends then decide to engage in a naked wrestling match. Lawrence's sensual description of the wrestling covers many pages: "So the two men entwined and wrestled with each other, working nearer and nearer"(270).

The match concludes with the friends holding each other's hand in near postcoital bliss. Both men then acknowledge their sensuality: " 'We are mentally, spiritually intimate, therefore we should be more or less physically intimate too—it is more whole.' 'Certainly it is' said Gerald. Then he laughed pleasantly, adding: 'It's rather wonderful to me' " (272). Finally, Birkin acknowledges his admiration for Gerald's body. " 'You have a northern kind of beauty, like light refracted from snow—and a beautiful, plastic form' " (273).

The scene between Gerald and Birkin can be contrasted with the encounter between Ursula and Miss Inger, in *The Rainbow*.[31] Ursula is intensely attracted to Miss Inger, but there is a clear asymmetry in the relationship. Miss Inger is older, experienced and a teacher. Ursula is a schoolgirl. Her infatuation with the teacher blossoms when they compete in a friendly swimming match: "Miss Inger touched the pipe, swung herself round, and caught Ursula round the waist, in the water, and held her for a moment against herself. The bodies of the two women touched, heaved against each other for a moment, then were separate" (314).

Ursula and Miss Inger soon become lovers. Lawrence describes the affair with strikingly erotic imagery. Yet the story is told from Ursula's adolescent perspective. Ursula's young lust however, turns into nausea: "But a heavy, clogged sense of deadness began to gather upon her, from the other woman's contrast. And sometimes she thought Winifred was ugly, clayey" (319). For women, losing one's beauty emerges as a threat that men do not have to face. The mirror functions as the reality symbol for a relationship marked by age discrepancy. Lesbian relationships then have much less continuity, in Lawrence's companion novels, than male-to-male desire. In fact, Lawrence titles the chapter between Winifred and Ursula "Shame."

Contrarily, the title "Gladiatorial" suggests a combat, but ends, paradoxically, in a strengthening of Gerald and Birkin's friendship. Although the sexual activity between the men may be muted, its physicality is not. Lawrence stresses the erotic nature of Gerald's and Birkin's relationship in the abandoned first chapter called *The Prologue*.[32] This posthumously published piece is important to understanding Lawrence's work for two major reasons. First, the chapter is an explicit description of male-to-male desire. Second, Lawrence expresses the social dilemma of such "dark love."

The men's attraction to each other is immediate. "Birkin and Gerald Crich felt take place between them, the moment they saw each other, that sudden connection which sometimes springs up between men who are very different in temper. There had been a subterranean kindling in each man. Each looked towards the other, and knew the trembling nearness." (489) Lawrence refers to their relationship as "transcendental intimacy," but always with the "interchange of spiritual and physical richness" (490). The relationship between Gerald and Birkin is much more satisfying than the relationship between Hermionie and Birkin.

In fact, the narrator describes a split within Birkin where he is physically attracted to men and spiritually drawn to women: "although he was always drawn to women, feeling more at home with a woman than a man, yet it was for men that he felt the hot, flushing, roused attraction which a man is supposed to feel for the other sex" (501). The narrative continues to delineate Birkin's physical attraction to both northern and the "dark-skinned, supple night-smelling men." Nonetheless, Birkin feels a tremendous division within himself. What prohibits his acting on such clearly homosexual drives?

The narrative explicitly locates Birkin's division as a product of society. Birkin's homosexual desire is innate: "a man can no more slay a living desire in him, that he can prevent his body from feeling heat and cold. He can put himself into bondage, to prevent the fulfillment of the desire, that is all" (504). Birkin cannot prevent what is to him a natural desire. He is held in bondage by a society that does not tolerate such same sex desire:

> This was the one and only secret he kept to himself, this secret of his passionate and sudden, spasmodic affinity for men he saw. He kept this secret even from himself. He knew what he felt, but he always kept the knowledge at bay. His priori were: "I should not feel like this," "and it is the ultimate mark of my own deficiency, that I feel like this." Therefore, though he admitted everything, he never really faced the question. He never accepted the desire, and received it as part of himself. He always tried to keep it expelled from him. (505)

Birkin's secret ultimately drives him to the abyss of despair. Hermonie is, consequently only a small foothold in a world that denies Birkin fulfillment of his sexual desires, and his dissatisfaction with women inevitably pushes him "into a bottomless sea" (506).

Lawrence does not publish the original first chapter for reasons not unlike E.M. Forster's decision not to publish *Maurice* or his own decision not to publish early versions of the Whitman essay.[33] After the censorship battles over *The Rainbow* Lawrence did not want another protracted censorship fight. The aesthetic discussion to discard *The Prologue*, however, is fortuitous. Its tone is entirely different than the novel's finely wrought, balanced narration. *The Prologue* is much closer to Lawrentian essays than his fiction. The voice is didactic and expository, but this style itself lends credence to Birkin's dilemma and Lawrence's sensitivity to homosexual desire despite his official denouncements of same-sex eroticism. Consequently, one cannot consider The Prologue as part of what ultimately becomes *Women in Love*. Nonetheless, *The Prologue*, like Lawrence's letters and essays contributes to the author's overall thinking about the work and necessarily informs Lawrence's own complex views on sexuality.

In terms of Sedgwick's model of triangular desire, the bond between Birkin and Gerald clearly displaces all Birkin's other bonds. The novel, however, appears to complicate a triangular model by representing two parallel sets of relationships between Birkin and Ursula and Gudrun and Gerald. Yet the novel definitely privileges the male-to-male relationship. Consequently, the chapter "Gladiatorial" can be read as a resurfacing of *The Prologue* or a return of the repressed. Craft makes a similar point arguing:

> In *Women in Love* as finally published, the desires that the prologue so emphatically lodges within Birkin's "own innate being" (504) have been transported across gender, into "the soul of a woman" whose body "just happens" to be female. The result for the narrative is an enabling distortion that can be expressed in another convenient formula, this one my own: *where Birkin's desire had been, there Gudrun's body shall be* . . . (Craft, 174)

The reader might recall here that the chapter "Man to Man" concludes with the narratives declaration of unspoken male love:

> The eyes of the two men met again. Gerald's, that were keen as a hawk's, were now suffused with warm light and with unadmitted love, Birkin looked back as out of darkness, unsounded and unknown, yet with a kind of warmth, that seemed to flow over Gerald's brain like a fertile sleep. (*WL*, 210)

The passages' sexual undertones are difficult to deny and the star equilibrium appears to be the deeper male bond Lawrence describes in the 1919 Whitman essay. Actually, the narrative indicates the temporary achievement of star equilibrium only at the moment of anal penetration: "He would be night-free, like an Egyptian, steadfast in perfectly suspended equilibrium, pure mystic nodality of physical being. They would give each other this star-equilibrium, which alone is true freedom" (*WL*, 319).

This indicates the transfer of the deep homosexual bond to a heterosexual relationship. Nonetheless, the novel pushes toward the transforming love possible between two men only to terminate in Gerald's death among the snowy alpine, a scene reminiscent of "The Prussian Officer." In the novel's shifting relationships Gerald's rivalry with Birkin becomes a rivalry with Loerke, "a conflict in spirit between the two men" (*WL*, 449) who, in the end, reigns triumphant. Gudrun agrees to go to Dresden and leave Gerald behind. Loeke, the pederast, "could penetrate into depths far out of Gerald's knowledge, Gerald was left behind like a postulant in the anteroom of this temple of mysteries, this woman" (451). Gerald's death among the snow then leaves Birkin contemplating a lost love just as he stands next to his wife. The final exchange between Birkin and Ursula over the now-dead Gerald clarifies where the novel's true affection belongs:

> "Did you need Gerald?" she asked one evening.
> "Yes," he said. "You are enough for me, as far as woman is concerened. You are all women to me. But I wanted a man friend, as eternal as you and I are eternal."
> "Why aren't I enough?" she said. "You are enough for me. I don't want anybody else but you. Why isn't it the same with you?"
> "Having you, I can live all my life without anybody else, any other sheer intimacy. But to make it complete, really happy, I wanted eternal union with man too: another kind of love," he said.
> "I don't believe it," she said. "It's obstinacy, a theory, a perversity."
> "Well—" he said.
> "You can't have two kinds of love. Why should you!"
> "It seems as if I can't," he said. "Yet I wanted it."
> "You can't have it, because it's false, impossible," she said.
> "I don't believe that," he answered. (*WL*, 481)

This love that Birkin elegizes over appears to be the love of comrades that Lawrence discusses in his reading of Whitman's *Calamus* (*SCAL*, 153–161). This love will, Lawrence claims for Whitman, build a new world. Yet, as Lawrence notes the deep love of man-to-man, deeper than the love of man to woman, slides into death, "[F]or the great mergers, woman at last becomes inadequate. For those who love to extremes, Woman is inadequate for the last merging. So the next step is the merging of man-for-man love. And this is on the brink of death. It slides over into death" (154). Just so,

Women in Love ends with Gerald's merging into death and Birkin's elegy expressing that heterosexual love cannot be enough. Although Gerald dies in sight of a cross, there will be no salvation. As indicated in my discussion of *The Escaped Cock*, Lawrence rejects salvation, and Whitman, for Lawrence, exhibits the "morality of the soul living her life, not saving herself" (157). The novel provides no resolution, only an elegiac despair. What exactly this other kind of love might be remains somehow inconclusive. Certainly, heterosexual love remains inadequate for Birkin and, consequently suggesting, as supplement, a homosexual love that never quite materializes. As Craft writes, "*Women in Love* thus expires upon the posthumous instantiation of a disgruntled heterosexuality whose terminal oscillations ('You can't have it/I don't believe that') dialogically rehearse the catastrophic homosexual loss that both founds this heterosexuality and cofounds its powers of satisfaction and completion" (Craft, 189). This impossible desire of Birkin remains as Ursula comments "This impossible desire of Birkin remains as Ursula comments 'perverse' and thus turns away from any convention or social organization critics might tighten around Lawrence's alleged celebration of the phallus, a symbol Gudrun finds so boring" (*WL*, 463).

THE FOX, THE PHALLUS, AND THE PLAY OF DESIRE

Lawrence's great novella, *The Fox* (1918–1922), allows me to bring together various readings of sexual desire.[34] As Eve Kosofsky Sedgwick argues sexual orientation remains the most salient dimension of sexuality and any analysis of sexuality in modern culture requires a discussion of sexual orientation.[35] *The Fox* interrogates the binary division of sexual orientation from multiple perspectives.

Sedgwick, for instance, maps the sexual orientation axis in relationship to transitivity, an integrative, universalizing model, and separatism, a minoritizing model (88). In *The Fox*, Banford and March appear to be living self-sufficiently on a farm. March plays the masculine role ("she would be the man about the place.") within the dyad. Historically, March would be considered the "mannish woman" or "mannish lesbian." These two women, however, do not represent an essentialist lesbian identity. For the appearance of the young soldier, Henry, triangulates Banford and March's homosocial bond into an ambiguous model of desire.

Henry's arrival elicits March's apparent heterosexual desire, "All the time, while she was active, she was attending to the youth in the sitting room, not so much listening to what he said, as feeling the soft run of his voice" (15). Banford, on the other hand, appears jealous of Henry's presence and she sees him as a rival for March. In fact she reacts to Henry's suggestion that he marry March as, "a bird that had been shot." In terms of Sedgwick's triangular model the female now mediates the rivalry between a male and female, not the ordinary rivalry between two men.

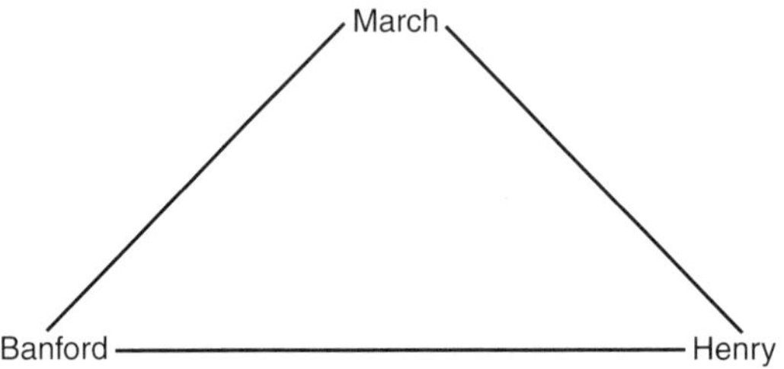

Henry appears to play the role later played by the gypsy and Mellors in *The Virgin and the Gypsy* and *Lady Chatterley's Lover* respectively. Henry would awaken the sexually dormant March, but does he awaken her heterosexuality? In order to achieve his rescue of March, Henry must plot his rival's death. Henry demands that March submit to his male destiny, "He wanted a new connection. He wanted her to give herself without defenses, to sink and become submerged in him" (69). Interestingly, Henry's manhood emerges only in relationship to March and his response to March wearing a dress. Does the secret of sexual difference that March's dress appears to disclose actually symbolize sexual difference along the sexual orientation axis?

Early in the story Henry appears, in the narrator's description, drawn to March's boyish face, "Her figure, like a graceful young man's, piqued him" (23). Later, when March appears in a dress, Henry's sexuality appears to fail him. His sexual paralysis subverts any easy association of Henry with heterosexual desire: "He held her hands in his, but he did not make love to her. Since he realized that she was a woman, and vulnerable, accessible, certain heaviness had possessed his soul. He did not want to make love to her. He shrank from any such performance, almost in fear" (53). In effect, *The Fox* shatters any model of straight desire and eludes any stable alignment of sex-gender roles.

In addition, to being hunted, March hunts or at least stalks the fox in her "male way." Yet, the fox, like March, appears to be an ambiguous symbol. Henry appears to be a double for the fox and, yet, ironically, it is Henry now who hunts March. In fact, March comes under Henry's spell just as she came under the fox's spell: "March, already under the influence of his strange, soft, modulated voice, stared at him spell-bound" (14). On the other hand, the fox symbolizes aspects of femininity. In Freudian terms, the fox would act as a fetish and the fox's fur as symbolic of the vagina. The narrative links the fox to the shadows, that is, a place of secrets and mystery. In this chain of associations Henry's killing the fox leads to March's exploration of his fur or a symbolic exploration of Banford:

> White and soft as snow his belly: white and soft as snow. She passed her hand softly down it. And his wonderful black-glinted brush was full and frictional, wonderful. She passed her hand down this also, and quivered. Time after time she took the full fur of that tail between her hands and passed her hand slowly downwards. Wonderful sharp thick splendour of tail! Wonderful! And he was dead! She pursed her lips, and her eyes went black and vacant. Then she took the head in her hand. (41)

The sensual language could be describing March reaching a sexual climax. Further sexual connotations linking March and the fox's fur emerge in her dream. March seeks, in the dream, to cover the dead Banford with the fox's fur. Consequently, March appears to displace her sexual desire for Banford onto the fox. Indeed, March seems to wish for Banford's death as much as Henry does, but Banford's death releases March's homosexual desire as much as her heterosexual desire.

If, in Freudian terms, the fetish signifies the missing penis (i.e., the fox's wonderful tail), the penis can never be recovered for the story's vaginal symbols are endless. The symbol of the bottomless pit most graphically evokes a free-floating vaginal fear or castration complex: "Yet pluck flower after flower—it is never the flower, the flower itself—its canyx is a horrible gulf, it is the bottomless pit" (69). The phallus, sign of unity and coherence, in other words, heterosexual order, can never be found.

Consequently, Lillian Faderman's attempt to read *The Fox* as Lawrence's indictment of lesbian sexuality requires considerable use of manufactured evidence.[36] The story does not, as I have shown, identify March as a lesbian. Although March may desire lesbian sex she may simply desire a sexual outlet irrespective of gender. Her masculine identity simply complements Banford's more traditional femininity. Faderman's contention that Lawrence, "teaches that lesbians are morbid and must be either killed of captured" (350) depends on the unsupported supposition that March is a lesbian. The critic's conclusion that Lawrence's moral is: "women cannot find satisfaction with each other, to try to do so is sick, and some terrible disaster will befall those who test this truth" (351), operates as a projection of the critic's own value system. Lawrence's representation of sexuality, like the fox, remains slippery and entirely outside the critics' straightjacket.

The entire novella operates in a liminal space. Its setting on the edge of a wood demarcates a space between two worlds and two genders. The trope of inversion, however, appears inadequate to resolve the stories knots of desire. March is neither a woman trapped in a man's body, her dress dispels that illusion, but nor is she a man trapped in a woman's body. The desire running underneath the characters shares Freud and Reich's instinctual force and operates independent of any genital organization. Homosexual bodies, like heterosexual bodies, exist, ultimately, in a circuit of desire that disrupts and dispels sexuality's supposed unitary orientation.

CONNIE'S JEWELS OR READING WITH IRIGARAY

In the fourth chapter of *Lady Chatterley's Lover* a group of Clifford Chatterley's intellectual friends gather to discuss issues relevant to modern England. The chapter unfolds as a modern version of Plato's *Symposium*, with talk of sex replacing talk of love. In representing Plato's dialogue, Lawrence re-inscribes the entire patriarchal vision of love engendered by Plato's text. The chapter satirizes both the Cambridge intellectuals and their philosophical forefather; and Lawrence's prose, of course, adds to the accumulation of sexual discourse. How can the narrative escape the talk about sex that the chapter presents as the essence of sexual modernism? To answer this, further consideration must be given to Connie's place in the dialogue: What does her silence represent? Is she simply a passive observer (women, after all, and this goes back to Plato, don't participate in intellectual discussions)? Or is Connie a romantic muse (the literati require her warm, physical beauty to inspire their talk)? These questions are the foreground to my rereading of chapter 4 as the point at which the novel reverses the reader's expectations and engenders another form of sexual discourse, which is covered over by the male intellectuals.

Hammond, a successful writer, begins the discussion by noting that all the talk about sex is what makes sex a problem. In the exchange with Charlie May and Tommy Dukes, Hammond's position represents a traditional Christian perspective; he believes that sex has its place and time (i.e., in the bedroom and within marriage). Behind Hammond's conservative perspective rests a financial belief, for Hammond, in the chapter, is equated with marriage and marriage with property ownership. Dukes make the point in the following fashion: "[i]f you begin to be unsuccessful you'd begin to flirt—like Charlie, who isn't successful. Married people like you and Julie have labels on you like travelers' trunk. Julie is labeled Mrs. Arnold B. Hammond—just like a trunk on the railway that belongs to somebody." (32).

Against this Christian, bourgeois view of sex Charlie May, an Irish writer, promotes a modern, emancipated view of sexuality. May places value entirely on the satisfaction of a physical need, and he experiences sex as a physical conversation in his response to Clifford, "Lascivious! Well, why not? I can't see I do a woman any more harm by sleeping with her than by dancing with her—or even talking with her about the weather. It's just an interchange of sensation instead of ideas, so why not?" (33). Lawrence's prejudice creeps in through the characterization of May as Celt; nonetheless, both Hammond and May represent an important pole of modern sexuality: conservative and liberal.

Clifford speaks least of all in this chapter; the narrator presents him as uneasy and effeminate throughout the characters' discussion. When pressed by Dukes to offer his opinion about sex, Clifford gives the following stammering reply: " '[I] suppose marry-and-have-done-with-it would pretty well stand for what I think" (35). Clifford is pure intellect: he sees sex as a marital duty, but one he cannot fulfill. He understands intimacy as primarily intellectual and he goes on to say that sex can be a "great thing" because "it perfects the intimacy." Clifford, in turn, becomes most closely associated with material success following this chapter. Although presented as Connie Chatterley, Clifford's wife is always his property and title (i.e., Lady Chatterley).

Tommy Dukes summarizes the dialogue's characterization of love as follows: "Love's another of those half-witted performances, today. Fellows with swaying waists fucking little jazz girls with small boy buttocks like two-dollar studs? Do you mean that sort of love? Or the joint-property, make-a-success-of-it, my husband-my wife sort of love? No, my fine fellow, I don't believe in it at all!" (39). His criticism closely parallels Lawrence's own criticism of both repressive, Victorian sexuality and emancipated, modern sexuality. Yet Dukes offers no alternative and condemns himself as a "mental lifer" (40). If Dukes is, at least in part, Lawrence's spokesman, the novelist includes himself in the mental life represented by the production of even more sexual discourse (i.e., writing the novel).

This discussion deploys the discursive field of sexuality. Luce Irigaray's work stresses the exclusion of women from this discourse and this exclusion is very true of Lawrence's text. Connie is, as Irigaray would say, a commodity in exchange between men. Her presence appears to be the occasion for discourse, and her silence subtends male speculation. The chapter unravels as an exhibition of phallic, that is, homosexual economy, which Irigaray describes as:

> The use of and traffic in women subtend and uphold the reign of masculine hom(m)o-sexuality, even while they maintain that hom(m)o-sexuality in speculations, mirror games, identifications, and more or less rivalrous appropriations, which defer its real practice. Reigning everywhere, although prohibited in practice, hom(m)o-sexuality is played out through the bodies of women,

matter, or sign, and heterosexuality has been up to now just an alibi for smooth workings of man's relations with himself, of relations among men.[37]

Connie is circulated among this male symposium just as she will later be exchanged between Clifford and Mellors.

If Connie speaks she will potentially signify impropriety, that is, no longer a lady, and disrupt the homosexual economy. In talking about Irigaray, Judith Butler describes: "The feminine as the unspeakable condition of figuration, as that which, in fact, can never be figured within the terms of philosophy proper, but whose exclusion from that propriety is its enabling condition."[38] This comment suggests that Connie has no language to articulate her sexuality (the book is after all called *Lady Chatterley's Lover* and not Lady Chatterley). Connie must remain at the text's margin to preserve and remind the men that they are men and also that a woman's place is peripheral to their intellectual posturing. In other words, Lawrence maintains clear gender lines. These men are not becoming effeminate, but nonetheless, Lawrence's inscription of Connie's sexuality challenges the novel's discursive field.

Luce Irigaray, like Deleuze and Guattari, deconstructs the Oedipal model of desire. Her valorization of flow in the essay "The Mechanics of Fluids," however, sexualizes that flow in an attempt to articulate female sexuality, which she claims, "can be found only at the price of crossing back through the mirror that subtends all speculation" (*CS*, 77). Irigaray here disrupts Platonic notions of desire and identity by dislodging the notion of a centering idea or structure for desire. In Irigaray's reading, feminine pleasure is always multiple and can never be reduced to the phallocentric logic of identity: "What she says is never identical with anything, moreover; rather, it is contiguous. It touches (upon). And when it strays too far from that proximity, she breaks off and starts over at 'zero' in her body-sex" (29). Irigaray privileges a tactile sexuality and style of writing: "It [writing of women/sexuality of women] comes back in touch with itself in that origin without ever constituting in it as some sort of unity. Simultaneity is its 'proper' aspect—a proper(ty) that is never fixed in the possible identity-to-self of some form or other. It is always fluid, without neglecting the characteristics of fluids that are difficult to idealize: those rubbings between two infinitely near neighbors that create a dynamics" (79).

Although, Irigaray's style articulates a feminine sexuality her text is never essentialist.[39] In fact, her lyrical text *Elemental Passions* is a nuptial quest, exploring in a seamless fluidity, relationships between men and women.[40] The text enacts the woman's body as "fluid and ever mobile" and its challenge for the man who appears to "encounter proximity when it is framed by property" (24). The male always attempts to enclose and limit the woman's movement, turning a fluid into a solid and reducing difference to distinction. Yet, Irigaray challenges the male to explore the difference: "Not in me but in our difference lies the abyss. We can never be sure of bridging the gap between us. But that is our adventure. Without this peril there is no you. If you turn it into a guarantee, you separate us" (28). This risk would involve the male in a tactile sexuality of proximity that threatens to shatter his identity, but opening him to new vistas of a relationship.

The relationship between Mellors and Connie explores this tactile experience. In fact, Mellors, who is excluded from Clifford's symposium, asserts this tactile sexuality as the outside of British sexuality: " 'But even he [the Buddha] fought shy of the bodily awareness, and that natural physical tenderness, which is best, even between men; in a proper manly way. Makes 'em really manly, not so monkeyish. Ay! It's tenderness, really; it's cunt-awareness. Sex is really only touch, the closest of all touch. And it's touch we're [the English] afraid of' " (*LCL*, 277). Lawrence attempts in this passage to approximate Irigaray's description of fluid sexuality but he remains muddled. The touch is masculine with overtones of suppressed homosexuality, but simultaneously, a reflection of "cunt awareness," a term of unclear reference in its curious denotation of tenderness with the vagina. Lawrence needs Mellors and Connie to separate in order to stress their "difference" and maintain Mellors's masculinity. Additionally, Mellors makes this comment in dialect suggesting this tactile aesthetic is outside his own British experience.

Nonetheless, there are textual places describing Connie and Mellors lovemaking in a tactile, flowing language: "His hand passed over the curves of her body, firmly, without desire, but with soft, intimate knowledge" (178). This narration follows Mellors's poem to Connie's vagina: " 'Cunt! Eh, that's the beauty o'thee, lass!' " (172). Lawrence oscillates between the softness of touch and the hardness of Mellors's erection: "He held her close, but he said nothing. He would never say anything. She crept nearer to him, [nearer, touch] only to be near the sensual wonder of him. And out of this utter, incomprehensible stillness, she felt again the slow, momentous, surging rise of the phallus again, the other power" (175). The softness of touch is appropriated by Mellors's multivalent penis but as soon as he becomes hard the couple melts into liquid: "And this time his being within her was all soft and iridescent, purely soft and iridescent, such as no consciousness could seize. Her whole self quivered unconscious and alive, like plasma" (*LCL*, 175). This passage marks the discursive limits of sexuality; only silence remains. Although, Lawrence cannot entirely write outside the limits of his own historical situation, there are moments when the novel, as above, approximates Irigaray's textuality.

The symbolic marriage between Connie and Mellors, as John Thomas and Lady Jane (210–211) and Lawrence's extended description of mystical marriage as the sexual expression whereby: "Two rivers of blood, are man and wife, two distinct streams, that have the power of touching and communing and so renewing, making new and another, without any breaking of the subtle confines, any confusing or commingling" (*A Propos of Lady Chatterley's Lover*, 325), approximate Irigaray's comment: "The limitlessness lies in relationship. In the gift without return he receives from the sustaining mother earth" (*EP*, 53). The relationship is a touching, which does not merge (i.e., turn fluid into solid) and respects the difference in the adventurous, gamble of the abyss.

The exploration of a tactile sexuality in the relationship between Connie and Mellors does not sufficiently address the question of Connie's sexuality. She does not accept the exalted idea of touching and her consciousness registers her ironic appreciation: "She liked to hear what they had to say, especially when Tommy was there. It was fun. Instead of kissing you, and touching you with their bodies, they revealed their minds to you. It was great fun! But what cold minds!" (35). The men, in Connie's view, at this point in the novel, are entirely frigid. But how does the woman's sexuality speak?

In the middle of *The History of Sexuality* (77–80) Foucault retells the fable of Diderot's *Les Bijoux indiscret*, but he never finally allows the jewels to speak, and can only trace the discourse around the woman's invisible sexuality. Contrarily, Luce Irigaray writes the sexuality of women in her marvelous essay "Quant nos levres se parlent."[41] This test rewrites *The Symposium* from an entirely feminine perspective, in which women dialogue among themselves and each other in a polyphony of desire independent of male constructions. Irigaray's lyric expresses the woman's self-touching pleasure, a monologue that always communicates in dialogue, the two lips speaking to themselves and each other. Two lips remain silent in their endless sexual caress, but also speak to the other through the speaking lips. The single body is plural even within the individual body, vaginal lips always communicating the woman's pleasure; but the "you" is also the other women. The text is open always to other lips, other touches, in an orchestration of desire that nowhere cites the Oedipal organization of desire. This exchange of desire belongs to neither patriarchy nor capitalism.[42]

Lawrence cannot write any such text. That would require a new novel composed from Connie's perspective and in 1928 no such novels by a male would be possible. Yet, Lawrence does leave traces of such a text and its alternative desires: for example, the relationship between Connie and her sister and each of their relationships to men prior to marriage. Constance and Hilda Reid are aggressively sexual and able to use men as a "tool" (9) for their own pleasure. "In the actual sex-thrill within the body, the sisters nearly succumbed to the strange male power. But quickly they recovered themselves, took the sex thrill as a sensation, and remained free" (9). Of course even this sexual assertion on the part of the sisters is swallowed up by discourse: "It marked [the sex act] the end of a chapter" (8) and Lawrence quickly encloses the sisters' sexuality through marriage.

The other mark of alternative sexuality comes with Connie's pregnancy (Hilda comes back into her life at this late date). An entirely new relationship of touch emerges with the possibility of Connie's relationship to her child. Mellors only truly approaches a tactile sexuality when Connie becomes pregnant: "He kissed her belly and her mound of Venus, to kiss down to the womb and the fetus within the womb" (278) and when Mellors penetrates Connie he realizes: "that this was the thing he had to do, to come into her tender touch, without losing his pride or his dignity or his integrity as a man" (279). Fatherhood brings Mellors into a new dimension of sexuality, just as motherhood will for Connie. Luce Irigaray has expressed this non-discursive, tactile sexuality in the proximity between mother and daughter.[43] The relationship between mother and fetus is another sign of post-discursive realities. Peggy Phelan commenting about the pregnant body writes:

> The central failure of discursive representation—the illegibility of the materiality of a pregnant body within a visual economy, which everywhere marks the boundary between self and other. Embodied in and by what is and is not one body, the visibly pregnant woman makes the possibility of a continuous subjectivity real. This possibility is everywhere repressed by the institutional arrangements of law, medicine, and politics—all of which presuppose singular social subjects as the foundational units of their discursive economics. (They assume fluency in singularity rather than sociality.)[44]

This brings up an entirely different sense of the sexual body as double and outside the visible economy. Pregnancy merges the man and woman while protecting the couple's separateness. They remain united as parents, a permanent commingling, but separate as individuals. The couple's merging is localized and temporary yet containing its trace through the couple's divergence. Consequently, Irgarary's valorization of tactile sexuality accommodates Lawrence's own complex representation of sexuality's vicissitudes. Chapter 4 takes up the problematic inscription of nondescriptive sexuality, but first I trace the serpentine path of desire throughout *Lady Chatterley's Lover* and show how the narrative's historical structure subsumes radical sexuality into a capitalist system that precludes both a genuine revolution and an individual transformation.

4. Industrial Love: Sexuality in *Lady Chatterley's Lover* ↩

Pull down my native village to the last brick

D.H. Lawrence, Nottingham and the Mining Countryside

A PARADIGM OF INDUSTRIAL LOVE

Chapter 5 of *Lady Chatterley's Lover* embodies, in miniature, the novel's larger structure. Connie and Clifford go for a stroll from the park to the wood, and the slightly hazy, off focus atmosphere suggests a dream state. This dream metaphor returns at the conclusion of chapter 12, which in turn, precedes Clifford and Connie's next trip to the wood: "As she ran home in the twilight, the world seemed a dream; the trees in the park seemed bulging and surging at anchor on a tide, and the heave of the slope to the house was alive" (*LCL*, 178). The landscape's vitality reflects Connie's sexual satisfaction following her sexual initiation with Mellors, and the dream opens up a world of possibility experienced in the wood. Chapter 5, contrary to chapter 12, suggests the entirely dreamlike nature of Connie's erotic reveries: "The hard air was still sulphureous, but they were both used to it. Round the near horizon went the haze, opalescent with frost and smoke, and on the top lay the small blue sky; so that it was like being inside an enclosure, always inside: Life always a dream or a frenzy, inside an enclosure" (*LCL*, 41).

The "frenzy" suggests sexual intensity and erotic release, but here the dream is within an enclosure. The dream does not open out to possibility; it is enclosed by the real world. On the most immediate level, the sulphureous atmosphere, that is, industrial pollution encloses and suffocates the dream. And on a deeper level, the dream represents the wood, and the wood represents a vision of history: "Clifford loved the wood. He loved the old oak trees. He felt they were his own through generations. He wanted to protect them; a place cut off from the world" (*LCL*, 42). Beyond Clifford's legacy stretches England's great past: "The wood was a remnant of the great forest where Robin Hood hunted, and this riding was an old, old thoroughfare coming across the country." This magic wood, a dream of history, is enclosed by modern, industrial England.

The wood is, however, not inviolate. Clifford comes upon the clearing noticing its barren spot: "The chair chuffed slowly up the incline, rocking and jolting on the frozen clods. And suddenly on the left came a clearing, where there was nothing but a ravel of dead bracken, a thin and spindly sapling leaning rickety here and there, big sawn stumps showing their tops and their grasping roots, lifeless and patches of blackness where the woodmen had burned the brushwood and rubish" (*LCL*, 42). This rupture in the wood symbolizes the inevitability of history's march; the war necessitates the destruction of nature and tradition. Clifford, in some sense, repudiates his own tradition here; he sees himself as part of England's great, literary past, imagining himself in his motorized chair part ". . . of Knights riding and ladies on palfreys." Yet Clifford's father, in fact, broke the land's continuity with the past:

> This was one of the places that Sir Geoffrey had cut during the war for trench timber. The whole knoll, which rose softly on the right of the riding, was denuded and strangely forlorn. On the crown of the knoll where the oaks had stood, now was bareness and from there you could look out over the trees, to the colliery railway and the new works at Stacks Gate. Connie had stood and looked: it was a breach in the pure seclusion of the wood. It let in the world. But she didn't tell Clifford. (*LCL*, 42)

The "clearing" brings to the foreground a number of complex ironies. The wood becomes fuel for the war, and Sir Geoffrey allows for its violation. In the war, Clifford loses use of his lower self, and in turn his impotency from the war injury literally ends the passage of the family name. The violation of the wood brings conclusion to family history and the British legacy, ending a dream of greatness and romance. Furthermore, this clearing, symbolic of the past's pastness, also opens out to the "colliery railway, and the new works at Stacks Gate." The railway tracks replace the ancient pathways, and the breach in nature, opened by the clearing, lets in the modern, industrial world. The ironies spiral as Connie and Clifford reach the clearing.

Clifford brings up the question regarding his desire to have a son in order to maintain family tradition (*LCL*, 43). He assumes the desired child will be a son, yet ironically, he cannot have a child. The attempt to replant the clearing will never replace the broken tradition, and the desire to have a child can only be a dream. Clifford makes his great speech on the integrated life in this chapter. He attempts to replace the historical tradition with a slowly built, interwoven marriage, a poor substitute for his real dream. Immediately following his talk about a son, Connie feels the "emotional bruise" that completely severs the couple's emotional intimacy. The irony compounds when Connie meets Mellors here for the first time.

Mellors will be the man with whom Connie has child, but the child will not continue any tradition. His presence brings along a number of conflicting, associations. Mellors carries a gun, "a soldier!" and speaks both as a gentleman and a collier. The division in Mellors' language reflects his divided identity: torn between the British Empire and its tradition (as an officer in India) and the industrial future. Mellors isolates himself in the wood as a gamekeeper and Connie associates Mellors with the wood's freedom and the sexual release from marital bondage. Yet, the sexual freedom and refuge Mellors represents for Connie also represent the violation of her marriage. Mellors brings his past with him into the wood, exemplifying the modern world not only enclosing the dream (the wood), but also intruding inside the dream itself. When asked about the gamekeeper, Clifford replies, ". . . son of a collier" (48). The outside (industrial world) is already inside (the wood).

The wild England Clifford wants to preserve has been replaced and virtually effaced by the England of Tevershall. The Wragby estate is an anachronism; Tevershall is the image of England's future. As Connie realizes, "Mellors had come out of all this" and her future with him cannot separate itself from this contemporary reality. The fact that her relationship with Mellors exists almost entirely within the wood indicates its dreamlike status and enclosure within the industrial world.

Chapter 5 concludes with Connie and Clifford leaving the wood for their respective worlds. He returns to the world of intellectuals and mental life:

There was Clifford's success: the bitch goddess! It was true, he was almost famous, and his books brought him a thousand pounds. His photograph appeared everywhere. There was a bust of him in one of the galleries, and a portrait of him in two galleries. He seemed to be most modern of modern voices with his uncanny, lame instinct for publicity he had become, in four or five years, one of the best-known of the young "intellectuals." Where the intellect came in, Connie did not quite see. (*LCL*, 50)

Connie's consciousness records an important characteristic of Clifford's notoriety: his intellectual leadership really means little. He is motivated by success and success requires skill in presentation, not intelligence or talent. Clifford cultivates his own ego, engineering his own fame. The artist becomes a public relations expert; and capitalism, the novel implies, swallows up art.

Connie's disenchantment with Clifford's superficial intellect extends to her discontent with her first adulterous lover's male ego. She elicits from Michaelis his own sense of inadequacy when she brings Michaelis to orgasm, and in return, she asks him about his concern for her pleasure (*LCL*, 54). Connie's interest is more with Michaelis's attitude than his performance, for she has already become accustomed to giving herself orgasms. What matters is Michaelis's lack of concern with her pleasure, which is a result of his own sexual inadequacy. In the modern sexual dialectic, Connie's desire for control demands Michaelis's poor performance; he cannot give her an orgasm. Sexuality is a "house of cards"; and Connie realizes with certainty that here sex is a game just like the game of success. Connie may be physically active, but the male ego controls the game. She no longer wants to play a distorting mirror for the male ego; but if both the social world and the personal world are games, her despair is understandable. Underneath modernism's sham lies only nothingness, as seen when the chapter ends with Connie's moment of nausea: "Nothingness! To accept the great nothingness of life seemed to be the one end of living. All the many busy and important little things that make up the grand sum-total of nothingness!" (*LCL*, 55).

Graham Holderness, in a study of the relationship between industrialism and a natural sexuality, attempts to describe Lawrence's novel in a dualistic fashion, which isolates reality from the ideal.[1] He sees Mellors's and Connie's relationship as entirely antithetical and prior to industrialism. The distinction between the two worlds of capitalism, on one hand, and man's essential natural self, on the other, is artificial. Holderness's analysis misreads the novel's structure outlined above; in no sense do the colliers represent anything like "live, truly human, relations." The colliers are about to go on strike; the modern economy and mine owners crush the colliers. If Mellors represents man's fundamental sensual nature, he curiously removes himself from human relationships; he identifies with the wood not the mines, but Clifford owns the wood. Clifford's effort to preserve the wood comes out of his own personal loss (i.e, inability to father a son). He very quickly identifies, through Mrs. Bolton, with industry and replaces the past with the future of the mines. He becomes an industrial leader associating with the business class, and he gives up writing only for the security of the commercial world. Clifford no longer wants to repeat the past. Holderness commits a most basic error by ascribing Lawrence's personal view to the narrator's consciousness. The novel's framework allows no separation between the historical world and the pastoral world; and the rupture of the wood signifies the inevitable march of historical time and the irretrievable nature of the past. Each character exists within the historical world and any attempt to escape it leaves them back in the web of history.

THE SEXUAL AWAKENING

Connie's changing experience of her body must also be mediated by her historical consciousness. The novel explores Connie's paradoxical, sexual awakening in an extended passage form in chapter 12. Connie's consciousness explores this particular sexual experience (*LCL*, 171–175). Mellors directs the action: "Lie down then!" he says, and Connie's body recoils from his commanding position. Her muscles tighten in a physical reaction to her mental resistance. The sexual act is as rapid as the brief, staccato-like, four-paragraph description; Mellors's haste and rapid orgasm leave Connie frustrated. The passage suggests that orgasm is incompatible with mental activity, just as Connie's mental activity satirizes the sexual act. The parody of "divine love" brings forth Platonic images regarding Connie's divided self: her body is split from her mind. Her mind, or disembodied self, appears above the couple observing her physical self, in the sexual act, from a distance. This objective view of sexuality suggests a distant scientific perspective: the technological camera looking down on the animal self's ridiculous coupling.

Connie's observations prompt some important linguistic considerations. Throughout the sex act, Connie and Mellors remain apart, just as Connie remains apart from herself. The absence of physical reciprocity represents the couple's failure to communicate as well as Connie's inability to reach orgasm. She conveys their emotional distance even as the two remain physically entangled:

> And yet, when he had finished, soon over, and lay very, very still, receding into silence and a strange motionless distance, far, farther than the horizon of her awareness, her heart began to weep. She could feel him ebbing away, ebbing away, and leaving her there like a stone on a shore. He was withdrawing. His spirit was leaving her. He knew.
>
> And in real grief, tormented by her own double consciousness and reaction, she began to weep. He took no notice, or did not even know. The storm of weeping swelled and shook her, and shook him. (*LCL*, 172)

Connie's urge to "heave her loins, and throw the man out" shows her desire to disentangle physically when she has already, from the beginning, distanced herself emotionally. The physical closeness does not indicate any real intimacy; Connie experiences "a strange, motionless distance" and failure to communicate, "receding into silence" (172). The failure of language contributes to the sexual failure, in fact, during the postcoital moment; she explains the poor communication through her hatred of Mellors's dialect. The narrator describes her disengagement from Mellors as follows: ". . . [H]e took his hand away from her breast and lay still, not touching her. And now she was untouched. She took an almost perverse satisfaction in it. She hated the dialect: the *thee* and the *tha* and the *thysen*" (173). Connie's pleasure in letting go, uncoupling, brings the difference of language to the forefront. Language represents the immediate gulf between Connie and Mellors; and this linguistic separation connotes class division. What Connie grieves is the apparent impossibility of their union; she intimates that the two will never be one. Connie achieves her sense of vitality through her body, but intellectually she realizes the sexual union's temporary nature.

The scene, however, does not conclude with Connie's dark imaginings. The initial sex act leads to her inner turmoil, which in turn, modulates into another extended lovemaking scene. Thus, the entire novelistic unit frames two sexual acts within one extended erotic scene. Connie's emotional distance and physical frustration leave her empty. Consequently, as Mellors begins to pull completely away from her limp body, she reaches up, out of both sexual desire and emotional need, pulling him back on top of her sexually charged body and initiating one of the novel's most intensely described sexual experiences:

> "It was so lovely!" She moaned. "It was so lovely!" But he said nothing, only softy kissed her, lying still above her. And she moaned with a sort of bliss, as a sacrifice, and a newborn thing. And now in her heart the queer wonder of him was awakened. A man! The strange potency of manhood upon her! Her hands strayed over him, still a little afraid of that strange, hostile, slightly repulsive thing that he had been to her, a man. And now she touched him, and it was the sons of god with the daughters of men. How beautiful he felt, how pure in tissue! How lovely, how lovely, strong, and yet pure and delicate, such stillness of the sensitive body! Such utter stillness of potency and delicate flesh! How beautiful, how beautiful! Her hands came timorously down his back, to the soft, smallish globes of the buttocks. Beauty! what beauty! a sudden little flame of new awareness went through her. How is it possible, this beauty here, where she had previously only been repelled? The unspeakable beauty to the touch, of the warm, living buttocks! The life within life, the sheer, warm, potent loveliness. And the strange weight of the balls between his legs! What a mystery! What a strange heavy weight of mystery,

that could lie soft and heavy in one's hand! The root, root of all that is lovely, the primeval root of all full beauty. (*LCL*, 174–175)

In this scene, the narrator signals Connie's triumph over her mental resistance through continual reiteration of her body's sensuality. This is not a passive waiting; her body is heaving with sexual desire and anticipation. She opens herself to any possibility, including violence: "It might come with the thrust of a sword," she thinks. Her desire reveals itself in images of flame. She risks, what Mailer would call the existential self, in the sexual act.[2] Connie and Mellors's sexual union brings forth this original, revelatory nature of sexuality. She totally lets herself go, making the true power of orgasm possible: "she dared to be gone in peace, she held nothing. She dared to let go everything, all herself, and be gone in the flood" (174). Connie gives up consciousness to the bodily experience. The narrator emphasizes the "dare" of her act, and as Connie throws herself into the sensual experience, she loses her individual self in a merging with Mellors.

Lawrence's challenge is to convey Connie's sexual experience in a language that does not destroy an essentially noncommunicative experience. He conveys Connie's sexual experience through wave-like images: her body heaves upward to meet Mellors's thrusts and she undulates, rocking back and forth with him inside her, like undulating waves rising and falling in an endless, natural rhythm. Lawrence achieves something approximate to Connie's sexual rhythm through the language's rhythm; the passage cannot be cited without some violence to its linguistic flow. The wave-like images are particularly effective in breaking down Connie's personality structure and discovering her archetypal being where she becomes a "plasm," an elemental part of the world. Only when Connie loses herself to the plasm can she become new: "She was gone, she was not and she was born: a woman" (175).

For Lawrence, the sexual experience must be biological. Thus, Connie's birth becomes a rebirth into the body. The entire passage works as an initiation ritual. Connie and Mellors merge not only with nature, through their fused bodies, but with the cosmos: ". . . And now she touched him, and it was the sons of god with the daughters of men" (174). Connie achieves, what Lawrence describes as the true unconscious, a pristine, vibrant consciousness: "We must discover, if we can, the true unconscious, where our life bubbles in us, which is innocent of any mental alteration, this is the unconscious. It is pristine, not in any way ideal. It is the spontaneous origin from which it behooves us to live."[3] Connie, of course, cannot only be "plasm like." She must return to consciousness, but she now perceives the world through the body's primacy. The narrator records Connie's new awareness through her physical response to Mellors.

The narrative also displays Clifford's rebirth, which concerns, "a man's victory; over the coal, over the very dirt of Tevershall pit" (108). Reading metaphor[4] against the narrative grain, however, inadequately accounts for the text's continual displacement of metaphor. For instance, if Connie undergoes rebirth through the fire of sex, then, as I indicate above, Clifford also undergoes a rebirth through the fire of the pit. He seeks a new technology to replace the emptiness art had left him with:

> The idea of a new concentrated fuel that burnt with a hard slowness at a fierce heat was what first attracted Clifford. There must be some sort of external stimulus to the burning of such fuel, not merely air supply. He began to experiment, and got a clever young fellow who has proved brilliant in chemistry, to help him.
>
> And he felt triumphant. He had at last got out of himself. He had fulfilled his life-long secret yearning: to get out out of himself. Art had not done it for him. Art had only made it worse. But now, he had done it. (108–109)

Anne Fernihough's compelling reading of Lawrence's aesthetics alongside Heidegger's *The Question Concerning Technology* notes how Clifford turns coal into a mineral deposit and makes the earth a standing reserve.[5] Nothing, in this Heideggerian reading, exists in itself, but only for use value, that is, the earth becomes a mineral for generating the coal industry's profit margin. Consequently, Connie and Mellors's coupling must always be read in relationship to the novel's representation of capitalist expansion, which I now examine through close textual readings.

SEX AND CAPITAL

Lady Chatterley's Lover, of course, represents many orgasms, but most of them are solitary experiences. The depiction of Connie and Mellors's simultaneous orgasm then marks a key point in the narrative. The narrator describes the encounter as: ". . . the voice out of the uttermost night, the life-exclamation. And the man heard it beneath him with a kind of awe, as his life sprang out into her. And as it subsided, he subsided too and lay utterly still, unknowing, while her grip on him slowly relaxed, and lay still. Still, unknowing, while her grip on him slowly relaxed, and she lay inert" (*LCL*, 134).

The essential quality of this scene is the simultaneity of the couple's orgasm. Connie gives up her habitual active sexuality and surrenders herself to the male; she releases herself from consciousness (i.e., mental-like), thus participating in pure bodily intensity. Mellors, too, surrenders himself entirely to the body's pleasure, oblivious to the world and his partner. Each partner's reckless, selfish surrender to pleasure allows the simultaneous orgasm to happen. Yet, ironically, the simultaneous orgasm leaves the couple mentally separate; their bodies have joined in a more fundamental, almost primordial sense through the interpenetration of sexual energies. This orgasm, in Lawrence's perspective, releases the couple from mental life and restores them momentarily to a natural (unconscious) union with the physical world. The sense of pure loss, "both lost" (139), signifies the couple's release from the material world. The couple's simultaneous orgasm, however, appears to impregnate Connie and thus return her to the material world. And although the child is Connie and Mellors's, she is still the wife of Clifford, the capitalist.

According to the narrator, Connie's new sense of life brings a sense of history with it. The experience may be one of true beauty and loveliness, but it is also unquestionably a burden. The restoration of Connie to her true (i.e., natural) self, the novel implies, includes sex, creativity (motherhood), and tenderness (sex with a man she loves, leading to conception). Mellors contributes to this newness through his restoration of tender masculinity: ". . . 'Thank God she's not a bully, nor a fool. Thank God she's a tender, aware woman.' And as his seed sprang into her, his soul sprang towards her too, in the creative act that is far more than procreative" (*LCL*, 279). The above passage represents the couple's final lovemaking; and the question to raise with Mellors, as with Connie, is whether this new touch represents a "creative act that is far more than procreative" (279)? If the couple's sexuality transcends the procreative, they might also transcend capitalism. Yet, ultimately, Clifford remains in control of both Mellors and Connie: he employs Mellors on his estate, and the child Connie will bear belongs to Clifford's world. The divorce first talked about in chapter 5 may not happen; and Connie and Mellors's natural marriage would then remain purely symbolic. Their child will be born into a world of division and strife.

Something must also be said of Lawrence's phallic marriage: the mystical marriage of two blood circuits. Lawrence's attempt to write a phallic novel and forge a new blood consciousness rests on his depiction of Mellors's and Connie's relationship. They are to grow toward this new touch, a restoration of humanity's primordial connection to the natural world and the cosmos. Yet in chapter 5, through Connie's consciousness, the most telling destruction of man's connection to his true self and natural surroundings is recorded. Connie's following observation to herself follows one of Clifford's disquisitions:

> . . . They were not the leafy words of an effective life, young with energy and belonging to the tree. They were the hosts of fallen leaves of a life that is ineffectual.

> So that it seemed to her everywhere. The colliers at Tevershall were talking again of a strike. And it seemed to Connie there again, it was not a manifestation of energy, it was the bruise of the war, that he had been in abeyance, slowly rising to the surface and creating the great ache of unrest, the stupor of discontent. The bruise was deep, deep, deep—the bruise of the false and inhuman war. It would take many years for the living blood of the generations to dissolve the vast black clot of bruised blood, deep inside their souls and bodies. And it would need a new hope. (*LCL*, 50)

The tree metaphor connects the underground, earth, and sky, the connection broken most emphatically by the world war. The war leaves, Lawrence suggests, a bruise in the very circulatory system of England. The regeneration of England requires a new blood consciousness, something to heal the war's lasting wound; this new blood connection will be the "new hope." The novel must realize this new hope through Mellors's and Connie's vibrant relationship. And although the couple does enact a symbolic, natural marriage and merge their bloodstream in simultaneous orgasm, do they ever achieve a phallic marriage? Does the new touch really happen?

The answer must be no. As I have been demonstrating, the phallic reality is a dream enclosed and choked off by industrial reality. Michael Squires, writing on the novel's three versions, describes the emphasis placed on relationships in the final version.[6] Squires believes the idea of phallic marriage becomes important only in version three: "Once Lawrence imagines Mellors outside class boundaries, the novel's central struggle is no longer between Connie and the Keeper, but between their commitment to each other and the external forces that erode it" (Squires, 1983: 50). Changing a class struggle to a divorce struggle is doubly significant; the struggle for divorce anticipates the decaying nature of the modern family. Lawrence downplays the class struggle because of its futility, thus the novel clearly demonstrates the business owners' complete control over the colliers.

Squires is incorrect, however, to say Lawrence imagines Mellors outside class boundaries. He comes from the mining class and by the novel's conclusion he has returned to a place virtually identical to Tevershall. Although Mellors lives on a farm, connecting him with nature, the Butler and Smitham Colliery Company own the farm, and he lives on a street called "Engineer Row." As Mellors writes to Connie: "The pits are working badly—this is a colliery district like Tevershall, only prettier" (*LCL*, 299). Mellors never escapes his class identification; he does not identify with the class struggle because it no longer seems worthwhile.

Mellors records England's gradual economic movement toward a largely consumer culture: "That's our civilization and our education: bring up the masses to depend entirely on spending money, and then the money gives out" (*LCL*, 299). The country is on the verge of economic depression; the working class works only to become part of the middle class through its purchases, and the colliers are now "dead to life."

Mellors's final letter to Connie evokes a pastoral paradise (*LCL*, 299). By this point, his dream is no longer a dream; he lapses into sentimental nostalgia preparing him for another bitter, rancid attack on the evil of money. But Mellors is part of the world he criticizes; he comes from the collier district and he returns, by the conclusion of the novel, to the collier district. Meeting Connie simply returns Mellors to the reality he wants to leave.

One can glimpse the impossibility of Connie and Mellors's dream through a wonderful Lawrence poem, *The End, The Beginning*. This beautiful lyric finishes with a restive sorrow:

> And if there were not an absolute, utter forgetting
> and a ceasing to know, a perfect ceasing to know
> and a silent, sheer cessation of all awareness
> how terrible life would be!
> how terrible it would be to think and know, to have consciousness!
> But dipped, once dipped in dark oblivion
> the soul has peace, inward and lovely peace.[7]

This imagined peace can only be dreamed, for the beauty of sex and the magical release of consciousness through orgasm is momentary. Connie and Mellors experience this "dark oblivion" and "lovely peace" following their simultaneous orgasm, but once over, they return to mental consciousness:

> . . . Till at last he began to rouse and become aware of his defenseless nakedness. And she was aware that his body was loosening its clasp on her, he was coming apart. But in her breast she felt she could not bear him to leave her uncovered. He must cover her now forever.
>
> But he drew away at last, and kissed her, and covered her over, she lay looking up to the boughs of the tree, unable as yet to move. He stood and fastened up his breeches, looking round. All was dense and silent, save for the awed dog, that lay with its paws against its nose. He sat down again on the brushwood, and took Connie's hand in silence. (*LCL*, 134)

As they awake to discover their nakedness, Mellors withdraws from Connie and the recognition of shame enters the relationship, that is, "he must cover her forever" (174). The couple's most powerful orgasm, the transfigurative moment, returns them to the net of history. The "awed dog" represents nature and causes Mellors to take Connie's hand again but in silence. The new touch, the new hope, the tenderness and phallic dream will never and can never happen.

Mellors's letter to Connie, which ends the novel, speaks of "the peace of fucking" (301). The real peace of the couple is the child Connie will bear; yet Mellors refers to this child as a side issue (*LCL*, 300). He wants to think that they have fucked the flame into being, and that the memory of their wonderful fucking will sustain their separation. In reality, Mellors is isolated, and the child may not hold the couple together.

Indeed, as Hinz and Teunissen argue, Mellors's letter is bitterly ironic.[8] He becomes just what he protests against: a man of high mental consciousness praising Christian virtue. Mellors ends the novel a man of words: "John Thomas say good-night to Lady Jane, a little droopingly, but with a hopeful heart" (302). The goodnight is a good-bye. He signs the symbolic name because he is writing fiction, and thus the phallic Mellors ends the man of language. The novel concludes with Mellors's separation from Connie, and with the letter—sent to the wind, unanswered, evanescent as a dream.

5. Notes About a Postmodern Sexuality: Between Bataille and Baudrillard ✑

Supposing a bomb were put under the whole scheme of things, what would we be after? What feelings do we want to carry through into the next epoch?

D.H. Lawrence, *Surgery for the Novel-or a Bomb*

LOOKING FOR THE POSTMODERN

Radical Modernism has operated, in this text, as a site of frontier thinking within modernity. What happens on the other side of modernity brings up the inevitable problem of postmodernity and other questions of nomenclature. Whether postmodernism simply spurs on academic careers or offers a genuine account of some hypothesized epistemological shift almost seems beside the point. As Jameson points out, postmodernism has become part of the intellectual climate and even entered the mainstream culture.[1] Nonetheless, I raise here a few concerns about this amorphous concept/theory/periodization. First, Professor Jameson's position linking postmodernism with late capitalism, however brilliant the overall argument, remains, to my mind limiting. Although culture has certainly shifted since the decline in monopoly capitalism, especially in relationship to the digital revolution, new forms such as hypertexts, music videos, and cyberpunk narratives do not necessarily represent any real break from modernity. In fact, Jameson's use of the temporal qualifier "late" suggests to me that capitalism may be soon overcome, when I see only a broad horizon across the globe. Likewise, the term late modernism means very little in relationship to our age's lack of historical perspective. If Jameson wants to claim, "postmodernism thinks the present historically" that suggests, at best, a social science perspective.

Where is the break between modernism and postmodernism? The surrealist revolution, for instance, has numerous antecedents including Freud's dream analysis, Rimbaud's poetry, Lautremont's *Chants de Malador*, Stindberg's theatre and cubism. Contemporary novelists have hardly done away with narrative nor could they. I would argue, on the contrary, that only Joyce's *Finnegan's Wake* represents a true break from modernist traditions and nothing after the wake (what could be after a wake?) offers anything but variations on modernist techniques.

Consequently, my position approximates Jürgen Habermas's argument that modernism remains an unfinished project (see introduction earlier).[2] My choice of Reich and Lawrence then supports the claim that modernism stresses a radical liberation and utopian element that has not and may never mature. On the other hand, I do grant a "postmodern aesthetics" credibility through my agreement with Lyotard's claim that postmodernism occurs within modernism, "a work can become modern only if it is first postmodern. Postmodernism thus understood is not modernism at its end but in the nascent state, and this state is constant."[3] The postmodern artist as Lyotard writes, must work without rules, "in order to formulate the rules of what will have been done" (81). Freud, Reich, and Lawrence all invented rules as they went and from this perspective they are, perhaps, in this limited aesthetic sense, somewhat postmodern. At this point, George Bataille's work also marks a critical frontier of radical aesthetics. Contrarily, Jean Baudrillard, another figure discussed below, questions the very idea of a frontier, and argues instead, that the contemporary age must be understood as a simulation. This chapter then talks around the "postmodern," though Lawrence, Bataille, and Baudrillard, as Mark Taylor writes about religion since both religion and the postmodern are ever elusive and in hiding, but also, nonetheless, every where present.[4]

George Bataille, as Leslie Anne Boldt-Irons suggests, fits into neither the modern nor the postmodern camp (in this he is like his precursor Sade).[5] More importantly, Bataille's modernity frequently touches the same ground as Lawrence's modernity. Both writers' preoccupation with sexuality and its relationship to the sacred bring them, like Freud and Reich too, into contact with the primitive. Mark Taylor makes an important observation about this affiliation of the modern with the primitive, "the origin is the end for which modernity longs. The primitive, in other words, represents the desire for the modern" (Taylor, 1999: 53). This paradoxical connection between the new and the old generates the first part of this chapter. Lawrence's controversial story "The Woman Who Rode Away" will be read in the context of Bataille's writings on the relationship between violence, sexuality, and the sacred. In addition, Bataille's work, an object of reflection for much poststructuralist thought, allows me to further explore the notion of frontier thinking. Finally, this chapter concludes with a discussion of Jean Baudrillard's valorization of the simulacra as a postmodern emblem.

LE GRAND MORT: WHERE THE WOMAN RODE

The Women Who Rode Away (1924) tells the story of waste, violence, and the sacred.[6] The protagonist, a 33-year-old woman from Berkeley, appears dissatisfied and psychologically dead, locked in marriage to a 53-year-old workaholic husband. The husband, a successful silver miner now turned rancher, regards his younger wife with much sexual suspicion and, as a result, holds her in "invincible slavery" (40). Only talk of nearby Indians, "[finds] a full echo in the woman's heart" (42). The moment her husband leaves the village on business the woman decides to visit the Chilchuis on her own.

Strangely, the woman gives barely a thought to either her husband or two young children during the arduous journey. "She felt it her destiny to wander into the secret haunts of these timeless, mysterious, marvelous Indians of the mountains" (42). Upon encountering three Indians the woman's desire to know the "other" turns, ironically, into her captivity. The story allows no possibility for bridging the two cultures. When the quartet camps for the night the woman experiences, "a long, long night, icy and eternal, and she aware that she had died" (49). The story unfolds then, in a sense, from the woman's posthumous perspective.

At no time do the Indians consider the woman other than an element in their ritual system, "they were so impersonal, absorbed in something that was beyond her. They never saw her as a personal woman: she could tell that. She was some mystic object to them, some vehicle of passion too remote for her to grasp" (67). The tribe incorporates the woman into a sacrificial rite necessary to regenerate their world. In the tribe's mythologized history the white man steals the sun and the white woman steals the moon leaving Indian gods hidden and their culture wasted. Consequently, the "white woman got to die and go like a wind to the sun, tell him the Indians will open the gate to him" (65).

Sacrifice then has a historical rationale, but, interestingly, the woman seems a willing victim, "she knew she was a victim: that all this elaborate work upon her was the work of victimizing her. But she did not mind. She wanted it" (67). Perhaps, subconsciously, the woman gives herself as a gift to the Chilchui. Mark Taylor writing about Bataille observes the function of such a sacrifice, "Since the most radical form of self-sacrifice is the sacrifice of self, every sacrifice harbors a faint trace of that ultimate sacrifice, which ends in death" (Taylor, 72). Unquestionably, the woman suffers a most violent death at the equinox, which the narrator describes as, "the mastery that man must hold, and that passes from race to race" (71). Although Lawrence does not end the story with the actual sacrifice the suspension of the act simply diverts any possible sensationalism. Mark Kinkead-Weekes stresses how the story's open-ended conclusion both creates the maximum disturbance for a reader and still allows for multiple readings.[7]

How should one read this violent sacrifice? The narrator describes the entire experience in sexual terms, but does this mean that the sacrifice represents a murder and symbolizes women's victimization at the knife, that is, the penis of male authority? The interpretation of the story as symptomatic of Lawrence's alleged misogyny requires biographical speculation and, additionally, confuses the teller with the tale. George Bataille's work, on the other hand, provides a framework for understanding the story's deeper layer of significance. What Leslie Anne Boldt-Irons writes about Bataille's fiction also applies to Lawrence's story, "the victim of sacrifice within the text is the discontinuous notion which is ruptured and returned to continuity."[8] In turn, the text's reader also experiences a kind of sacrifice, "the reader both meditates upon the sacrifice of the discontinuous notion (a reflection upon its initial mise-en-abime) and experiences it as his or her own return to continuity (a second mise-en-abime which affords reflection from the initial mise-en-abime, since conscious reflection upon the latter is now problematic)" (96). The reader experiences then both the woman's sacrifice and the earlier ruination of Chilchui culture demanding the woman's subsequent sacrifice.

The story's overall economy discloses both the husband's world or work, that is, everything is put to use value, and the Indian culture discarded by the white man's colonization. The narrative presents this postcolonial world as a mausoleum, which, as Peter Balbert remarks shows that, "death is not only common, it becomes a redundant aspect of the landscape, a familiar waste product."[9] The husband, in fact, treats his wife as a dead object, part of "his works" and a "secret vein of ore in his mines" (41). The husband "admired his wife to extinction" (40) indicating her essential ghost-like status. However, Balbert, in his defense of Lawrence against feminist attacks, incorrectly reads the story as a critique of Indian life. Quite the opposite, the narrative directs its critique against the European civilization, which exterminates native cultures.

A countermovement in the story concerns the restoration of the sacred to the Chilchui. The Indian gods rise only as the western God dies, " 'when a white woman gives herself to our gods, then our gods will begin to make the world again, and the white man's gods will fall to pieces' " (61). As one culture achieves continuity's ecstatic experience of the sacred another culture falls into the discontinuity of alienated life and capitalistic acquisitiveness. Tragically, the two cultures cannot thrive together. Lawrence, like E.M. Forster, in *A Passage to India* (1924), exposes the damage wrecked upon "the other" while simultaneously disclosing, in Bataille's framework, the ecstasy of the impossible.[10]

TRANSGRESSION/SEXUALITY

Bataille's work understands human society as mediated through structures of prohibition and taboo.[11] The transgression of a taboo signals its existence and moral importance. These taboos generally revolve around sexuality and death. Eroticism, not sexuality, ruptures the taboo and provides a couple with an experience of unity, that is, continuity in an otherwise discontinuous society. This erotic experience is, in Bataille's view, sacred. In general, society organizes itself around the denial of eroticism, and maintains a purely utilitarian economy of work and reproductive sexuality. Contrary to these homogenous impulses, are the heterogeneous experiences of eroticism and crime (i.e., the accused share), which can be individual or national (e.g., war). The essay entitled: "The Notion of Expenditure," expresses Bataille's approach to utilitarian social reality: "The most appreciated share of life is given as the condition of productive social activity," with: "an interest in considerable losses, in catastrophes that, while conforming to well defined needs, provoke tumultuous depressions, crises of dread, and in the final analysis, a certain orgiastic state" (117).

Transgression brings about this later experience of loss: "In the human sphere, sexual activity has broken away from animal simplicity. It is in essence a transgression, not after the taboo, a return to primitive freedom."[12] The greatest experience of loss, in Bataille's thinking, is death, which he considers, paradoxically, the most luxurious form of life: "The movement of human life event tends toward anguish, as the sign of expenditures that are finally excessive, that go beyond what we can bear. Everything within us demand that death lay waste to us . . ." (*AS*, 85).[13] The apotheosis of violent death and violent life is represented by the experience of sacrifice: "It is the common business of sacrifice to bring life and death into harmony, to give death the upsurge of life, life the momentousness and the vertigo of death opening on to the unknown. Here life is mingled with death, but simultaneously death is a sign of life, a way into the infinite" (*E*, 91).

Finally, Bataille develops his notion of sovereignty in response to an economy of loss; that is, the luxurious, excessive lifestyle of a leisure class: "What is sovereign in fact is to enjoy the present time without having anything else in view but this present time" (*AS*, 199). He translates this experience of sovereignty into aesthetic practice: "sovereign art signifies, in the most exact way, access to sovereign subjectivity independently of rank. This does not imply the meaninglessness of the behaviors that raised men above themselves as well as above animals, but rather their complete dislocation and their constant calling into question" (*AS*, 423). The writer then inscribes waste, loss, violence, and eroticism as his/her sovereign mark.

Along with Nietzsche, Bataille's oeuvre has engaged a plethora of poststructuralist commentary including that of Jacques Derrida, Jürgen Habermas, and Michel Foucault. Thus Bataille operates like Freud, Reich, and D.H. Lawrence as a frontier thinker whose work acts as an epicenter of modernity and sexual discourse.

TRANSGRESSION/ECRITURE

Derrida approaches Bataille through a close replication of Bataille's reading of Hegel.[14] This strategy reinterprets Bataille just as Bataille reinterprets Hegel: "In the course of this repetition a barely perceptible displacement disjoints all the articulations and penetrates all the points welded together by the imitated discourse. A trembling spreads out which then makes the entire old shell crack" (260). This wound in Hegelian dialectics uncovers "the limit of discourse and the beyond of absolute knowledge" (261). For Derrida, eroticism is within discourse, but as the site of "absolute loss." Eroticism or poetic figures of discourse mark the limit of reason and open the text to the unknown. Bataille's dilemma, in Derrida's reading, is how to write sovereignty in a language, which is always servile. This writing becomes possible only through excess: "It draws upon, in order to exhaust it, the resource of meaning," and "the writing of sovereignty places discourse in relation to absolute non-discourse" (270). Derrida's reading of Bataille, then, opens out to his own writing this loss of meaning which: "Must assure us of nothing, must give us no certitude, no result, no profit. It is absolutely adventurous, is a chance and not a technique" (273). This destruction of the servility of meaning becomes the transgression of the book enabling Derrida's grammatological play.

Habermas also focuses on Bataille's concept of sovereignty, but unlike Derrida, he stresses some of the political ramifications sovereignty carries with respect to fascism.[15] With respect to epistemology, Habermas uncovers

Bataille's attempt to break from the rationalist tradition through an analysis of heterogeneous social groups. These marginalized figures are then connected with Bataille's attempt to unbound subjectivity: "With the form of expression that leads back again into the intimacy of a life context that has become alien, confined, cut off, fragmented" (214). Ultimately, Habermas locates an impasse between Bataille the writer and Bataille the philosopher. Through pornography, Habermas claims, Bataille can affect the experience of sacrifice, but philosophically he cannot break out of the linguistic universe. For Habermas, Bataille's theory fails to deliver a true radical critique of reason. This conclusion runs counter to Derrida's argument by failing to see how closely Bataille's writing, even his pornography (i.e., the erotic in its most violent, disruptive shape) reflects his philosophy of excess. In the Derridean re-reading, as Susan Suleiman remarks: ". . . the transgressive content of a work of fiction must be read primarily as a metaphor for the transgressive use of language effected by modern writing."[16]

Foucault's essay on Bataille reiterates the above arguments in its emphasis on language.[17] He stresses the turning point in Bataille's thinking, from transgression as an exterior to an interior experience: "By denying us the limit of the limitless, the death of God leads to an experience in which nothing may again experience the exteriority of being, and consequently to an experience which is interior and sovereign" (32). In modernity, the "limitless reign of the limit" replaces the "limit of the limitless." Foucault's reading destroys the dialectical nature of transgression and domesticates its position to the pure crossing of limits, which he compares to a flash of lightening (35).

This linguistic reading of transgression marks, in Foucault's understanding, the limits of the enlightenment tradition and brings dialectical thought to closure. The departure from rational discourse is "non-positive affirmation" and contestation; and "affirmation that affirms nothing, a radical break of transitivity" (36). "The principle of non-positive affirmation refers to the disruption of the boundaries of conventional identity and the resultant questioning of accepted notions of the normal and natural." This contestation does not bring philosophy to a closure, but does end: "the philosopher as the sovereign and primary form of philosophical language" (42).

Thus Foucault, like Derrida and Habermas, reveals Bataille as marking the limit of enlightenment thought and the closure of rationale discourse. These readings empty out Bataille's dialectics, and turn his sacred image of transgression as a moral and ultimately unifying principle, into a purely linguistic transgression. Finally, what lies on the other side of this closure, Foucault remarks, remains unspoken: "But in spite of so many scattered signs, the language in which transgression will find its space and the illumination of its being lies almost entirely in the future" (33).

CONNIE'S ABJECTION AND THE CLOSURE
OF SEXUALITY

Lawrence is not the future Foucault gestures toward, but, like Bataille, he brings sexual discourse to an end game. Clifford, for example, represents the productive, utilitarian economy that Bataille castigated. He is the consummate capitalist and in a famous speech outlines this homogeneous life-philosophy:

> "Don't you think one can just subordinate the sex thing to the necessities of a long life. Just use it, since that's what we're driven to? After all, *do* these temporary excitements matter? Isn't the whole problem of life the slow building up of an integrated personality through the years? living an integrated life? There's no point in a disintegrated life. If lack of sex is going to disintegrate you, then go out and have a love affair. If lack of a child is going to disintegrate you, then have a child if you possibly can. But only do these things so that you have an integrated life, that makes a long harmonious thing. And you and I can do that together—don't you think?—if we adapt ourselves to the necessities and at the same time weave the adaptation together into a piece with our steadily-lived life. Don't you agree? (*LCL*, 45)

Clifford always subordinates sexuality to reflection and knowledge produces the social norm. The relationship between Connie and Mellor's transgresses the taboo of marriage. Their illicit sexuality creates the eroticism praised by Bataille as an experience of loss. The narrative enacts the dialectical movement between taboo (Clifford's productive world) and transgression (the couple's ecstatic, illicit sexual experience of expenditure).

Each of the Connie's orgasms marks a loss. The most intense of these ecstatic experiences is her night of animal passion:

> Though a little frightened, she let him have his way, and the reckless, shameless sensuality shook her to the very foundations, stripped her to the very last, and made a different woman of her. It was not really love. It was not voluptuousness. It was sensuality sharp and searing as fire, burning the soul to tinder.
>
> Burning out the shames, the deepest, oldest shames, in the most secret places. It cost her an effort to let him have his way and his will of her. She had to be a passive, consenting thing, like a slave, a physical slave. Yet the passion licked round her, consuming, and when the sensual flame of it presses through her bowels and breast, she really thought she was dying: yet a poignant, marvellous death. (*LCL*, 246–247)

This encounter bears no trace of romanticism. Connie's experience of anal intercourse becomes, paradoxically, a liberating moment. This transgression involves what Bataille calls the dejecta; that is, those forms of animal sexuality: "excluded from a bright world which signified humanity" (*AS*, 62). Humanity, Bataille claims, rejects the natural and consequently consigns both sexuality and excretion (human waste products) to secrecy and filth. Lawrence represents Connie's abject body as the source of the novel's heterogeneity.

Doherty reads this scene as an exemplification of Lawrence's use of metaphor and how it, "exchanges simple word-substitutions for extended figural networks that subsume old vestigial images into fresh mythical constellations, recharging them with force and signification."[18] The narrative association of coal mining with the anus, in Doherty's reading, becomes redeployed through Mellors's phallic hunting of Connie and ends up signifying, "fresh virginal continents, getting at the very heart of the jungle of herself' " (113). Although the scene does clearly link Connie's bowels with the earth (i.e., "smelt out the heaviest ore of the body into purity" (*LCL*, 247)) the power of sodomy's fire and Mellors's alleged alchemical magic remains inscribed within a larger narrative that frustrates any genuine sexual resolution of the novel's protracted historical crisis.

This "phallic hunting" is marginalized in relationship to Clifford's growing economic strength. Lawrence's effort to reimagine the sacred in this moment of ecstatic sexuality marks the closure of sexuality as the figure of transgression. Connie and Mellor's next encounter leads to her pregnancy and their likely homogenization into a utilitarian economy. The novel ends, in fact, with a dead, perhaps, obsolete sexuality. Thus Bataille writes the end of sexuality's sacred and social possibilities and, Lawrence brings to closure the individual's experience of transgression.

In summary, writing transgressively brings an end to the end. For Bataille, transgressive writing mirrors eroticism. The ecstatic orgasm shatters reality's ordered discourse and marks the silence surrounding continuity. What happens when writing reaches the limit, the absolute limit? The orgasm of the little death, as Marc LaFountain argues, acts as a simulacrum.[19] The absolute limit can be simulated only through transgressive writing that incites eroticism, but transgression disappears when the limit is disclosed. This impasse marked by both Bataille and Lawrence brings this text to one limit of radical thought. The concluding remarks distribute some potential avenues for thinking on the other side of the limit this text has described.

SEXUALITY AND THE SIMULACRA

What happens to sexuality in the post-humanist world? The social theorist Jean Baudrillard asks this question in his essay, "Transpolitics,

Transsexuality, and Transaesthetics."[20] Indeed, Baudrillard's entire oeuvre interrogates the modernist tradition. He describes the modernist enterprise as an orgy:

> To characterize the present, I would say that it is the post-orgy state of affairs. The orgy could be viewed as the epitome of the whole explosive movement of modernity, the movement of liberation in all domains: political liberation, sexual liberation, liberation of productive forces, liberation of destructive forces, liberation of women, liberation of the child, liberation of unconscious desires, the liberation of art. It is the assumption of all the models of representation, of all the models of anti-representation. The orgy was total. It was an orgy of the real, of the rational, of the sexual, of the critical, of the anti-critical, of growth and growth crises. We explored all the paths of production and of virtual overproduction of objects, signs, messages, and ideologies, pleasure. Today, if you want my opinion, everything has been liberated. "<u>Les jeux sont faits</u>" (the die are cast), and we find each other together in front of this collective crucial question: <u>What are we going to do after the orgy?</u> (21–22)

Sexuality has, in other words, exhausted itself with its modernism. What remains for sexuality when the orgy is over?

In *Overexposed*, Sylvère Lotringer traces the history of contemporary sexology and provides some possible answers to Baudrillard's question.[21] He finds that private life has evaporated and the secrets of sexual life are only social secretions (171). Sexuality is entirely externalized and "if, as Foucault insisted modern society is perverse, then postmodernity is obscene. Crudely exposing everything sexual, it merely destroys the excitement" (172). Lotringer's most startling discovery is that sexuality has become a bore, and pleasure, in the postmodern age: "turns into a chore, and a bore. Instead of enhancing the deepest mysteries in human kind, it turns us into dogs" (177).

Baudrillard makes similar discoveries. He describes the postmodern sexual order as artificial, with "an indifference to jouissance, that is to say, to sex as pleasure and joy" (*T*, 19). Baudrillard characterizes the postmodern period as the age of the simulacra; everything in this cultural phase is simulated: "After jouissance (sexual pleasure), comes the artifice" (*T*, 20). Baudrillard's metaphor for this simulated sexuality is the transsexual:

> The transsexual is based on artifice whether it is a question of anatomy (changing sex) or a question of variations of dress, gesture or morphological codes that are characteristics of transvestites. In all cases, whether it is a surgical process or transvestism, it is a question of artifice. Today the destiny of the body is to become prosthesis; it is therefore logical that the model of

sexuality may become transsexuality and that transsexuality becomes everywhere the place and space of seduction. (*T*, 20)

The two key elements in his analysis of transsexuality are the body as prosthesis and the space of seduction.

Baudrillard talks about the prosthetic body toward the end of his book *De la séduction*.[22] He makes specific reference to the science fiction/fact of cloning:

> The person cloned does not engender himself: he comes to bud from a segment. One might speculate on the wealth of these plant-like branchings that dissolve Oedipal sexuality in favour of a non-human sex—but the fact remains that both the Father and Mother have disappeared, and in favour of a <u>matrix/code</u> [the word "<u>matrice</u>" means both "matrix" and "womb"]. No more mothers, just a matrix. And henceforth it is the matrix of the genetic code that will "give birth" without end in an operative manner purged of all contingent sexuality. (*S*, 169)

The entire family structure disappears in this artificial mode of reproduction; even the family's symbolic apparatus collapses. This "bio-cybernetic vision" also destroys the Lacanian mirror stage because the role of the other ceases to function. Likewise, Lacan's valorization of the phallic signifier ends up, in the worlds of Arthur and Marilouise Kroker, "the post-modern penis which becomes an emblematic sign of sickness, disease and waste. Penis-burnout for the end of the world."[23] Baudrillard is very careful not to replace the symbolic phallus with a feminine sexuality, for he specifically criticizes Irigaray on this account (*S*, 9–11). Rather, he replaces the Oedipal structure with the image of a digital Narcissus (i.e., a masturbatory technology). This technological myth does not operate as an oppositional, anti-Oedipal force similar to its embodiment in Deleuze and Guattari or Marcuse, but rather as the after image of sexuality's closure.[24]

The other key element in Baudrillard's analysis of sexuality is the place and space of seduction.[25] He associates seduction with the feminine, but not necessarily the female gender, for if male subjectivity disappears in the postmodern age, so too, does the female. The feminine is associated with the transsexual, and this individual is, in Baudrillard's view, an indeterminate gender and post-sexual. The transsexual is part of an "erotic simulacra" an image of reversibility; Baudrillard considers seduction precisely as the continual reversibility of gender. Seduction then, is not sexual "but an ironic, alternative form, one that breaks the referentially of sex and provides a space, not of desire, but of play and defiance" (*S*, 21).

Baudrillard defines seduction in contrast to production: "Seduction is that which is everywhere and always opposed to production; seduction withdraws something from the visible order and so runs counter to production, whose project is to set everything up in clear view, whether it be an object, a number, or a concept." This statement criticizes Foucault's analysis of the production of sexual discourse as already out of date. For Baudrillard, everything has already been said, but what remain are the seductive strategies of play, and these strategies belong, in part, to the invisible world of myth and ritual. Although close to Bataille's valorization of loss, Baudrillard desexualizes Bataille's theory. Orgasm, for Baudrillard, is not loss, but the very mark of visibility; that is, the emblem of pleasure (*S*, 20). Unlike Bataille, Baudrillard writes against the power of jouissance: "Sexual pleasure too is reversible, that is to say that, in the absence of denial of the orgasm, superior intensity is possible. It is here, where the end of sex becomes aleatory again, that something can be called seduction or delight" (*S*, 18).

The word radical comes to take, in Baudrillard's work, a new meaning: the reversibility of sexuality. Again, power, in his view, belongs to the "culture of premature ejaculation" and functions as an element of the libidinal economy. Contrarily, seduction has no measurable value, no telos, and always defers the orgasm. He associates seduction with the fractal stage of simulation, where value "radiates in all directions, filling in all interstices, without bearing reference to anything whatsoever except by mere contiguity" (*T*, 15). Ultimately, Baudrillard wants to restore mystery to the cybernetic world, but he does this precisely when seduction too passes into its fractal stage.

Although Baudrillard also calls the fractal stage the viral stage, he writes nowhere, in the above texts, about AIDS, and this erasure is troubling. Elaine Showalter, for example, draws close parallels between the nineteenth-century fin de siècle and contemporary apocalyptic thinking.[26] What Baudrillard calls the fractal stage she refers to as sexual anarchy. What emerges in Showalter's vision is not a transsexual figure, but rather a resurgence of authoritarian thinking about the family and consequently, the attempt to establish normative social values at the expense of minorities; that is, race, gender, and class.

The Krokers help put Showalter's fin-de-millennium fears in a context that illuminates Baudrillard's post-orgiastic, techno vision of sexuality. They discuss the "unhappy consciousness at being trapped in bodies which are pleasure palaces first and torture chambers later . . ." (Krokers, 14). The modernists' orgiastic body becomes the postmodernists' AIDS-riddled, disappearing body. The self must become bionic since the secretions of sex carry the potential mark of death; this bionic body is the hyperbody of health spas. The Krokers see postmodern sexuality as:

> The result is the production of a <u>cynical</u> sex, of sex itself as an ideological site of disaccumulation, loss and sacrifice as the perfect sign of a nihilistic culture where the body promises only its own negation; where the previously reflexive connection between sexuality and desire is blasted away by the seductive vision of <u>sex without organs</u>—a hyper-real, surrogate, and telematic sex like that promised by the computerized, phone sex of the Minitel system in France—as the ultimate out-of-body experience for the end of the world; and where the terror of the ruined surfaces of the body translates immediately into its opposite: <u>the ecstasy of catastrophe and the welcoming of a sex without secretions as an ironic sign of our liberation.</u> (15)

The postmodern self is liberated from sexuality itself. Ultimately, we are, as Baudrillard writes, now a network linked to the invisible sexuality of anonymous voices on the other end of a phone line or computer terminal.[27] This disenchanted, political form of seduction appears as our collective destiny, yet the hope remains that a more enchanted sexuality, inspired by revisions of D.H. Lawrence and others, will emerge from the ruins of the post-human configurations of desire.

Conclusion: Reassessing the Radical in Modernism ⸻

The louder the din of human destruction, the quieter the world becomes. People save themselves by simply closing their eyes.

Wilhelm Reich, October 19, 1935

In writing about Jean Genet, Leo Bersani makes an important observation about radical modernism, "Beckett and Genet belong to a radical modernity anxious to save art from the pre-emptive operations of institutional culture."[1] A self-identified gay artist and lifelong criminal, Genet would appear to have little in common with Freud, Reich, or D.H. Lawrence. Nevertheless, each of the figures discussed in this text are, in different ways, clearly outside the institutional mainstream. Reich and Lawrence lived, for the most part, nomadic lives. Professional organizations forced Reich to move from country to country during the 1930s. Finally, in the year of Freud's death, Reich immigrated to the United States. Similarly, Lawrence wandered across the southwestern United States, Mexico, and Europe during the final years of his life. Lawrence had nothing but contempt for the Bloomsbury group in London and preferred to remain in self-imposed exile rather than participate in the established British culture of his day. Blacklisting forced Reich to self-publish his late works and Lawrence, in order to avoid censorship, had to utilize a private publisher for both *Lady Chatterley's Lover* and his volume of poetry, *Pansies*. Although Freud's relationship to the culture of his time was more ambiguous than either Reich's or Lawrence's outsider positions, Freud also began his career breaking from established medical authority. His support of lay analysis maintained an adversarial relationship to the institutional framework of the university system.[2] Yet, ironically, Freud also founded the institution of psychoanalysis, which quickly met with defection from its early supporters, Adler and Jung.

Interestingly, Freud's problematic relationship with mainstream culture has remained as such throughout the twentieth century; whereas contemporary history has rendered both Reich and Lawrence nearly invisible to the academic and institutional network of late modern culture. The radical may be, in other words, a vanishing figure. D.H. Lawrence, for example, has been pillaged ever since the publication of Kate Millet's *Sexual Politics* in the late 1960s. Despite being, perhaps, the greatest male writer of twentieth-century England, the poststructuralist movements of the century's second half have scarcely touched on Lawrence's work. Contrarily, Lawrence's great contemporaries, James Joyce and Virginia Woolf, have been the occasion for entire industries of critical commentary. These cultural disequilibria require some exploration.

Joyce Wexler's "D.H. Lawrence through a Postmodernist Lens" and Earl Ingersoll's *D.H. Lawrence, Desire and Narrative* both fall short, in my view, to adequately represent Lawrence from a contemporary perspective.[3] Wexler's article, published in *The D.H. Lawrence Review*, focuses on the expatriate novels of the 1920s: *The Lost Girl, Aaron's Rod, Mr. Noon, Kangaroo,* and *The Plumed Serpent.* Wexler attempts to rehabilitate Lawrence's generally, most poorly regarded fiction by applying a postmodernist perspective to the works. The method has some potential merit, but its value remains limited to a highly specialized audience likely to read *The D.H. Lawrence Review.* More significantly, Wexler makes almost arbitrary assumptions about the differences between modernism and postmodernism (48–49). For instance, metafiction, which Wexler appears to consider postmodern, has been an integral part of the novel since its beginning.[4] Could there be a more playful, metafiction than *Tristram Shandy?* There is nothing uniquely postmodern about Lawrence's fiction in the 1920s and, more important, common sense would tell any reader that *Women in Love* will always be infinitely superior to *Kangaroo* no matter how much the revisionist argues for the minor works' canonization (itself a not very postmodernist position).

Fortunately, Ingersoll's full-length study does tackle Lawrence's masterpieces. Ingersoll relies primarily on Jacques Lacan to guide his postmodern reassessment of Lawrence. Unfortunately, Lacan represents only a textual approach to writing that rarely extends the formalist commentary of early modern critics like I.A. Richards. Terminology does not, by itself, offer any sense of Lawrence's larger vision. In addition, Lacan's overvaluation of the visual completely contradicts Lawrence's own attack on visual primacy. As a result, though Ingersoll makes some excellent comments on *The Trespasser* and *Women in Love*; he elides Lawrence's own tactile sensibility.

In "Morality and the Novel" (1925) Lawrence attacks what he calls man's "Kodak vision." Technolologically enhanced sight leads men to see, in

Lawrence's opinion, only what the camera sees and then take that reproduction as reality.[5] "The identifying of ourselves with the visual image of ourselves has become an instinct; the habit is already old. The picture of me, the me that is seen, is me" (165). Here, Lawrence describes what Reich and Marcuse call second nature; a constructed reality so ingrained in our consciousness that men take the construction as natural. Lawrence juxtaposes this Kodak vision with a Cézanne still life, which Lawrence claims, can only be understood, "with your blood and your bones" (167). For Lawrence, Cézanne represents the avant-garde whereas the photographer represents the status quo.

In "The Novel and Feelings" (1925) Lawrence articulates his version of a physical non-repressive civilization symbolized by the "old Adam." "So great is the Freudian hatred of the oldest, old Adam, from whom God is not yet separated off, that the psychoanalyst sees Adam as nothing but a monster of perversity . . . (204–205)." In Lawrence's mind repression produces the guilt ridden modern man. Man's deeper nature, however, remains buried under "thousands of shameful years," untamed, guilt free and ready to act. That which for Freud would be a regression to primitive chaos, unbounded instinct, becomes, in Lawrence, a recovery of "the primeval, honorable beasts of our being" (205).

Lawrence's vision of a non-repressive civilization represented in *St. Mawr* has been discussed in chapter 4. My point here is to draw attention to the problematic value of using Lacan as an entry into Lawrence's "postmodernity." A larger issue concerns the use of Lacan as a return to Freud and what place Freud plays in the contest between assimilation and dismissal played out by contemporary thinkers. Of the three figures in this study Freud has received by far the most attention from postmodernists. This attention, however, has tended to be mediated through Lacan. Lacan, in turn, commands little emphasis from within the larger psychoanalytic community, but tremendous attention from the fields that continue to engage Freud's thought: feminism, philosophy, literary criticism, and various textual theories. The 1998 conference on Freud held at Yale University testifies to Freud's academic allure. Ironically, the conference commenced with Frederick Crews launching a sustained assault on the value of both Freud, in particular, and psychoanalysis, more generally.[7] Professor Crews's challenge, a derivative challenge as I will soon show, goes to the heart of my own project and thus engages some closing comments on psychoanalysis, radicalism, and science.

Frederick Crews established his own name with a very Freudian work entitled *The Sins of the Father*. Subsequently, the good professor saw the error of his early thinking and in the 1980s initiated an attack on Freud that continues into the twenty-first century.[8]

The kernel of Crews's argument is simple. Freud offers circular thinking, in Crews's interpretation, absent of empirical validity. Consequently, for Crews, psychoanalysis is no better than magic; a side show with nothing real to offer.

Many objections to Crews project come to mind. First, Professor Crews has been a professor of English. He cannot offer a scientific critique within the nonscientific domain of literary criticism and he does not have the training to offer a scientific critique of Freud's science. An equally basic objection to Crews concerns his tendency to treat psychoanalysis as mono-lithic. The field has spawned many divergent thinkers and theories from Adler and Jung to Winnicott and Klein. Any reading of psychoanalysis must account for its various reformations.

Crews does correctly point out that Freud has been largely excluded from departments of psychology and from the practice of psychiatry. This observation, however, has dubious value. Psychiatry, to begin with, has evolved into an almost pharmacological branch of chemistry and thus largely abdicates its therapeutic role (other than for medication management). Likewise, psychology's place within the university system must be read within the larger context of the university's economic superstructure, that is, how research money and grants are allocated for various studies. In other words psychology's "science" has many contaminating factors.

Finally, Crews's love affair with standards of proof should be juxtaposed with Kurt Göedel's 1931 revision of Alfred North Whitehead and Bertrand Russell's *Principia Mathematica*. Göedel offered a proof showing the impossibility of demonstrating certain important propositions in arithmetic, "there is an endless number of true arithmetical statements which cannot be formally deduced from any given set of axioms by a closed set of rules of inference."[9] Gödel's incompleteness theorem shows the inherent limitations of the axiomatic method for pure mathematics. Where then do psychology's standards of proof lie?

Ultimately, Crews's pop critique of Freud dervives from Adolph Grünbaum's more rigorous attack on Freud in his monumental, *The Philosophical Foundations of Psychoanalysis: A Philosophical Critique of Freud*. Grünbaum cogently argues that Freud's theories rely on extra-clinical evidence such as dreams, slips of the tongue, artwork, and the like. Further, for Grünbaum, Freud's theories do not adequately account for his patients' cures which can, the philosopher maintains, be attributed to factors other than psychoanalytic insight. A psychoanalytic cure, of course, necessarily resists the controlled standards of proof operating in the natural sciences. The innumerable variables that contribute to a patient's improvement, including the simple passage of time, can never be isolated from contaminating factors. What Grünbaum, and later, Crews, really object to, however, is Freud's challenge to positivism.

Paul Robinson beautifully dismantles Grünbaum's critique by showing how the philosopher of science's hostility to Freud operates within a larger cultural reaction to Freud's more skeptical positions:

> It was revolt against the uncertainties and ambiguities that the modernist legacy burdened us with, above all the sense that the self is unreliable, indeed largely unknowable. The anti-modernist persuasion longs for confidence about what cannot be known; it wants to believe that the choice between correct and incorrect behavior is unambiguous; it holds that definite conclusions can be confidently reached on the basis of unimpeachable evidence.[10]

Interestingly, Jacques Derrida attributes psychoanalysis's power precisely to the essential ambiguity Robinson articulates as forming the core of Freud's legacy. For Derrida, psychoanalysis moves between archeological and philolytic motifs.[11] Derrrida discusses psychoanalysis's border position in relationship to the history of reason:

> ... on the one side, an Enlightenment progressivism which hopes for an analysis that will continue to gain ground on initial obscurity to the degree that it removes resistances and liberates, unbinds, emancipates, as does every analysis, and, on the other side, a sort of fatalism or pessimism of desire that reckons with a portion of darkness and situates the unanalyzable as its very resources. (Derrida, 1996: 16)

In other words, as Derrida continues, "being determined, if one can say that, only in adversity and in relation to what resists it, psychoanalysis will never gather itself into the unity of a concept or a task" (20). Resistance to analysis, then, signifies a belief in positivism, a nostalgia or certainty doubling as a totalitarian master narrative, which Freud's writing dislodges.

Again, Robinson describes just how Freud needs to be placed, "on the rich interstices of art and science. Freud remains a border thinker, neither fish nor fowl, always at risk of seeming caught in a hopeless contradiction and destined to be fought over perpetually by the representatives of the two great intellectual traditions that have dominated modern culture" (266).

This assessment of Freud's legacy brings me back to the larger question of radicalism and revolt. Julia Kristeva has recently argued that analytic interpretation, "reveals the inauthenticity of the writing subject: the writer is a subject in process, a carnival, a polyphony without possible reconciliation, a permanent revolt."[12] A revolt, most certainly against positivism. Kristeva's reading helps return Reich to the psychoanalytic fold. More even than Freud, Reich evokes "the rhythmic, melodic articulations" of a trans-verbal semiotic (Kristeva, 259). Reich forcefully welds biology to psychoanalysis and allows for the possibility of social reform simultaneous with individual transformation. Kristeva sees "cure" as a patient's self-beginning, a gift from the analyst to the patient, which, ultimately, the patient affirms in his or her self-beginning; a utopian gesture which asserts a future that does not repeat the past and hence overcomes the ultimate resistance

In finishing, theory can move toward either a grand totalization like string theory in the natural sciences or maintain a constant oppositional stance toward prevailing wisdom. A radical modern always adopts, often in spite of him/herself, the latter stance. Ultimately, psychoanalysis, like Marxism, has traveled far over the last hundred years. Edward Said's superb essay on "Traveling Theory" allows for a final reflection on my own methodology.[13] Said examines how theory from one period and community applies to another country and another time. He traces a theory's transformation across four dimensions; point of origin (circumstances of an idea's birth), distance (time of composition to time of reception and the changing contexts of the time travel), conditions of acceptance, and the accommodated idea, that is, how the theory is currently used. Said travels along with Lukács's "History of Class Consciousness" (Hungary, 1929) via Lucien Goldman's *Le Dieu Cache* (Paris, 1955) to Raymond Williams's work in Cambridge during the 1970s. He discovers that Lukács brilliant theory of reification undergoes, "conversion of insurrectionary, radically adversarial consciousness into an accommodating consciousness and homology" (236).

Said urges the mapping of a theory's terrain, paths of dissemination, and interpretive history. This kind of detailed history of psychoanalysis remains to be written. Reich and Marcuse, I would argue, represent the last vestige of a sexual radicalism that refuses accommodation. Beginning, ironically, with Freud's own work in the 1920s and extending to the present, psychoanalysis has, like Marxism, undergone conversion, for the most part, to institutional status. If psychoanalysis ever achieves the status, of the natural sciences or even medical sciences then I will, perhaps, offer an ironic applause. An empirical outcome may be the end of radicalism for any human science. Fortunately, neither Freud nor Reich nor D.H. Lawrence lived to see the magic of science and technology's pharmacological manipulation of sexuality. In the end the value of all three figures cannot be measured in terms of natural science or empirical verification. What matters for Freud, Reich, and Lawrence is the representation and pursuit of a critical vision, since, as Said notes, "and what is critical consciousness at bottom if not an unstoppable predilection for alternatives?" (247).

Notes ∾

All quotes from Freud are taken from *The Standard Edition of the Complete Psychological Works of Sigmund Freud* (S.E.), trans. James Strachey in collaboration with Anna Freud, assisted by Alex and Alan Tyson, London: The Hogarth Press 1953–1974, 24 volumes.

All quotations of D.H. Lawrence are taken, unless otherwise specified, from *The Cambridge Edition of The Works of D.H. Lawrence*. When relevant, original publication dates are provided alongside recent editions for the reader's ease of reference.

INTRODUCTION: RADICAL MODERNISM

1. D.H. Lawrence, *Lady Chatterley's Lover*, ed. Michael Squires, Cambridge: Cambridge University Press, 1993/1928.
2. Paul de Man, *Allegories of Reading: Figural Language in Rousseau, Nietzsche, Rilke, and Proust*, New Haven: Yale University Press, 1979, 80–81.
3. Michel Foucault, "Nietzsche, Genealogy, History," in *The Foucault Reader*, ed. Paul Rabinow, New York: Pantheon Books, 1984, 83.
4. Michel Foucault, *The Order of Things: An Archaeology of the Human Sciences*, New York: Random House Inc., 1970, 340–344.
5. Karl R. Popper, *Conjectures and Refutations: The Growth of Scientific Knowledge*, New York: Harper and Row Publishers, 1963, 34.
6. Wilhelm Dilthey, *Introduction to the Human Sciences: An Attempt to have a Foundation for the Study of Society and History*, trans. Ramon J. Betanzos, Detroit: Wayne State University Press, 1989.
7. Sigmund Freud, "The Claims of Psychoanalysis to Scientific Interest," *S.E. XIII*, 163–190.
8. Jürgen Habermas, "Modernity: An Unfinished Project," reprinted in: *Habermas and the Unfinished Project of Modernity: Critical Essays on The Philosophical Discourse of Modernity*, ed., Maurizio d'Entreves and Seyla Benhabib, Cambridge: MIT Press, 1997, 38–55.
9. Frederic Jameson, *A Singular Modernity: Essay on the Ontology of the Present*, London: Verso, 2002, 24.
10. Perry Anderson, "Marshall Berman: Modernity and Revolution," in *A Zone of Engagement*, London: Verso, 1992, 44.

136 *Notes*

11. Anthony Giddens, *The Consequences of Modernity*, Palo Alto: Stanford University Press, 1990.

12. *Oeuvre Completes des Manuscrits de Charles Fourier*, Paris: Editions Anthropos, 1966–1968. Charles Pellarin documents Fourier's strange and paradoxical life, *sa vie et sa theorie*, Paris: Librairie de l'Ecole Societaire, 1843.

13. Roland Barthes, *Sade/Fourier/Loyola*, trans. Richard Miller, Baltimore: Johns Hopkins University Press, 1971, 114.

14. Stephen Frosh, *The Politics of Psychoanalysis: An Introduction to Freudian and Post-Freudian Theory*, New Haven: Yale University Press, 1987, 269.

15. Philip Rieff, *The Triumph of the Therapeutic: Uses of Faith after Freud*, Chicago: University of Chicago Press, 1966, 71.

16. Paul Ricoeur, *Freud and Philosophy: An Essay on Interpretation*, trans. Denis Savage, New Haven: Yale University Press, 1970, 30.

17. Karl Marx, "Contribution to the Critique of Hegel's Philosophy," in *Early Writings*, trans. and ed. T.B. Bottomore, New York: McGraw-Hill Book Company, 1963, 52.

18. Ibid., 12.

19. "The distinguishing feature of Communism is not the abolition of property generally, but the abolition of bourgeois property. But modern bourgeois private property is the final and most complete expression of the system of producing and appropriating products that is based on class antagonisms, on the exploitation of the many by the few. In this sense, the theory of the Communists may be summed up in the single sentence: Abolition of private property." Karl Marx and Friedrich Engels, *The Communist Manifesto*, Harmondsworth: Penguin Books Ltd., 1967, 96.

20. Herbert Marcuse, *Eros and Civilization, Revised Edition*, New York: Vintage Books, 1966.

21. Sigmund Freud, "Civilization and Its Discontents (1930)," *S.E. XXI*, 122.

22. D.H. Lawrence, *Study of Thomas Hardy and Other Essays*, ed. Bruce Steele, Cambridge: Cambridge University Press, 1985, 199–206.

23. D.H. Lawrence, "The Overtone," in *St. Mawr and Other Stories*, ed. Brian Finney, Cambridge: Cambridge University Press, 1983, 4–17.

24. Ibid.

25. The letter is quoted in: Mabel Dodge Luhan, *Lorenzo in Taos*, New York: Alfred Knopf, Inc., 1932, 13–15.

26. George Lukács, "The Old Culture and the New Culture," in *Marxism and Human Liberation: Essays on History, Culture and Revolution*, ed. E. San Juan Jr., New York: Dell Publishing Co., Inc., 1973, 11.

27. D.H. Lawrence, "A Propos of 'Lady Chatterley's Lover' " (1929), ed. Michael Squires, 308.

28. *The Letters of D.H. Lawrence, Volume 7*, 1928–1930, ed. Keith Sagar and James T. Boulton, Cambridge: Cambridge University Press, 1993, 106.

29. Hans-Georg Gadamer, *Truth and Method, 2nd Edition*, trans. Joel Weinsheimer and Donald G. Marshall, New York: Continuum, 2000/1960, 551–579.

30. D.H. Lawrence, *The Letters of D.H. Lawrence, vol. 2: June 1913–October 1916*, ed. George J. Zytarnuk and James T. Boulton, Cambridge: Cambridge University Press, 1981, 266.
31. Julia Kristeva, *Intimate Revolt: The Powers and Limits of Psychoanalysis*, trans. Jeanine Herman, New York: Columbia University Press, 2002, 12.
32. D.H. Lawrence, *Psychoanalysis and the Unconscious*, Harmondsworth: Penguin Books, 1971/1921, 212.
33. Perry Anderson uses the word curvilinear to describe Marx's account of social development, see above, note 10.

1   THE ANALYTIC RADICAL: FREUD AND MODERN SEXUALITY

1. Michel Foucault, *The History of Sexuality Volume I: An Introduction*, trans. Robert Hurley, New York: Random House, Inc., 1978.
2. Jeffrey Weeks, *Sex, Politics and Society: The Regulation of Sexuality Since 1800*, London: Longman Group Ltd., 1981.
3. Steven Marcus, *The Other Victorians: A Study of Sexuality and Pornography in Mid-Nineteenth Century*, England, New York: Basic Books, 1964, 283–284.
4. Lawrence Birkin, *Consuming Desire: Sexual Science and the Emergence of a Culture of Abundance, 1871–1914*, Ithaca: Cornell University Press, 1988, 40–71.
5. Jeffrey Weeks, *Sexuality and Its Discontents: Meanings, Myths and Modern Sexualities*, London: Routledge, Kegan Paul, 1985, 64.
6. Richard von Krafft-Ebing, *Psychopathia Sexualis with Special Reference to the Antipathic Sexual Instinct: A Medico-Forensic Study*, trans. F.J. Rebman, Brooklyn: Physicians and Surgeons Book Company, 1927.
7. Paul Robinson, *The Modernation of Sex: Havelock Ellis, Alfred Kinsey, William Masters and Virginia Johnson*, New York: Harper and Row, Inc., 1976, 3–4.
8. Sigmund Freud, "Three Essays on the Theory of Sexuality (1905)," *S.E. VII* (1901–1905), 1.
9. Sigmund Freud, *The Origins of Psychoanalysis: Letters to Wilhelm Flies, Drafts and Notes 1887–1902*, ed. Marie Bonaparte, Anna Freud, and Ernst Kris, trans. Eric Mosbacher and James Strachey (New York: Basic Books, Inc., 1954), letter dated January 11, 1997, 184–187.
10. Sigmund Freud, "Fetishism (1927)," *S.E. XXI* (1927–1931), 155.
11. Sigmund Freud, "Formulations Regarding the Two Principles in Mental Functioning (1911)," *S.E. XII* (1911–1913), 218–226.
12. Sigmund Freud, "Instincts and Their Vicissitudes (1915)," *S.E. XIV* (1914–1916), 14.
13. Sigmund Freud, "The Ego and the ID (1923)," *S.E. XIX* (1923–1925), 175–204
14. Sigmund Freud, " 'A Child is Being Beaten,' A Contribution to the Study of the Origin of Sexual Perversion (1919)," *S.E. XVII*, 184–185.

15. Jean Laplanche, *Life and Death in Psychoanalysis*, trans. Jeffrey Mehlman, Baltimore: Johns Hopkins University Press, 1976, 91.

16. Sigmund Freud, "Constructions in Analysis (1937)," *S.E. XXIII* (1937–1939), 259.

17. Sigmund Freud, "The Economic Problems in Masochism (1924)," *S.E. XIX*, 157–170.

18. Sigmund Freud, "Beyond the Pleasure Principle" *(1920), S.E. XVIII (1920–1922), 7–64*, trans. James Strachey, New York: W.W. Norton and Company, 1961, 7.

19. Leo Bersani, *The Freudian Body: Psychoanalysis and Art*, New York: Columbia University Press, 1989.

20. Paul Ricoeur, *Freud and Philosophy: An Essay on Interpretation*, trans. Denis Savage, New Haven: Yale University Press, 1970, 151.

2   THE SOCIAL RADICAL: REICH AND SEXUAL UTOPIA

1. Steven Marcus, "Over-Soul as Orgone: The Strange Case of Wilhelm Reich," in *Emerson and His Legacy: Essays in Honor of Quentin Anderson*, ed. Stephen Donadio, Stephen Railton, and Ormond Seavey, Carbondale: Southern Illinois University Press, 1986, 130–146. Harold Bloom uses the term visionary company to characterize the English romantic tradition of *The Visionary Company: A Reading of English Romantic Poetry*, Ithaca: Cornell University Press, 1971.

2. Philip Rieff, "The Therapeutic Martyr: Reich's Religion of Energy," *The Triumph of the Therapeutic*, Chicago: University of Chicago Press, 1966, 141–188.

3. Charles Rycroft, *Wilhelm Reich*, New York: Viking Press, Inc. 1969.

4. Cf. David Boadella, *Wilhelm Reich: The Evolution of His Work*, Chicago: Henry Regency Co., 1973, and Ola Raknes, *Wilhelm Reich and Orgonomy*, New York: St. Martin's Press, 1970.

5. Cf. Bertell Ollman, *Social and Sexual Revolution: Essays on Marx and Reich*, Boston: South End Press, 1979, and Paul A. Robinson, *The Freudian Left: Wilhelm Reich, Geza Roheim, Herbert Marcuse*, New York: Harper & Row, Inc., 1969.

6. Mary Higgins and Chester M. Raphael, eds., *Reich Speaks of Freud*, trans. Therese Pol, New York: Farrar, Strauss and Giroux, 1967, 22–23. This book is a transcript of an interview conducted between Dr. Kurt R. Eissler and Dr. Reich on October 18 and 19, 1952 in Rangeley, Maine.

7. Wilhelm Reich, *The Function of the Orgasm: Sex-Economic Problems of Biological Energy* trans. Vincent R. Calfagno, New York: Farrar, Straus and Giroux, 1942, 124.

8. Wilhelm Reich, *Passion of Youth: An Autobiography, 1987–1922*, ed. Mary Boyd Higgins and Chester M. Raphael, trans. Philip Schmitz and Jerri Tompkins, New York: Farrar, Straus, Giroux, 1988, 6.

9. The most balanced and thorough biography of Reich is: Myron Sharaf, *Fury on Earth: A Biography of Wilhelm Reich*, New York: St. Martin's Press, 1983.

10. Sigmund Freud, *Project for a Scientific Psychology* printed in: *The Origins of Psychoanalysis: Letters to Wilhelm Fliess, Drafts, and Notes: 1887–1902*, ed. Marie Bonaparte, Anna Freud, Ernst Kris, and trans. Erich Mosbacher and James Strachey, New York: Basic Books, Inc., 1954, 356.

11. A comprehensive analysis of Freud's project can be found in: Karl H. Pribram and Merton M. Gill, *Freud's "Project" Reassessed: Preface to Contemporary Cognitive Theory and Neuropsychology*, New York: Basic Books, Inc., 1976. Pribram and Gill place Freud's theory within the frame of both modern cybernetic theory and Freud's own later psychological development.

12. Sigmund Freud, "Sexuality and the Aetiology of the Neurosis (1898)," *S.E. III* (1893–1899), 268.

13. Sigmund Freud, *The Interpretation of Dreams* (1899), *S.E. V* (1900–1901), 603. "When I described one of the psychical processes occurring in the mental apparatus as the 'primary' one, what I had in mind was not merely considerations of relative importance and efficiency; I intended also to choose a name which would give an indication of its chronological priority. It is true that, so far as we know, no psychical apparatus exists which possesses a primary process only that such an apparatus is to that extent a (theoretical fiction). But this much is a fact: the primary processes are present in the mental apparatus from the first, while it is only during the course of life that the secondary processes unfold, and come to inhibit and overlay the primary ones; it may even be that their complete domination is not attained until the prime of life. In consequence of the belated appearance of the secondary processes, the core of our being, consisting of unconscious wishful impulses, remains inaccessible to the understanding and inhibition of the preconscious; the part played by the latter is restricted once and for all to directing along the most expedient paths the wishful impulses that arise form the unconscious. These unconscious wishes exercise a compelling force upon all later mental trends, a force that those trends are obliged to fall in with or which they may perhaps endeavor to divert and direct to higher aims. A further result of the belated appearance of the secondary process is that a wide sphere of mnemic material is inaccessible to preconscious cathexis."

14. Reich's diagram on human sexual responsiveness can be seen in *The Function of Orgasm* (107–108) and then compared to the kind of research studies conducted by William H. Masters and Virginia E. Johnson, *Human Sexual Response*, New York: Bantam Books, 1981/1966.

15. For a serious consideration of Reich's work within an anti-Cartesian tradition see: Thomas Hana, *Bodies in Revolt: A Primer in Somatic Thinking*, New York: Holt, Rhinehart, and (Winston, 1967), 122–137. Additionally, Arthur Efron provides a fine overview of Reich's reading of the body: "The Reichian Tradition: A View of the Sexual Body," *Journal of Mind and Behavior*, vol. 6, nos 1 and 2 (Winter/Spring 1985), 57–72.

16. Wilhelm Reich, *Cosmic Superimposition*, trans. Therese Pol, New York: Farrar, Straus, and Giroux, 1949, 222.

17. Wilhelm Reich's view on the relationship of language and the body can be found in the third edition of *Character Analysis*, trans. Vincent R. Carfagno, New York: The Noonday Press, 1945, 355–398 ("The Expressive Language of the Living").

18. Reich's classic essay on contact and the difference between active and reactive living is: "Psychic Contact and Vegetative Current," in *Character Analysis*, 285–354.

19. Cf. Sandor Ferenczi, "The Further Development of an Active Therapy in Psychoanalysis," in *Further Contributions to the Theory and Technique of Psychoanalysis*, trans. Jane Isabel Sultie, London: Hogarth Press, 1926, 198–217. Ferenczi's active therapy involves giving the patient directives or tasks, including paradoxical tasks such as performing activities a particular phobia prevents from doing.

20. Wilhelm Reich, *Ether, God and Devil*, trans. Therese Pol. New York: Farrar, Straus and Giroux, 1949.

21. The orgone accumulator was an invention Reich used to capture orgone energy for healing purposes. Organic and metallic materials would be layered inside a wooden shell or other nonmetallic material. Reich discusses the orgone accumulator in chapter six of *Ether, God and Devil* (139–161). Unfortunately, Einstein dismissed Reich's experiments and collaboration of Reich's work has often been published by his own organization making independent verification a problem still to be overcome.

22. Sontag attacks Reich, among others, for using cancer as a metaphor translating a life-threatening physical illness into a subjective, psychological realm capable of expressing in projected form man's particular anxieties. For Sontag Reich's cancer research is a work of science fiction. Reich does not exactly use cancer in Sontag's sense but considers the illness as psychosomatic. Cf. Susan Sontag, *Illness as Metaphor*, New York: Random House, Inc., 1977 and Wilhelm Reich, *The Cancer Biopathy*, New York: Farrar, Straus & Giroux, 1973.

23. Wilhelm Reich, *Children of the Future: On the Prevention of Sexual Pathology*, ed. Mary Higgins and Chester M. Raphael, trans. Derek and Inge Jordan and Beverly Placzek, New York: Farrar, Straus and Giroux, 1967, 7–21.

24. T. Berry Brazelton and Bertrand G. Cramer, *Earliest Relationship: Parents, Infants, and the Drama of Early Attachment*, New York: Perseus Publishing, reprint edition, 1991.

25. The groundbreaking studies on mother–infant attachment and birth environment can be found in: Marshall H. Klaus and John H. Kennel, *Bonding: The Beginnings of Parent-Infant Attachment*, New York: New American Library, 1983. Also see. Evelyn B. Thoman, "Changing Views of the Being and Becoming of Infants," in *Origins of the Infant's Social Responsivenes*, ed. Evelyn B. Thoman, Hillsdale, NJ: Lawrence Erlbaum Associates, 1979, 445–459 and Arthur Efron, "Reinventing the Asexual Infant: On the Present 'Explosion' in Infant Research," ibid., 89–126, for detailed studies on infant research.

26. John Bowlby, *A Secure Base: Parent-Child Attachment and Healthy Human Development*, New York: Basic Books, Inc., 1988.

27. Wilhelm Reich, *The Sexual Revolution: Toward a Self-Regulating Character Structure*, trans. Therese Pol, New York: Farrar, Straus and Giroux, 1962, 39.

28. Karl Marx and Friedrich Engels, in *Writings of the Young Marx on Philosophy and Society*, ed., and trans. Loyd D. Easton and Kurt H. Fuddat, New York: Doubleday and Co. Inc., 1967, 421–422.

29. Ira H. Cohen, *Ideology and Unconsciousness: Reich, Freud, and Marx*, New York: New York University Press, 1982, 151–153.

30. Wilhelm Reich, *The Mass Psychology of Fascism, Third Edition*, trans. Vincent R. Carfagno. New York: The Noonday Press, 1970, 19.

31. Christopher Lasch's *The Culture of Narcissism: American Life in An Age of Diminishing Expectations, Revised Edition*, New York: W.W. Norton, 1991, 218–236, remains a classic study of the family under siege from outside experts.

32. Reich, "On Natural Work Democracy," in *The Mass Psychology of Fascism*, 360–395.

33. Sigmund Freud, "Civilization and Its Discontents," *Standard Edition Vol. XXI*, New York: W.W. Norton & Company, 74.

34. Janine Chasseguet-Smirgel and Bela Grunberger, *Freud or Reich? Psychoanalysis and Illusion*, trans. Claire Pajacskowska, New Haven: Yale University Press, 1986.

35. Wilhelm Reich, "The Imposition of Sexual Morality," in *Sex-Pol: Essays, 1929–1934*, ed. Lee Baxandall, trans. Anna Bostock, Tom DuBose, and Lee Bazandall, New York: Random House, Inc., 1966, 89–250.

36. Erich Fromm, "The Oedipus Complex and the Oedipus Myth," in *The Family: It's Function and Destiny*, ed. Ruth Nanda Anshen and *of Psychoanalysis: Essays on Freud, Marx, and Social Psychology*, Greenwich, CO: Fawcett Publications, Inc., 1970, 101–136. For Malinsowski's influential work see: Bronislaw Malinowski, *Sex and Repression in Savage Society*, New York: Routledge, 2001 and *The Sexual Life of Savages in Northwestern Melanesia*, New York: Routledge, 1987.

37. Cf. Jean-Pierre Vernant and Pierre Vidal-Naquet, *Mythe et tragédie en Grèece ancienne*, Paris: Maspero, 1972.

38. Sigmund Freud, " 'Civilized' Sexual Morality and Modern Nervous Illness (1908)," *S.E. IX* (1906–1908), 181–204.

39. Morris Berman, *The Reenchantment of the World*, Ithaca: Cornell University Press, 1981.

40. Heinz Hartman, *Ego Psychology and the Problem of Adaptation*, New York: International Universities Press, 1939. Marcuse's trenchant dismantling of Hartman and other ego psychologists can be found in chapter, "Critique of Neo-Freudian Revisionism," *Eros and Civilization*, 217–248.

41. Robert S. Corrington, *Wilhelm Reich: Psychoanalyst and Radical Naturalist*, New York: Farrar, Straus and Giroux, 2003.

42. Wilhelm Reich, *The Murder of Christ*, New York: Farrar, Straus and Giroux, 1966.

43. D.H. Lawrence, *The Escaped Cock*, ed. Gerald M. Lacy, Los Angeles: Black Sparrow Press, 1973.

44. D.H. Lawrence, *The Letters of D.H. Lawrence, vol. 6: March 1927–November 1928*, ed. James T. Boulton and Margaret H. Boulton with Gerald Lacy, Cambridge: Cambridge University Press, 1991.

45. D.H. Lawrence, "The Risen Lord," *Assorted Articles*, New York: Martin Seeker, 1930, 105–117.

46. D.H. Lawrence, *The Complete Poems*, ed. Vivian de Sola Pinto and F. Warren Roberts, New York: Penguin Books, 1977.

47. D.H. Lawrence, *The Letters of D.H. Lawrence: vol. 7: November 1928–February 1930*, ed. Keith Sagar and James T. Boulton, Cambridge: Cambridge University Press, 1993.

48. The classic study of how cocks function as symbols of manhood remains: Clifford Geertz's, "Deep Play: Notes on the Balinese Cockfight," *The Interpretation of Cultures*, New York: Basic Books, 1973, 412–454. The novella's religious symbols are adequately unpacked by: James C. Cowan, "Allusions and Symbols in D.H. Lawrence's *The Escaped Cock*," in ed. *Critical Essays on D.H. Lawrence*, Dennis Jackson and Fleda Brown Johnson, Boston: G.K. Hall & Co., 1988.

3 THE SEXUAL RADICAL: D.H. LAWRENCE'S EMBODIED FICTION

1. D.H. Lawrence, "On Being a Man," *Reflections on the Death of a Porcupine*, ed. Michael Herbert, Cambridge: Cambridge University Press, 1988/1915, 211–212.

2. Paul Poplawski, *Writing the Body in D.H. Lawrence: Essays on Language, Representation, and Sexuality*, ed. Paul Poplawski, Westport: Greenwood Press, 2000, xiii.

3. Peter Brooks, *Body Work: Objects of Desire in Modern Narrative*, Cambridge: Harvard University Press, 1993.

4. Wilhelm Reich, *The Mass Psychology of Fascism*, trans. Vincent R. Carfagno, New York: Farrar (Straus and Giroux, 1970/1934).

5. Maria Aline Ferreira, " 'Glad Wombs' and 'Friendly Tombs': Reembodiments in D.H. Lawrence's Late Works," in Poplawski, *Writing the Body in D.H. Lawrence*, 174.

6. D.H. Lawrence, *The Prussian Officer and Other Stories*, ed. John Worthen, Cambridge: Cambridge University Press, 1983, 1–21.

7. Barbara Mensch, *D.H. Lawrence and the Authoritarian Personality*, New York: Palgrave Macmillan, 1991.

8. T.W. Adorno, Else Frenkel-Brunswick, and Daniel J. Levinson, *The Authoritarian Personality*, New York: W.W. Norton & Company, 1993.

9. Hugh Stevens, "Sex and the Nation: 'The Prussian Officer' and 'Women and Love,' " *The Cambridge Companion to D.H. Lawrence*, ed. Anne Fernihough, Cambridge: Cambridge University Press, 2001, 57.

10. Simon Casey, *Naked Liberty and the World of Desire: Elements of Anarchism in the Work of D.H. Lawrence*, New York: Taylor and Francis, Inc., 2003.

11. Kingsley Widmer, *The Art of Perversity: D.H. Lawrence's Shorter Fiction*, Seattle: University of Washington Press, 1962.

12. D.H. Lawrence, "The Sick Collier," *The Prussian Officer and Other Stories*, ed. John Worthen, Cambridge: Cambridge University Press, 1983, 165–171.

13. Peter Middletown, *The Inward Gaze: Masculinity and Subjectivity in Modern Culture*, London: Routledge, 1992, 43–77.

14. D.H. Lawrence, *The Letters of D.H. Lawrence, vol. 2: June 1913–October 1916*, ed. George J. Zytarnuk and James T. Boulton, Cambridge: Cambridge University Press, 1981, 488–490.

15. D.H. Lawrence, *Phoenix II: Uncollected, Unpublished, and Other Prose Works*, Harmondsworth: Penquin Books, Ltd., 1936, 592–596.

16. Linda Williams, *Sex in the Head: Visions of Femininity and Film in D.H. Lawrence*, Detroit: Wayne State University Press, 1993.

17. D.H. Lawrence, "The Blind Man," *England, My England and Other Stories*, ed. Bruce Steele, Cambridge: Cambridge University Press, 1990/1920.

18. Ronald Granofsky, *D.H. Lawrence and Survival: Darwinism in the Fiction of the Transitional Period*, Montreal: McGill-Queen's University Press, 2003.

19. Michael L. Ross, "The Mythology of Friendship: D.H. Lawrence, Bertrand Russell, and 'The Blind Man,' " in *English Literature and British Philosophy; A Collection of Essays*, ed. S.P. Rosenbaum, Chicago: University of Chicago Press, 1971, 285–315.

20. Mauriza Boscagli, *Eye on the Flesh: Fashions of Masculinity in the Early Twentieth Century*, Boulder: Westview Press, Inc., 1996, 1.

21. D.H. Lawrence, *The Plumed Serpent*, ed. L.D. Clark, Cambridge: Cambridge University Press, 1987/1926, 353–371.

22. Eve Kosofsky Sedgwick, *Between Men: English Literature and Male Homosocial Desire*, New York: Columbia University Press, 1985.

23. René Girard, "Triangular Desire," *Deceit, Desire and the Novel: Self and Other in Literacy Structure*, trans. Yvonne Freccero, Baltimore: Johns Hopkins University Press, 1965, 1–52.

24. D.H. Lawrence, *Woman in Love*, ed. David Farmer, Lindeth Vasey, and John Worthen, Cambridge: Cambridge University Press, 1987/1920.

25. Gerard Doherty, *Theorizing Lawrence: Nine Tropological Themes*, New York: Peter Lang, 1999, 17.

26. Jonathan Dollimore, "D.H. Lawrence and the Metaphysics of Sexual Difference," *Sexual Dissidence: Augustine to Wilde, Freud to Foucault*, Oxford: Clarendon Press, 1991, 268–275.

27. G. Wilson Knight, " 'Through . . . Degration to a New Health': A Comment on Women in Love," in *D.H. Lawrence: The Rainbow and Women in Love: A Casebook*, ed. Colin Clarke, London: Macmillan and Co. Ltd., 1969, 135–141.

28. D.H. Lawrence, *Studies in Classic American Literature*, ed, Ezra Greenspan, Lindseth Vassey, and John Worthen, Cambridge: Cambridge University Press, 2003, 358–369 and 403–430.

29. Christopher Craft, "No Private Parts: On the Rereading of Women in Love," *Another Kind of Love: Male Homosexual Desirie in English Discourse, 1850–1920*, Berkeley: University of California Press, 1994, 140–191.

30. Mark Kinkead-Weekes, *D.H. Lawrence, Volume II: Triumph to Exile, 1912–1922*, Cambridge: Cambridge University Press: 1996,103.

31. D.H. Lawrence, *The Rainbow*, ed. Mark Kinkead-Weekes, Cambridge: Cambridge University Press, 1989/1915, 310–327.

32. D.H. Lawrence, "The 'Prologue' to Women in Love," appendix II, in *Women in Love*, 489–506.

33. George H. Ford, "Introductory Note to D.H. Lawrence's Prologue to Women in Love," in Clarke, 35–62.

34. D.H. Lawrence, *The Fox, The Captain's Doll, The Lady Bird*, ed. Dieter Mehl, Cambridge: Cambridge University Press, 1922/1918–1922.

35. Eve Kosofsky Sedgwick, *Epistemology of the Closet*, Berkeley: University of California Press, 1990.

36. Lillian Faderman, *Surpassing the Love of Men: Romantic Friendship and Love between Women from the Renaissance to the Present*, New York: William Morrow and Company, Inc. 1981.

37. Luce Irigaray, *This Sex Which is Not One*, trans. Catherine Porter, Ithaca: Cornell University Press, 1985, 172.

38. Judith Butler, *Bodies that Matter: On the Discursive Limits of "Sex,"* New York: Routledge, 1993, 37.

39. For a different reading of Irigaray see: Diana J. Fuss, " ' Essentially Speaking': Luce Irigaray's Language of Essence," *Hypation*, vol. 3, no. 3 (Winter 1989), 62–80.

40. Luce Irigaray, *Elemental Passions*, trans. Joanne Collins and Judith Still, New York: Routledge, 1982.

41. Luce Irigaray, "Quant nos leures se parlent," *This Sex Which Is Not One*, 205–218.

42. Irigaray follows her essay on the exchange of women with a vision of an alternative, noncommercial exchange between women: "Commodities among Themselves," *This Sex Which is Not One*, 192–204.

43. Luce Irigaray, *Speculum of the Other Woman*, trans. Gillian C. Gill, Ithaca: Cornell University Press, 1985, 34–45, 147–151, and 214–226.

44. Peggy Phelan, *Unmarked: The Politics of Performance*, New York: Routledge, 1993, 170.

4   INDUSTRIAL LOVE: SEXUALITY IN *LADY CHATTERLEY'S LOVER*

1. Graham Holderness, *D.H. Lawrence: History, Ideology, and Fiction*, London: William Heinemann Ltd., 1985, 36.

2. Norman Mailer, *The Prisoner of Sex*, Boston: Little and Brown, Co., Inc., 1971, 93–115.
3. D.H. Lawrence, *Psychoanalysis and the Unconscious*, Harmondsworth: Penguin Books, Ltd., 1921, 212.
4. Gerard Doherty, *Theorizing Lawrence: Nine Tropological Themes*, New York: Peter Lang, 1999, 15–31.
5. Anne Fernihough, *D.H. Lawrence: Aesthetics and Ideology*, Oxford: Clarendon Press, 1993.
6. Michael Squires, *The Creation of Lady Chatterley's Lover*, Baltimore: Johns Hopkins University Press, 1983, 50.
7. D.H. Lawrence, *The Complete Poems*, Harmondsworth: Penguin Books Ltd., 1978.
8. Evelyn J. Hinz and John J. Teumissen, "War, Love and Industrialism: The Ares/Aphrodite/Hephaestos Complex in Lady Chatterley's Lover," in Squires and Jackson, 197–221.

5   NOTES ABOUT A POSTMODERN SEXUALITY: BETWEEN BATAILLE AND BAUDRILLARD

1. Fredric Jameson, *Postmodernism or, The Cultural Logic of Late Capitalism*, Durham: Duke University Press, 1991, ix.
2. Habermas, "Modernity: An Unfinished Project," in Maurizio d'Entreves and Seyla Benhabib, *Habermas and the Unfinished Project of Modernity*. Cambridge: MIT Press, 1997, 38–55.
3. Jean Francois Lyotard, *The Postmodern Condition: A Report on Knowledge*, trans. Geoff Bennington and Brian Massumi, Minneapolis: University of Minnesota Press, 1984, 79.
4. Mark C. Taylor, *About Religion: Economies of Faith in Virtual Culture*, Chicago: University of Chicago Press, 1999, 48–79.
5. I refer to the introduction of *On Bataille: Critical Essays*, ed. Leslie Anne Bodlt-Irons, Albany: SUNY Press, 1995, for an excellent overview of Bataille's work.
6. D.H. Lawrence, *The Woman who Rode Away and Other Stories*, ed. Dieter Mehl and Christa Jansohn, 1995/1924.
7. Mark Kinkead-Weeks, "The Gringo Senora Who Rode Away," *D.H. Lawrence Review*, vol. 22, no. 3 (Fall 1990), 251–263.
8. Leslie Anne Boldt-Irons, "Sacrifice and Violence in Bataille's Erotic Fictions: Reflections from/upon the mise en abime," *Bataille: Writing the Sacred*, ed. Carolyn Bailey Gill, New York: Routledge, 1995, 96. The author deforms the French word abyme in order to stress Bataille's polyvalent terminology, i.e., his fiction also puts characters into the abyss.
9. Peter Balbert, *D.H. Lawrence and the Phallic Imagination: Essays on Sexual Identity and Feminist Misreading*, New York: St. Martin's Press, 1989.
10. See the introduction to the Cambridge edition for Lawrence's appreciation of Forster's novel.

11. Michel Foucault, "Preface to Transgression," *Language, Counter Memory, Practice*, trans. Donald F. Bouchard and Sherry Simon, Ithaca: Cornell University Press, 1980.

12. George Bataille, *Eroticism: Death and Sensuality*, trans. Mary Dalwood, San Francisco, City Lights Books, 1962.

13. George Bataille, *The Accursed Share Volumes II and III*, trans. Robert Hurley, New York: Zone Books, 1993, 84–86.

14. Jacques Derrida, "From Restricted to General Economy: Hegelianism Without Reserve," *Writing and Difference*, trans. Alan Bass, Chicago: University of Chicago Press, 1978, 251–277. Derrida follows his essay on Baitille with his own affirmation of play: "There are thus two interpretations of structure, of sign, of play. The one seeks to decipher, dreams of deciphering a truth or an origin, which escapes play, and the order of the sign, and which lives the necessity of interpretation as an exile. The other, which is no longer turned toward the origin, affirms play and tries to pass beyond man and humanism, the name of man being the name of that being who, throughout the entire history of metaphysics or of ontotheology, in other words, throughout his entire history has dreamed of full presence, the reassuring foundation, the origin and the end of play," in "Structure, Sign, and Play in the Discourse of the Human Sciences," 292.

15. Jürgen Habermas, "Between Eroticism and General Economics: George Bataille," *The Philosophical Discourse of Modernity*, trans. Frederick G. Lawrence (Cambridge: MIT Press, 1987), 211–237. Habermas makes an interesting reading of fascism, which he finds govermentalized sovereignty. He also talks about Bataille's "cosmically expanded energy ecology" and its potential discharge in either a "glorious" or "catastrophic" form. These remarks would make an interesting comparison with Wilhelm Reich's work and Lawrence's political vision, a subject for an entire paper.

16. Susan Rubin Suleiman, "Transgression and the Avant-Garde: Bataille's histoire de l'oeil," *Subversive Intent: Gender, Politics, and the Avant-Garde*, Cambridge: Harvard University Press, 1990, 72–87.

17. Michel Foucault, "Preface to Transgression," ibid.

18. Doherty, *Theorizing Lawrence: Nine Tropological Themes*, New York: Peter Lang, 1999, 109.

19. Marc J. LaFountain, "Bataille's Eroticism, Now: From Transgression to Insidious Sorcery," in *Philosophy and Desire*, ed. Hugh J. Silverman, New York: Routledge, 2000.

20. Jean Baudrillard, "Transpolitics, Transsexuality, Transaesthetics," trans. Michel Valentin, in, *Jean Baudrillard: The Disappearance of Art and Politics*, ed. William Stearns and William Chalowpka, New York: St. Martin's Press, 1987, 9–26. Hereafter cited in text as T.

21. Sylvere Lotringer, *Overexposed: Treating Sexual Perversion in America*, New York: Pantheon Books, 1988.

22. Jean Baudrillard, *Seduction*, trans. Brian Singer, New York: St. Martin's Press, 1990, 157–178.

23. Arthur and Marilouise Kroker, eds, *Body Invaders: Panic Sex in America*, New York: St. Martin's Press, 1987, 95, hereafter cited in the text as Krokers.

24. Herbert Marcuse, "The Images of Orpheus and Narcissus," *Eros and Civilization*, New York: Vintage Books, 1962, 144–156.

25. Jean Baudrillard, *Forget Foucault*, New York: Semiotext (e), Inc., 1987, 21. Baudrilliard maintains that Foucault's description of power is interchangeable with Deleuze's description of desire: "For in those days [high modernism] Reichians and Freudo-Marxists and desire and power were under opposite signs; today micro-desire (that of power) and micro-politics (that of desire) literally merge at the libido's mechanical confines: all one has to do is miniaturize, (18–19). Thus the two poles of radicalism are imploded in Baudrilliard's thought. He also implicitly argues against Irigaray in the following description: "This compulsion toward liquidity, flow, and an accelerated circulation of what is psychic, sexual, or pertaining to the body is the exact replica of the force that rules market value: capital must circulate; gravity and any fixed point must disappear; the chain of investments and reinvestments must never stop; value must radiate endlessly an in every direction. This is the form itself that the current realization of value takes. It is the form of capital, and sexuality as a catchword and a model is the way it appears at the level of bodies" (25). He replaces these obsolete theories with his own description of seduction outlined in my conclusion.

26. Elaine Showalter, "The Way We Write Now: Syphilis and AIDS," *Sexual Anarchy: Gender and Culture at the Fin de Siecle*, Harmondsworth: Penguin Books Ltd., 1990, 188–208.

27. Baudrillard's work leads to the complex world of virtual reality and cyborg sexuality. The most interesting summary of cyborg (i.e., post-genital) sexuality from a positive perspective is: Donna Haraway, "A Manifesto for Cyborgs: Science, Technology, and Socialist Feminism in the 1980s," in *Feminism/Postmodernism*, ed. Linda J. Nicholson, New York: Routledge, 1990, 190–233.

CONCLUSION: REASSESSING THE RADICAL
IN MODERNISM

1. Leo Bersani, *Homos*, Cambridge: Harvard University Press, 1995, 181.

2. Sigmund Freud, "The Question of Lay Analysis," *S.E. XX*.

3. Joyce Wexler, "D.H. Lawrence Through a Postmodernist Lens," *D.H. Lawrence Review*, vol. 27, no. 1 (1997–1998), 47–64; Earl G. Ingersoll, *D.H. Lawrence, Desire and Narrative*, Gainesville: University Press of Florida, 2001.

4. Robert Alter, *Partial Magic: The Novel as a Self-Conscious Genre*, Berkeley: University of California Press, 1975.

5. D.H. Lawrence, *Study of Thomas Hardy and Other Essays*, ed. Bruce Steele, Cambridge: Cambridge University Press, 1985, 161–168.

6. Ibid.; 196–206.

7. Frederick Crews, "Unconscious Deeps and Empirical Shallows," in *Whose Freud? The Place of Psychoanalysis and Contemporary Culture*, ed. Peter Brooks and Alex Woloch, New Haven: Yale University Press, 2000, 19–32.

8. Frederick Crews, *Sins of the Father: Hawthorne's Psychological Themes*, Berkeley: University of California Press, 1966; *Skeptical Engagements*, New York: Oxford University Press, 1986; *Memory Wars: Freud's Legacy in Dispute*, New York: New York Review of Books, 1997; and *Unauthorized Freud: Doubters Confront a Legend* (editor), New York: Penguin USA, 1999.

9. Ernest Nagel and James R. Newman, *Gödel's Proof*, New York: New York University Press, 1958, 98–99.

10. Paul Robinson, *Freud and His Critics*, Berkeley: University of California Press, 1993.

11. Jacques Derrida, *Resistances of Psychoanalysis*, trans. Peggy Kamuf, Pascale-Anne Brault, and Michael Nass, Stanford: Stanford University Press, 1998, 27–28.

12. Julia Kristeva, *Intimate Revolt: The Powers and Limits of Psychoanalysis*, trans. Jeanine Herman, New York: Columbia University Press, 2002, 258.

13. Edward W. Said, "Traveling Theory," *The World, the Text and the Critic*, Cambridge: Harvard University Press, 1984, 226–247.

Bibliography

Adorno, T.W., Else Frenkel-Brunswick, and Daniel J. Levinson. *The Authoritarian Personality*. New York: W.W. Norton & Company, 1993.

Alter, Robert. *Partial Magic: The Novel as a Self-Conscious Genre*. Berkeley: University of California Press, 1975.

Anderson, Perry. *A Zone of Engagement*. London: Verso, 1992.

Balbert, Pete. *D.H. Lawrence and the Phallic Imagination: Essays on Sexual Identity and Feminist Misreading*. New York: St. Martin's Press, 1989.

Barker-Benfield, J. *The Horrors of the Half Known Life: Male Attitudes Toward Women and Sexuality in 19th Century America*. New York: Harper and Row, Inc., 1976.

Barthes, Roland. *The Pleasure of the Text*. Trans. Richard Miller. New York: Hill and Wang, 1975.

———. *Sade/Fourier/Loyola*. Trans. Richard Miller. Baltimore: Johns Hopkins University Press, 1971.

Bataille, George. *The Accursed Share Volumes II and II*. Trans. Robert Hurley. New York: Zone Books, 1993.

———. *Eroticism: Death and Sensuality*. Trans. Mary Dalwood. San Francisco: City Lights Books, 1962.

———. *Visions of Excess: Selected Writings, 1927–1939*, ed. Allan Stockl. Minneapolis: University of Minnesota Press, 1985.

Baudrillard, Jean. *Forget Foucault*. New York: Semiotext (e), Inc., 1987.

———. *Seduction*. Translated by Brian Singer. New York: St. Martin's Press, 1990.

Berman, Morris. *The Reenchantment of the World*. Ithaca: Cornell University Press, 1981.

Bersani, Leo. *The Freudian Body: Psychoanalysis and Art*. New York: Columbia University Press, 1989.

———. *Homos*. Cambridge: Harvard University Press, 1995.

Birkin, Lawrence. *Consuming Desire: Sexual Science and the Emergence of a Culture of Abundance, 1871–1914*. Ithaca: Cornell University Press, 1988.

Boadella, David. *Wilhelm Reich: The Evolution of His Work*. Chicago: Henry Regency Co., 1973.

Bodlt-Irons, Leslie Anne, editor. *On Bataille: Critical Essays*. Albany: SUNY Press, 1995.

Boone, Joseph Allan. *Libidinal Currents: Sexuality and the Shaping of Modernism.* Chicago: University of Chicago Press, 1998.

Boscagli, Mauriza. *Eye on the Flesh: Fashions of Masculinity in the Early Twentieth Century.* Boulder: Westview Press, Inc., 1996.

Bowlby, John. *A Secure Base: Parent-Child Attachment and Healthy Human Development.* New York: Basic Books, Inc., 1988.

Brazelton, T. Berry and Bertrand G. Cramer. *Earliest Relationship: Parents, Infants, and the Drama of Early Attachment.* New York: Perseus Publishing, reprint edition, 1991.

Brooks, Peter. *Body Work: Objects of Desire in Modern Narrative.* Cambridge: Harvard University Press, 1993.

Butler, Judith. *Bodies that Matter: On the Discursive Limits of "Sex."* New York: Routledge, 1993.

Casey, Edward S. *Remembering: A Phenomenological Study.* Bloomington: Indiana University Press, 1987.

Casey, Simon. *Naked Liberty and the World of Desire: Elements of Anarchism in the Work of D.H. Lawrence.* New York: Routledge, 2003.

Chalowpka, William and William Stearns. *Jean Baudrillard: The Disappearance of Art and Politics.* New York: St. Martin's Press, 1987.

Clarke, Colin. Ed. *The Rainbow and Women in Love: A Casebook.* London: MacMillan and Co., Ltd., 1969.

Cohen, Ira H. *Ideology and Unconsciousness: Reich, Freud, and Marx.* New York: New York University Press, 1982.

Corrington, Robert S. *Wilhelm Reich: Psychoanalyst and Radical Naturalist.* New York: Farrar, Straus and Giroux, 2003.

Craft, Christopher. *Another Kind of Love: Male Homosexual Desire in English Discourse, 1850–1920.* Berkeley: University of California Press, 1994.

Crews, Frederick. *Memory Wars: Freud's Legacy in Dispute.* New York: New York Review of Books, 1997.

———. *Sins of the Father: Hawthorne's Psychological Themes.* Berkeley: University of California Press, 1966.

———. *Skeptical Engagement.* New York: Oxford University Press, 1986.

———. *Unauthorized Freud: Doubters Confront a Legend.* New York: Penguin USA, 1999.

———. *Whose Freud? The Place of Psychoanalysis and Contemporary Culture.* Ed. Peter Brooks and Alex Woloch. New Haven: Yale University Press, 2000.

Deleuze, Gilles and Felix Guattari. *Anti-Oedipus: Capitalism and Schizophrenia.* Trans. Robert Hurley, Mark Seem, and Helen R. Lane. New York: Viking Press, 1977.

de Man, Paul. *Allegories of Reading: Figural Language in Rousseau, Neitzsche, Rilke, and Proust.* New Haven: Yale University Press, 1979.

Derrida, Jacques. *Writing and Difference.* Trans. Alan Bass. Chicago: University of Chicago Press, 1978.

———. *Resistances of Psychoanalysis.* Trans. Peggy Kamuf, Pascale-Anne Brault, and Michael Nass. Stanford: Stanford University Press, 1998.

Dilthey, Wilhelm. *Introduction to the Human Sciences: An Attempt to have a Foundation for the Study of Society and History*. Trans. Ramon J. Betanzos. Detroit: Wayne State University Press, 1989.

Dollimore, Jonathan. *Sexual Dissidence: Augustine to Wilde, Freud to Foucault*. Oxford: Clarendon Press, 1991.

Doherty, Gerard. *Theorizing Lawrence: Nine Tropological Themes*. New York: Peter Lang, 1999.

Dyer, Geoff. *Out of Sheer Rage: Wrestling with D.H. Lawrence*. New York: North Point Press, 1997.

Ecles, C. *The Neurophysiological Basis of Mind: The Principles of Neurophysiology*. Oxford: Clarendon Press, 1953.

Eliot, T.S. *After Strange Gods: A Primer of Modern Heresy*. New York: Harcourt and Brace Co., 1934.

Ellis, David. *D.H. Lawrence: The Dying Game 1922–1930*. Cambridge: Cambridge University Press, 1998.

Faderman, Lillian. *Surpassing the Love of Men: Romantic Friendship and Love between Women from the Renaissance to the Present*. New York: William Morrow and Company, Inc., 1981.

Ferenczi, Sandor. *Further Contributions to the Theory and Technique of Psychoanalysis*. Trans. Jane Isabel Sultie. London: Hogarth Press, 1926.

Fernihough, Anne. *D.H. Lawrence: Aesthetics and Ideology*. Oxford: Clarendon Press, 1993.

Frosh, Stephen. *The Politics of Psychoanalysis: An Introduction to Freudian and Post Freudian Theory*. New Haven: Yale University Press, 1987.

Foucault, Michel. *The Foucault Reader*. New York: Pantheon Books, Inc.,

———. *The Order of Things: An Archaeology of the Human Sciences*. New York: Pantheon Books, 1970.

———. *Language, Counter-Memory, Practice*. Trans. Sherry Simon. ed. Paul Rabinow Ithaca: Cornell University Press, 1977.

———. *The History of Sexuality: Volume I: An Introduction*. Trans. Robert Hurley. New York: Random House, Inc., 1978.

Freud, Sigmund. *The Standard Edition of the Complete Psychological Works of Sigmund Freud*, 24 Volumes. Trans. James Strachey. London: Hogarth Press, 1953–1966.

———. (1895). "Project for a Scientific Psychology," *S.E. I*, 283–397.

———. (1898). "Sexuality and the Aetiology of the Neurosis," *S.E. III*, 263–285.

———. (1900). "The Interpretation of Dreams," *S.E. IV* and *V*, 1–626.

———. (1905). "Three Essays on the Theory of Sexuality," *S.E. VII*, 125–245.

———. (1908). " 'Civilized' Sexual Morality and Modern Nervous Illness," *S.E. IX*, 181–204.

———. (1911). "Formulations Regarding the Two Principles in Mental Functioning," *S.E. XII*, 218–226.

———. (1915). "Instincts and their Vicissitudes," *S.E. XIV*, 11–140.

———. (1919). " 'A Child is Being Beaten,' A Contribution to the Study of the Origins of Sexual Perversion," *S.E. XVII*, 177–204.

Freud, Sigmund. (1920). "Beyond the Pleasure Principle," *S.E. XVIII*, 1–64.

———. (1923). "The Ego and the Id," *S.E. XIX*, 175–204.

———. (1924). "The Economic Problems in Masochism," *S.E. XIX*, 157–170.

———. (1926). "The Question of Lay Analysis," *S.E. XX*, 183–258.

———. (1927). "Fetishism," *S.E. XXI*, 149–157.

———. (1930). "Civilization and Its Discontents," *S.E. XXI*, 59–145.

———. (1939). "Constructions in Analysis," *S.E. XXIII*, 256–269.

Fromm, Erich. *The Crisis of Psychoanalysis: Essays on Freud, Marx and Social Psychology*. Greenwich: Fawcett Publications, Inc., 1970.

———. *Of Psychoanalysis: Essays on Freud, Marx, and Social Psychology*. Greenwich, CO: Fawcett Publications, Inc., 1970.

Gadamer, Hans-Georg. *Truth and Method, 2nd Edition*. Trans. Joel Weinsheimer and Donald G. Marshall. New York: Continuum, 2000/1960.

Gallop, Jane. *Thinking through the Body*. New York: Columbia University Press, 1988.

Gay, Peter. *Freud: A Life for Our Time*. New York: W.W. Norton & Company, 1988.

Geertz, Clifford. *The Interpretation of Cultures*. New York: Basic Books, 1973.

Giddens, Anthony. *The Consequences of Modernity*. Palo Alto: Stanford University Press, 1990.

Gill, Carolyn Bailey, ed. *Bataille: Writing the Sacred*. New York: Routledge, 1995.

Girard, René. *Deceit, Desire and the Novel: Self and Other in Literary Structure*. Trans. Yvonne Frecrero. Baltimore: Johns Hopkins University Press, 1965.

———. *Things Hidden Since the Foundation of The World*. Trans. Stephen Bann and Michael Metteer. Stanford: Stanford University Press, 1978.

Granofsky, Ronald. *D.H. Lawrence and Survival: Darwinism in the Fiction of the Transitional Period*. Montreal: McGill-Queen's University Press, 2003.

Grünbaum, Adolph. *The Foundations of Psychoanalysis: A Philosophical Critique*. Berkeley: University of California Press, 1984.

Hanna, Thomas. *Bodies in Revolt: A Primer in Somatic Thinking*. New York: Holt, Rinehart, and Winston, 1970.

———. *The Philosophical Discourse of Modernity*. Trans. Frederick G. Lawrence. Cambridge: MIT Press, 1987.

Habermas, Jürgen. *Habermas and the Unfinished Project of Modernity: Critical Essays on The Philosophical Discourse of Modernity*. Ed. Maurizio d'Entreves and Seyla Benhabib, Cambridge: MIT Press, 1997.

Hartman, Heinz. *Ego Psychology and the Problem of Adaptation*. New York: International Universities Press, 1939.

Heath, Stephen. *The Sexual Fix*. New York: Schocken Books, 1984.

Higgins, Mary and Chester M. Raphael, eds. *Reich Speaks of Freud*. Trans. Therese Pol. New York: Farrar, Strauss and Giroux, 1967.

Holderness, Graham. *D.H. Lawrence: History, Ideology and Fiction*. London: William Heinemann Ltd., 1985.

Horkheimer, Max and Theodor W. Adorno. *The Dialectic of Enlightenment*. Trans. John Cummings. New York: Herder and Herder, 1972.

Ingersoll, Earl G. *D.H. Lawrence, Desire and Narrative*. Gainesville: University Press of Florida, 1975.

Irigaray, Luce. *Elemental Passions*. Trans. Joanne Collins and Judith Still. New York: Routledge, 1982.

———. *This Sex Which is Not One*. Trans. Catherine Porter. Ithaca: Cornell University Press, 1985.

———. *Marine Lover of Friedrich Nietzsche*. Trans. Gillian C. Gill. New York: Columbia University Press, 1991.

———. *Speculum of the Other Woman*. Trans. Gillian C. Gill. New York: Routledge, 1993.

Jackson, Dennis and Jackson, Freda Brown. *Critical Essays on D.H. Lawrence*. Boston: G.K. Hall and Co., 1988.

———. *Postmodernism or, The Cultural Logic of Late Capitalism*. Durham: Duke University Press, 1991.

Jameson, Frederic. *A Singular Modernity: Essay on the Ontology of the Present*. London: Verso, 2002.

Kellner, Douglass. *Jean Baudrillard: From Marxism to Postmodernism and Beyond*. Stanford: Stanford University Press, 1989.

Kermode, Frank. *The Sense of an Ending: Studies in the Theory of Fiction*. Oxford: Oxford University Press, 1966.

Kinkead-Weekes, Mark. *D.H. Lawrence, Volume II: Triumph to Exile, 1912–1922*. Cambridge: Cambridge University Press, 1996.

Knight, G. Wilson. *D.H. Lawrence: The Rainbow and Women in Love: A Casebook*. Ed. Colin Clarke. London: Macmillan and Co. Ltd., 1969.

Krafft-Ebing, Richard Von. *Psychopathia Sexualis: With Special Reference to the Antipathic Sexual Instinct, A Medico-Forensic Study*. Trans. F.J. Rebman. Brooklyn: Physicians and Surgeons Book Company, 1927.

Kristeva, Julia. *Intimate Revolt: The Powers and Limits of Psychoanalysis*. Trans. Jeanine Herman. New York: Columbia University Press, 2002.

Kroker, Arthur and Marilouise Kroker, Eds. *Body Invaders: Panic Sex in America*. New York: St. Martin's Press, 1987.

Lacan, Jacques. *Ecrits: A Selection*. Trans. Alan Sheridan. New York: W.W. Norton and Co., 1977.

Langbaum, Robert. *The Mysteries of Identity: A Theme in Modern Literature*. Chicago: University of Chicago Press, 1977.

Laplanche, Jean. *Life and Death in Psychoanalysis*. Trans. Jeffrey Mehlman. Baltimore: Johns Hopkins University Press, 1976.

Lasch, Christopher. *The Culture of Narcissism: American Life in An Age of Diminishing Expectations, Revised Edition*. New York: W.W. Norton, 1991.

Lawrence, D.H. *Apocalypse*. Harmondsworth: Penguin Books, Ltd., 1931.

———. *The Complete Poems*. Harmondsworth: Penguin Books, Ltd., 1978.

———. *England, My England and Other Stories* (1922), ed. Bruce Steele. Cambridge: Cambridge University Press, 1990.

———. *The Escaped Cock*. Ed. Gerald M. Lacy. Los Angeles: Black Sparrow Press, 1973.

Lawrence, D.H. *The Fox, The Captain's Doll, The Lady Bird* (1923), ed. Dieter Mehl. Cambridge: Cambridge University Press, 1992.

———. *Lady Chatterley's Lover* (1928), ed. Michael Squires. Cambridge: Cambridge University Press, 1993.

———. *The Letters of D.H. Lawrence.* 7 volumes. General Editor, James T. Boulton. Cambridge: Cambridge University Press, 1979–1993.

———. *Phoenix: The Posthumous Papers of D.H. Lawrence.* London: William Heinemann Ltd., 1936.

———. *Phoenix II: Uncollected, Unpublished, and Other Prose Works.* Harmondsworth: Penguin Books, Ltd., 1978.

———. *The Plumed Serpent (Quetzalcoatl)* (1926), ed. L.D. Clark. Cambridge: Cambridge University Press, 1987.

———. *The Prussian Officer and Other Stories* (1914), ed. John Worthen. Cambridge: Cambridge University Press, 1983.

———. *Psychoanalysis and the Unconscious.* Harmondsworth: Penguin Books, Ltd., 1926.

———. *The Rainbow* (1915), ed. Mark Kinkead-Weekes. Cambridge: Cambridge University Press, 1989.

———. *Reflections on the Death of a Porcupine*, ed. Michael Herbert. Cambridge: Cambridge University Press, 1988.

———. *Selected Letters.* Harmondsworth: Penguin Books, Ltd., 1950.

———. *Sex, Literature and Censorship Essays.* New York: Twayne Publishers, Inc., 1953.

———. *Sketches of Etruscan Places and Other Italian Essays* (1932), ed. Simonetta de Filippis, Cambridge: Cambridge University Press, 1992.

———. *St. Mawr and Other Stories* (1925), ed. Brian Finney. Cambridge: Cambridge University Press, 1983.

———. *Studies in Classic American Literature* (1924), eds. Ezra Greenspan, Lindseth Vassey, and John Worthen, Cambridge: Cambridge University Press, 2003.

———. *Study of Thomas Hardy and Other Essays* (1936), ed. Bruce Steele. Cambridge: Cambridge University Press, 1985.

———. *The Woman Who Rode Away and Other Stories* (1928), ed. Dieter Mehl and Christa Jansohn. Cambridge: Cambridge University Press, 1995.

———. *Women in Love* (1920), ed. David Farmer, Lindeth Vasey, and John Worthen. Cambridge: Cambridge University Press, 1987.

Lawrence, Frieda. *"Not I, but the wind . . ."* New York: Viking Press, Inc., 1934.

Leaves, F.R. *D.H. Lawrence: Novelist.* New York: Simon and Schuster, 1955.

Lichtman, Richard. *The Production of Desire: The Integration of Psychoanalysis into Marxist Theory.* New York: Free Press, 1982.

Lingis, Alphonso. *Libido: The French Existential Theories.* Bloomington: Indiana Press, Inc., 1985.

Lotringer, Sylvere. *Overexposed: Treating Sexual Perversion in America.* New York: Pantheon Books, 1988.

Luhan, Mabel Dodge. *Lorenzo in Taos.* New York: Alfred Knopf, Inc., 1932.

Lukács, George. *Marxism and Human Liberation: Essays on History, Culture and Revolution*. Trans. E. San Juan, Jr. New York: Dell Publishing Co., Inc., 1973.

Lyotard, Jean Francois. *The Postmodern Condition: A Report on Knowledge*. Trans. Geoff Bennington and Brian Massumi. Minneapolis: University of Minnesota Press, 1984.

MacLeod, Sheila. *Lawrence's Men and Women*. London: William Heinemann, Ltd., 1985.

Mailer, Norman. *The Prisoner of Sex*. Boston: Little and Brown Co., Inc., 1971.

Malinowski, Bronislaw. *Sex and Repression in Savage Society*. New York: Routledge, 2001.

———. *The Sexual Life of Savages in Northwestern Melanesia*. New York: Routledge, 1987.

Marcus, Steven. *Emerson and His Legacy: Essays in Honor of Quentin Anderson*, ed. Stephen Donadio, Stephen Railton, and Ormond Seavey. Carbondale: Southern Illinois University Press, 1986.

———. *The Other Victorians: A Study of Sexuality and Pornography in Mid-Nineteenth Century England*. New York: Basic Books, 1964.

Marcuse, Herbert. *Eros and Civilization: A Philosophical Inquiry into Freud*. New York: Vintage Books, 1955.

Marx, Karl. *Early Writings*. Trans. and ed. T.B. Bottomore. New York: McGraw-Hill Book Company, 1963.

Marx, Karl and Friedrich Engels. *The Communist Manifesto*. Hamondsworth: Penguin Books, Ltd., 1967.

———. *Writings of the Young Marx on Philosophy and Society*, ed. and Trans. Loyd D. Easton and Kurt H. Fuddat. New York: Doubleday and Co., Inc., 1967.

Masters, William H. and Virginia A. Johnson. *Human Sexual Response*. Boston: Little and Brown Co., 1966.

Mensch, Barbara. *D.H. Lawrence and the Authoritarian Personality*. New York: Palgrave Macmillan, 1991.

Middletown, Peter. *The Inward Gaze: Masculinity and Subjectivity in Modern Culture*. London: Routledge, 1992.

Millet, Kate. *Sexual Politics*. New York: Ballantine Books, 1969.

Moi, Toril. *Sexual/Textual Politics: Feminist Literary Theory*. London: Methuen and Co., Ltd., 1985.

Montagu, Ashley and Floyd Matson. *The Dehumanization of Man*. New York: McGraw-Hill Book, Co., 1983.

Moore, Harry T., ed. *A D.H Lawrence Miscellany*. Carbondale: University of Illinois Press, 1959.

Moore, Harry T. and F.J. Hoffman, eds. *The Achievement of D.H. Lawrence*. Norman: University of Oklahoma Press, 1953.

Nagel, Ernest and James R. Newman. *Gödel's Proof*. New York: New York University Press, 1958.

Nietzsche, Friedrich. *The Use and Abuse of History*. Trans. Adrian Collins. Indianapolis: Bobbo-Merrill Educational Publishing, 1949.

Ollman, Bertell. *Social and Sexual Revolution: Essays on Marx and Reich.* Boston: South End Press, 1979.

Phelan, Peggy. *Unmarked: The Politics of Performance.* New York: Routledge, 1993.

Poplawski, Paul. *Writing the Body in D.H. Lawrence: Essays on Language, Representation, and Sexuality.* Westport: Greenwood Press, 2000.

Popper, Karl R. *Conjuectures and Refutations: The Growth of Scientific Knowledge.* New York: Harper and Row Publishers, 1963.

Pribram, Karl H. and Merton M. Gill. *Freud's "Project" Reassessed: Preface to Contemporary Cognitive Theory and Neuropsychology.* New York: Basic Books, Inc., 1976.

Rabinow, Paul, ed. *The Foucault Reader.* New York: Pantheon Books, 1984.

———. *Seduction.* Trans. Brian Singer. New York: St. Martin's Press, 1990.

Raknes, Ola. *Wilhelm Reich and Orgonomy.* New York: St. Martin's Press, 1970.

Ricoeur, Paul. *Freud and Philosophy: An Essay on Interpretation.* Trans. Denis Savage. New Haven: Yale University Press, 1970.

Rieff, Philip. *The Triumph of the Therapeutic: Uses of Faith after Freud.* Chicago: University of Chicago Press, 1966.

Robinson, Paul. *Freud and His critics.* Berkeley: University of California Press, 1993.

———. *The Freudian Left: Wilhelm Reich, Geza Roheim, Herbert Marcuse.* New York: Harper & Row, Inc., 1969.

———. *The Modernation of Sex: Havelock Ellis, Alfred Kinsey, William Masters and Virginia Johnson.* New York: Harper and Row, Inc., 1976.

Ross, Michael L. *English Literature and British Philosophy: A Collection of Essays,* ed. S.P. Rosenbaum. Chicago: University of Chicago Press, 1971.

Rycroft, Charles. *Wilhelm Reich.* New York: Viking Press, Inc., 1969.

Said, Edward W. *The World, the Text and the Critic.* Cambridge: Harvard University Press, 1984.

Sedgewick, Eve Kosofsky. *Between Men: English Literature and Male Homosocial Desire.* New York: Columbia University Press, 1985.

———. *Epistemology of the Closet.* Berkley: University of California Press, 1990.

Sharaf, Myron. *Fury on Earth: A Biography of Wilhelm Reich.* New York: St. Martin's Press, 1983.

Showalter, Elaine. *Sexual Anarchy: Gender and Culture at the Fin de Siecle.* Harmondsworth: Penguin Books, Ltd., 1990.

Silverman, Hugh J., ed. *Philosophy and Desire.* New York: Routledge, 2000.

Smirgel, Janine Chasseguet- and Bela Grunberger. *Freud or Reich? Psychoanalysis and Illusion.* Trans. Claire Pajacskowska. New Haven: Yale University Press, 1986.

Solso, Robert L. and Dominic W. Massaro, eds. *The Science of the Mind: 2001 and Beyond.* New York: Oxford University Press, 1995.

Sontag, Susan. *Illness as Metaphor.* New York: Random House, Inc., 1977.

Stearns, William and William Chalowpka, ed. *Jean Baudrillard: The Disappearance of Art and Politics.* Trans. Michel Valentin. New York: St. Martin's Press, 1987.

Stevens, Hugh. *The Cambridge Companion to D.H. Lawrence*, ed. Anne Fernihough. Cambridge: Cambridge University Press, 2001.

Suleimann, Susan Rubin. *Subversive Intent: Gender, Politics, and the Avant-Garde*. Cambridge: Harvard University Press, 1990.

Squires, Michael. *The Creation of Lady Chatterley's Lover*. Baltimore: Johns Hopkins University Press, 1983.

Squires, Michael and Cushman, Keith, eds. *The Challenge of D.H. Lawrence*. Madison: University of Wisconsin Press, 1990.

Squires, Michael and Jackson, Dennis, eds. *D.H. Lawrence's "Lady": A New Look at Lady Chatterley's Lover*. Athens: University of Georgia Press, 1985.

Taylor, Mark. *About Religion: Economies of Faith in Virtual Culture*. Chicago: University of Chicago Press, 1999.

———. *Altarity*. Chicago, University of Chicago Press, 1987.

———. *Erring: A Postmodern A/Theology*. Chicago: University of Chicago Press, 1987.

Vattimo, Gianni. *The End of Modernity: Nihilism and Hermeneatics in Postmodern Culture*. Trans. Jon R. Snyder. Baltimore: Johns Hopkins University Press, 1985.

Vernant, Jean-Pierre and Pierre Vidal-Naquet. *Mythe et tragédie en Grèce ancienne*. Paris: Maspero, 1972.

Weeks, Jeffrey. *Sex, Politics and Society: The Regulation of Sexuality Since 1800*. London: Longman Group, Ltd., 1981.

———. *Sexuality and Its Discontents: Meanings, Myths and Modern Sexualities*. London: Routledge, Kegan Paul, 1985.

Widmer, Kingsley. *The Art of Perversity: D.H. Lawrence's Shorter Fiction*. Seattle: University of Washington Press, 1962.

Williams, Linda. *Sex in the Head: Visions of Femininity and Film in D.H. Lawrence*. Detroit: Wayne State University Press, 1993.

Williams, Raymond. *The English Novel: From Dickens to Lawrence*. New York: Oxford University Press, 1990.

Index